TOM S

And ...

Thermo-Ion Jetpack

BY

Victor Appleton II

Made in The United States of America

Tom Swift And His
Thermo-Ion Jetpack

By Victor Appleton II

Like many people who've imagined the future, Tom Swift—and even his father, Damon—have dreamed of the days when those personal jet backpacks we've heard about since the 1940s would become reality.

So, when a famous movie director from Hollywood comes to Tom to create the real thing—he demands reality in his science fiction films without resorting to special effects—it intrigues the young inventor enough to try to see what he might create. It's a lot harder than it appears at first!

He must convince the director that his plans to have a 1940's period piece with leather jackets and bullet-nosed SCUBA tank-shaped rockets has to be updated to match what he believes might be deliverable as a working device.

When the suit is hijacked by the stuntman and ends up shooting him into space, it becomes a search and rescue mission with a very short window for success.

In the end, it is up to Bud Barclay to save the day and fly the dangerous suit for the film. But, a sudden attack might be sending him on a collision course with death.

Can Tom rescue his best friend and save the movie?

This book is dedicated to the folks who gave us Commando Cody, but especially the special effects team of the Lydecker brothers, Howard and Theodore, who made the flying scenes seem magical and possible. Only with the advances in television resolution did the wires ever appear. And, if you were lucky enough to see these serials on a big movie screen, those flying sequences actually made the dialog and plot tolerable.

Bud spent more than a minute admiring the sleek, steampunk appearance of the Hollywood jet pack illustration. CHAPTER **1**

TABLE OF CONTENTS

AUTHOR'S NOTE

Tom Swift is capable of anything the author's imagination—and willingness to suspend disbelief on the part of the reader—can come up with. Like many things falling into the lengthy list of, "Just because you *can* do something, does it make any sense to do actually it?" comes the things this 18th novel deals with.

But, no spoiler here. Let's look at this in a slightly different light.

Just because you have enjoyed one or more of this series, should you really keep purchasing the books and the collections of short stories?

The answer is obvious. Obviously you *should*. And, you can. While not as inexpensive as the original books in the first two series, these are priced to please, orderable via almost any computer or mobile device (not too certain about Blackberry) and come in relatively plain cardboard wrappers so you can claim that, "Oh, that's just my order for a signed first edition of Dostoevsky's *Notes From The Underground!*"

Actually, if they are your friends I believe they would rather see you carrying around a good Tom Swift novel than one of those indecipherable Russian books that may or may not have been translated correctly. Heck. For all you know old Dosty's *The Idiot* might have originally been titled, *The Fool Who Bought This Story*.

Copies of all of this author's works may be found at:

http://www.lulu.com/spotlight/tedwardfoxatyahoodotcom

My Tom Swift novels and collections are also available on Amazon in paperbound and Kindle editions. Barnes and Nobel sells Nook ebook editions of these same works.

Tom Swift and His Thermo-Ion Jetpack

FOREWORD

For a few decades I have toyed with the idea of how neat it might be to have access to an honest-to-gosh jet pack. I mean, back in the fifties we were practically promised they would be reality and in our garages by the turn of the 21st century. So, sixteen years after that, where the heck are they?

If Tom Swift can go to the Moon, then Mars and even outside our solar system, what has been stopping him from fulfilling this one simple thing?

Of course Tom has always had it in his skill set to devise something like this, but there has never been a truly good reason. We have enough troubles with teenager drivers and other idiots down here on the ground even when they are sober. Can you imagine the deadly combination of alcohol, drugs or other intoxicants and the ability to fly?

"Betcha I can buzz that 747 and pee right on their windshield!" one plastered wit would declare.

"Oh yeah? Betcha ya can't!"

Followed by a *zoom*, a *thunk*, a "did you see that?" a scream (perhaps), and a final *splat*!

Don't believe such idiots exist? **This photo is real!**

And so, perhaps it is best that things have waited until future days —whenever those might be!

Victor Appleton II

CHAPTER 1 /
HOLLYWOOD IS CALLING

TOM SWIFT, twenty-four year old inventor, spun around at the sound of footsteps crossing the hard concrete floor of the underground hangar where his *Sky Queen*—the triple-decker jet aircraft that had been one of Tom's first major inventions—had been sitting, idle, for nearly nine months.

He stepped to the door between his underground lab and small office in time to see his best friend, and brother-in-law, Bud Barclay, approaching.

What first grabbed Tom's attention was the manner in which Bud was walking across the concrete. It was more a periodic staccato than footfalls, and now he could see why.

Bud was attempting to tap dance across the floor, holding a thin aluminum rod in front of him as if it were a cane.

"Very good, flyboy, but you'll never make it in the revival of Masters of the Tap!"

Bud stopped and came walking over. "Hey, skipper! So, what's this rumor I hear about Swift Enterprises going all Hollywood?"

Enterprises, the four-mile-square research, experimental, production and airfield facility in the north of New York, was owned by Tom's family, run by his father, Damon Swift, and currently was the place of work for Tom, Bud, and Tom's sister, Sandy Swift-Barclay. Both Bud and Sandy were pilots with Bud being one of their top test pilots while Sandy split her time between working in the Communications department and providing test flights for prospective purchasers in any of the eleven aircraft currently in the company's production schedule.

Most recently Tom and a number of other Enterprises employees had been engaged in developing a team of nanobots to perform surgery on Mr. Swift who had developed an inoperable brain tumor.

That had come to a happy ending a few weeks earlier when the operation succeeded and Damon had been able to address a group of reporters and doctors, all of whom initially seemed intent on having the younger Swift brought up on charges for operating without a medical license. Some even thought he may have killed his own father in a botched operation. Once they saw that Damon not only lived through the radical surgery but was recovering extremely well, all had gone away grousing but grudgingly admitting there might be something to come from this barely charted field.

"We are not getting into the Hollywood thing, Bud. What we are doing, and by 'we' I guess I mean 'I,' is trying to make real a little something that has been a staple of good and bad science fiction for decades and decades, but has never been successfully realized, or not by much."

"What's that?"

Tom squinted his left eye and turned his head slightly. "If you won't laugh, because I know how you feel about such things given your family's little problem last year, I'm working on a viable jetpack."

Bud groaned. He had indeed had a small problem the previous year. A company his father invested heavily in out in his home state of California had come up with a sleek and only slightly bulky flying backpack they hoped to sell to the public. It was a combination of a ducted fan system with a small turbine jet engine that provided both power to the pair of fans plus some additional lift and thrust.

Made from bright yellow fiberglass and enameled aluminum, a healthy man of about five-foot-eight could lift its one hundred-ten pounds and walk to a takeoff point. The jet could spin up in under one minute and the takeoff checklist was mostly handled by a small onboard computer.

All in all, Bud had approached the opportunity to take a one-week leave of absence from Enterprises to act as test pilot in an upbeat manner. He had poured over all the specifications for weeks before he flew west; once he arrived on site everything checked out.

His three days of low, tethered hovering runs demonstrated how the built-in gyroscopic systems took nearly all the balance and weight distribution tasks over freeing the pilot to only handle the basic flying.

And, his attitude had only been made more happy when his first untethered flight—over water and at just twenty feet—had terminated in a light touchdown back at the launch platform.

The problem came the following day when, at a height of about five hundred feet, the jet turbine had snapped from its mounts, slammed into the back of his protective shield knocking the wind out of him, and the entire rig plummeted to the ground.

It was only about seventy feet above the hard surface when Bud's parachute deployed fully and he nearly slammed into the ground. He didn't exactly walk away and had to wear a clamshell cast on his right foot for five weeks while five tiny bones mended.

On arriving back in Shopton the evening of the crash, Bud declared, "Never, never, never again will I climb into anything built on a shoestring budget or by anyone other that the Swift companies!" That was a year ago.

Now, Tom pulled out a folder about an inch thick and slid it across the desk. On the cover it stated:

SKY MARSHAL 7

(Strictest Secret Movie Treatment, Monograph Studios)

...followed by a couple paragraphs of legal warnings telling whomever found or possessed the folder they would be subject to a one hundred-million dollar lawsuit if they gave out any information or lost the folder or stole the idea.

"Take a look at the top page inside and then study the next five or so," Tom suggested and took his seat again.

Bud settled in on the office sofa to read. The more he read the more his face turned into a grin and then a full smile.

"So, Hollywood has come knocking on your door to get involved in a try at reviving the old movie serials of the nineteen-forties and fifties, huh? And these space ranger flying detectives they mention do not fly around in airplanes I'm guessing."

"Nope. Take a listen to this phone call I got yesterday just about the time that package arrived." Tom pressed a key on his keyboard.

"*Hello, Mr. Swift. My name is Howard Gardner and I'm Senior Producer and head of acquisitions for Monograph Studios out here in sunny, Hollywood, California,*" came an overeager voice probably more used to spouting promotional drivel than talking to humans.

"Hello, Mr. Gardner. Before you go any further I need to be certain you wanted to speak to me and not my father. I'm Tom Swift."

"*Just the rascal I'm looking for. Listen, Monograph makes a lot of movies, and as our saying goes, 'We Make 'Em Better!' So, the reason I called today is to see if I can get some of your very valuable time. You are going to get a package from us today with a very valuable piece of property we are developing. That's movie talk for a script. I don't need to tell you how hush-hush it all is, so don't go squawking it around, if you know what I mean.*"

"Yes, I understand, Mr. Gardner, but please if you can get to the point. I have a package here from your studio that came this morning that our Security people opened but I also have a great number of things on my calendar today so I was not going to look inside until tomorrow."

"*Oh, that'd be a big mistake, Tommy boy. I can call you Tommy, can't I?*"

"No, I'd rather you did not do that. Tom will be fine."

"*Right. Sorry. So, anyways, we are going to be making a great and epic new movie serial, just like your granddad used to watch. We're calling it the name you will find on the folder in that package. And, please don't say it out loud. So, here's the thing; it harkens back to the days of heroes and villains who battle on the ground, under the sea and in the air. That's where you come in. We can get a good grip on the land and water bit, but we're having a bit of a problem with the air...*"

Tom pressed the key again to shut off the recorded conversation. "So, I wanted you to hear that to establish we *are* talking Hollywood and some man who is all 'used-car-salesman' and very little straight forward businessman."

"Sounds like one of those old time hawkers at a carnival trying to sell snake oil or some sugar pills to cure the rheumatiz." Bud cackled like a crazy old man.

Tom smirked. "Right. Here's the idea, though. They supposedly want to do things right and say they have the budget for it. They are building two submarine models, I think he said to quarter scale, and are renting two full-sized ones from the old Russian Navy. Not running, of course, but for the exterior shots. He told me they want to do the air scenes using actual flying backpacks. He seems to think the more flames coming out the better but we had a discussion about burning the pilot's legs."

Now, Bud's face showed the battle his brain was having. On the one hand Tom was proposing a flying backpack about which he knew nothing. On the other had Tom was proposing a *Swift-built* flying backpack that he knew nothing about, but that was sounding *very* intriguing.

He took a deep breath and let out a heavy sigh.

"And, they don't want a man or mannequin all dressed up hanging from the sort of wires they can erase in editing?"

"They do not," Tom told him. "In fact, the scope of what he tells me his cinematographer and camera operator want wouldn't allow a crane or even a helicopter up above and just outside of the shots. Also blue or green screen is out because he 'hates that look.'" Tom made finger quotes in the air to emphasize the last words.

"Okay. Tell Budworth all about it and let's see if I get the willies or my little heart goes pitta-pat."

Tom motioned his friend to come over to the drafting table and to take a seat.

Once he also sat he said, "I've got absolutely no idea where to start, Bud. What I have is this," and he slid over an open book. On the left page was a beautifully rendered color illustration of a man wearing what looked like the front end of an art deco steam locomotive on his head, with a backpack spewing flames and smoke out behind.

Bud spent more than a minute admiring the sleek steampunk appearance of the Hollywood jet pack art.

"Jetz! And not in the sense of jets inside the backpack," he stated finally. "That's beautiful. A bit too, well, *small* for one thing to be of much use, but I remember watching an old B movie serial about a guy named Colby or Cody who wore one of those. More of a bullet head helmet, but same idea."

"Yes. That would be the *Commando Cody* serials. This new one is a modern take on that. I've had a look at one old episode on line to see just what the Hollywood people seem to consider their target. And, you are right. I figure I could get maybe thirty seconds of flight time down in this size unless I use repelatrons, and that just isn't going to happen."

"Okay," Bud said almost sounding like he agreed. "But, why not?"

"No real lift control if they are on the back of the wearer for one. The flyer's body would want to find a balance point and swivel and bend to reach it throwing off all attempts at balance. For another thing, unless I created a full avionics system with computer, how could anyone be expected to make the constant adjustments to what the repelatrons push against."

"And my guess is that stopping would be a real bitch," Bud said.

Tom nodded. "Right. Even so, all that doesn't get to the massive power issues, meaning that sort of flying pack is out!"

"So, what's in?"

The inventor shook his head. "I'm not certain. For starters I don't know what era they need this to be built for. If it's still for a World War II era movie, I'll have to back out with a polite version of, 'You are crazy.' If I've convinced them on a futuristic movie world then perhaps I can build something like an exoskeleton with the necessary power, lift, thrust and maneuverability they need. Oh, and duration. One shot he intends to get will be over eight minutes long!"

"How long do you want to go for? Flight time, I mean."

Tom thought a moment. "At the very least, ten minutes and maybe double that to cover multiple takes without refueling or recharging."

Bud nodded but looked concerned. "Bud has a question, professor. Most movies that require robots, flying across planets, and other whiz-bang things get done in what I believe they call post editing. Special effects and things like that. So, why not for this movie?"

"The producer wants to go back to realism. He hates the artificial look of computer-generated video and has sworn his new movie will use none of it. That leaves him with trying to come up with a flying backpack that evidently features in about twenty percent of all scenes."

"And you can't give him that in the retro look, huh?"

Tom shook his head. "Not really. For one, look at the exposed body parts. Can you image taking a bird or even rain or hail right in the throat at several hundred miles per hour? Or the turbulence coming up under the pilot's chin at any sort of speed? It'd rip the helmet off, and maybe even more!"

"Ouch!"

"Yes. Ouch, choke, bleed and all that. This jet pack is going to have to be much larger in order to lift anyone. And, I'm still not onto any fuel supply that might last more than perhaps ten minutes. Possibly less. Oh, and can you spot the other problem?"

Bud went back to the illustration and looked it over. Then he came over to look at a picture the inventor had sitting on his desk. A moment later he tapped his finger on the page.

"Upright!" he declared swinging around to point at the larger picture, stating, "Not upright. Right?"

"Right. Oh, maybe if the man or woman flying is racing in one direction, but aerodynamically the human body doesn't give much lift. In some way I have to figure out how to get power pushing the flyer along plus enough of it going downward to give constant lift. Even then I fear the body's tendency to relax and sort of droop in the middle is going to ruin the effect. I mean, have you ever tried to do that exercise thing called the plank? Sixty seconds and your stomach muscles want to knot up!"

The flyer shook his head. "Tried it. Made the mistake of then going for sit-ups. It took Enterprises' two trainers and Hank Sterling sitting on me to get me flattened back out. Never, never, never again." He shook his head with conviction.

"Well, my guess is that anyone flying without some very stiff support system is going to have their legs drooping and also bending at the waist, all throwing off the balance and stability. If he really wants realism, then I believe Mr. Gardner is going to have to accept the realities of what such a flight system will need to include."

"Great, but I've got to run. Count me in on all the fun!"

"Oops," Tom said looking at his watch. "I have to go as well. I'm late for a meeting with dad."

Once he got to the office the two Swifts often shared, Tom described many of the things he and Bud had discussed. Mr. Swift nodded his agreement to all of them, but added one of his own.

"You may need to include an air supply for any pilot heading up very far. Actually," Damon Swift said as he watched his son's face to see if they were on the same page, "I'm seeing that the entire suit will need to be sealed for fast flights or there would be tearing and ripping of anything loose or open. And that, definitely, will require that you provide air."

"That's not on my initial list," Tom admitted, "but I would hope I might have thought about that sooner or later. Glad you are on the ball so I don't have to put things to chance!" He grinned at his father who returned it with a smile.

"Happy to be of any help, Son. So, do you have a good feeling about this? I mean from both a viability and company standpoint."

Tom shrugged. "I believe so, but there are still a lot of unknowns. I might need to head to California to talk with the two main men on this and see what they want and what they are willing to accept as the right thing to do."

"Let me know if I can do anything," his father offered before Tom headed back to his lab.

Bud and Sandy came to dinner at Tom and Bashalli's house. While the ladies played with Tom's young son, Bart, after dinner, Tom and Bud sat to one side of the spacious living room quietly talking about the Hollywood project.

"I don't know what you two are discussing," Sandy stated in a loud voice after about ten minutes, "but if you believe for a minutes Bashi and I will let you two head out to Hollywood without us, think again!"

Tom replied, "While I'd love to bring you two in on this, it actually is a confidential matter. So, Bud and I are going outside to talk about it and remove the temptation for you two to lean this way and open your ears!"

Both young men went over and kissed their wives before heading out the front door.

"Well!" Sandy harrumphed as the door closed. "Can you believe that? As if we'd *ever* listen in on a private conversation."

They sat there looking at each other for a few seconds before they both broke out in gales of laughter.

Outside, Tom and Bud ambled down to the sidewalk. They stopped and the inventor asked, "Are you up to a quick out and back trip to Los Angeles and a meeting with these movie guys?"

Bud brightened. "So, you're going to take the project on?"

With a small shake of his head, Tom told him, "I'm not sure, yet. It sounds like it might be fun, and it may even have practical uses later on, but I need more info than Mr. Gardner seemed willing to part with over the phone."

"Okay. I understand the need for a meeting, but what sort of uses for that pack do you have in mind? Other than this potential Hollywood blockbuster... or bust."

"I'm thinking about the dream for personal flying systems that has been around since the mid nineteen hundreds. Those movie serials helped get people thinking about them, and then the several false starts that were made up until about a dozen years ago when the last company to try went bankrupt. Even if personal flight systems are more dream that practicality, there have been several attempts to make jet packs for Army troops to use in areas too dense or dangerous to try to move across on foot."

"Oh, yeah. And there's always to need for police to follow criminals. I can see them soaring over Central Park..."

"Right. Helicopters are fine, but they have limitations and restrictions. And, they announce their presence. Well, that's future stuff, but for now I want to call our new West Coast friends and suggest a face-to-face for tomorrow. Can your schedule handle you being gone a day?"

Bud took out his new cell phone, a unit being built and sold by the Swift Construction Company. It featured a lot of high-technology he was still getting used to.

"Yo, phono?" The screen came on with a question mark. "If I have anything scheduled for tomorrow, see if it can re-set for the following day."

A few seconds later a pleasant voice told him, "You had two meetings scheduled for tomorrow afternoon. One with Hank Sterling and the other with Sandra Swift Barclay. I have notifying them both of the change."

Bud's eyes grew large as he tried to stammer out the command, "Don't call Sandy," but it was too late. The front door flew open and his wife was standing there, hands on hips. "How dare you have that darned yakkity phone person cancel our lunch, Bud?"

Giving Tom a rueful grin, he hastened to the front porch to explain. Tom could see him gesturing and trying to explain things. Soon, Sandy looked over her husband's head at her brother.

"Jerk!" she stated before turning and closing the door behind her.

Bud came back, slowly to Tom.

"Tomorrow is the anniversary of the day she and I first met, skipper. It's something that fell off my RADAR years ago, but I guess she holds it to be a sacred day, or something. What am I going to do?"

Tom laughed. "You go ahead and reschedule that meeting with Hank to tomorrow, clear the following day for our trip, and I'll go set things right with my sister. Just follow my lead."

When Bud came back inside three minutes later, Sandy flung herself into his arms. "Oh, Bud, Can you forgive me?"

As he stammered his forgiveness, Bud looked at Tom who just stood there smiling innocently.

"Tom just told me he goofed on the date and you didn't want to disappoint him. But, since he said it was really the day *after* tomorrow, that's okay. I'm sorry I lost it. Forgive me?"

She leaned in and gave him a big kiss.

"Sure. It was a goof all around; I told the phone to look at the wrong day."

"And," Tom added, "I can attest to the fact he really tried to override the phone but it was just too fast and contacted you in a split second. Maybe I need to reprogram things to give people a minute or so to change their minds?"

"If you want to keep my Bud out of trouble, you'd better do that, Tomonomo."

"It gets my almost undivided attention the day after Bud and I get back from California. And..." he said looking from his wife to his sister, "I promise that the next trip out there will include the two of you. If only there were some nice, older women who would want to babysit Bart. Hmmmm?'

Bud grinned. "Yeah, something like a couple grandmothers!"

The four of them laughed and little Bart giggled, stating, "Gramma!" That met with his approval as well.

CHAPTER 2 /
COULD YOU PERHAPS CHANGE THAT?

TWO MORNINGS later, Tom and Bud met on the tarmac above the underground hangar of the *Sky Queen*.

"Been quite a while since you had the old girl out for a spin. Think she'll remember who we are," Bud joked. The *Sky Queen*— Tom's first major invention and the world's first triple-decker aircraft—had been a staple of his flying adventures since he turned eighteen. Now, more than six years later and with enough miles on her to circle the globe at least twenty-nine times, the Flying Lab was starting to show her age, at least on the inside. Outwardly she was still a gleaming white thing of beauty.

Her sister aircraft, the *Super Queen*, was several years newer, faster and more versatile with its ability to use custom pods filled with mission-specific equipment, laboratories, and even field hospital units. Both ships could take off and land vertically using repelatron dish drives, both featured nuclear power generators to provide safe and consistent power for all systems, and both were surprisingly easy to fly.

They also could both reach supersonic speeds creating no noticeable sonic "booms" in the process partly due to design features and partly from the use of Tom's silentennas, or "sonic boom traps" as Bud called them.

But, the *Sky Queen* had older instrumentation and older amenities. And, as Bud stated, she had been parked for quite a while.

"If you think of her as a woman, then try not to think of her as somebody like Sandy. If she is like your wife—my sister—the fact that we've sort of ignored her will bite us on the behinds, and hard!" Tom told the flyer.

With a small alarm buzzer coming from the nearby small entrance building and then barely a whisper from the mechanism, the large flat doors covering the deep hangar dropped down a foot then began to move aside. Before they parted, railings popped up from the ground to surround the area, keeping anyone not paying attention from stumbling into the nearly eighty-foot-deep pit.

As the giant airship rose, a technician who had been cleaning her windscreen could be seen hanging from the right-hand side window.

"Hey, skipper! Hey, Bud!" he called out as he finished wiping the copilot's front window and the jet neared the top of its ride.

Without warning, and to the horror of the two young men, the tech lost his grip, suddenly slipped out of the window and began to tumble downward.

Tom wanted to rush forward but both the railing and the open pit stopped him. Bud let out a strangled cry of anguish as the man disappeared down into the hole. There was a thudding noise followed by a moan and a deep oath as the elevator rose to ground level and stopped.

There, lying across the top of a pile of what appeared to be empty cardboard boxes, was the technician. He cursed again and raised himself up to a sitting position.

"Of all the boneheaded junk I could do—" he chided himself before turning to look at the startled and speechless pair, "Oh, hi, skipper. Bud. Sorry about this. I sort of lost my grip."

Tom now stepped over the descending safety railing followed closely by Bud. As he ran to the man he tapped a small pin under his collar. The TeleVoc pin was a combination communication device and security measure that all Swift employees wore. It used silent communication technologies that relied on brainwaves and jaw and muscle movements to be translated into a simulation of the caller's voice. He mouthed the words, "Doc Simpson," as he reached the bottom of the now partly collapsed pile.

His call was answered as silently as it was made, and he described the situation. Doc "Voc'd" back stating that he was on his way.

"Stay still, Robbie," Tom ordered as the man appeared ready to slide off the pile. "Doc is coming to check you out and doesn't want you to injure yourself any more than you might have."

"But, I—" the man began to argue but saw Tom's determined look and stopped. "Right. Sorry, again, and I'll stay put. Didn't mean to give you two a scare."

Doctor Greg Simpson, Enterprises' chief physician, came on the run along with one of his nurses. They cautiously climbed onto the boxes to get to Robbie's side. A quick check showed that the man suffered nothing more serious than a bleeding abrasion on his left elbow from hitting and scraping it on the boxes.

"Lucky for you these boxes broke your fall and nothing else!"

"Lucky they were empty and not full of canned goods," Bud called up to them.

Doc had the nurse apply an antiseptic cream and a gauze bandage to protect the wound, and then they left to go back the Infirmary while Tom and Bud helped the technician to get off the pile and onto his feet.

"Go ahead and take a couple hours off, Robbie," Tom said. "You may have come through with just a scrape, but there can be serious after effects from all the adrenaline that shot through your body," Tom told him sensing an argument coming. "Bud and I have both been there so there is nothing to argue about. I might be a bit of a mother hen on this, but I've been injured enough times to know that once that adrenaline rush calms down, you might find that you have some major pains. Thanks, by the way, for cleaning the windscreens."

"I appreciate it, Tom," the tech told him as he handed his wiping cloth to the inventor and walked away with only a slight limp.

"Clarey the Klutz," Bud muttered after the man was out of earshot. "That man has taken more little spills and slips than Zimby Cox has crash landed airplanes!"

Tom had to snort a little at that thought.

Zimby was another of the Swift's test pilots—as well as an accomplished submariner and astronaut—who had, in his seven years with Enterprises, walked way from no fewer than eight crash landings of experimental aircraft, or ones that had been sabotaged by Tom and Damon Swift's enemies. One time had been at the hands of an inexperienced pilot who froze at the wrong moment.

But, he had survived them all with barely more damage than Robbie just received from his slip and fall.

As they entered the jet Tom patted the wall of the lower hull lovingly. "We're back again, old girl. Time to spread your wings." He tapped a code into a pad next to the hatch that turned on lights throughout the ship.

The two men climbed the first set of steep and narrow stairs to the middle deck and then moved forward fifty feet to the next set. At the top, now just thirty feet behind the cockpit, Tom noticed the woeful state of her carpeting. There were several tears in the durable floor covering and at least one spot where it had pulled completely away from the wall.

He looked around and could see many other small things that needed attending to. There were a few places where the movement of large equipment had scuffed the wall panels, one burnt out light—which Tom marveled at as all lights were long-life LEDs—and a missing identification plaque on one door.

If there is this amount of stuff in a few feet, I really wonder how much there is throughout the ship! Tom thought as he and Bud headed to the cockpit.

"Bud? Remind me to ask dad if I can put some money into a refurbishment. The old girl needs some sprucing up."

As they entered the cockpit an alarm went off and an outline of the aircraft popped up on one of the monitors. A flashing red dot could be seen at the place where they had entered the jet.

Tom was about to slip into the pilot's seat and turn on the video surveillance system when they both heard the unmistakable sounds of a man singing—slightly warbly and a tiny bit off key—the old western ballad, "Home on The Range."

"Chow!" they said together and then laughed.

Charles "Chow" Winkler had met Tom, and Tom had met Bud, when the two boys were barely sixteen out in New Mexico as Damon Swift was finishing construction of the Swift's nuclear research facility, the Citadel. The then fifty-year-old former chuck wagon cook had taken a liking to Tom immediately, and so had Tom to the colorful cook.

When the time came a few weeks later to return to Shopton and Swift Enterprises, Chow had practically begged to be allowed to come along.

Since that time he had come along on many of Tom and Bud's adventures on the ground, under the seas and even into space! He was a veteran of all forms of travel and made new friends wherever he went as readily as he collected interesting—or 'strange!' as Bud put it—recipes.

His cowboy boots clomped up the steps behind them and he called out, "Hey, Buckaroos! I hear as you're goin' out to Californy in a bit an' forgot ta invite the old Chow Hound along. What the heck are you two gonna eat if I don't come along?" He now entered the cockpit.

To emphasize his readiness to provide food, he rattled the large grocery bag he carried with his right arm.

"Not trying to leave you out on purpose," Tom explained. "It's just that we're going out early so we can have a mid-morning meeting there, and then head back home in time for dinner. I guess we planned to grab something quick on the way back to the airport. But, if you're packed and ready, come on along! Great to have you with us."

As soon as the giant jet took off and leveled out at forty-five thousand feet, Chow came forward again with a couple mugs of hot coffee and some sticky cinnamon rolls.

"Got a little snack fer ya. Enjoy! I'll have lunch waitin' once ya get back. Think that'll be around one or so?"

"Probably," Tom stated. "Why?"

"Wahl, I got an old acquaintance who's got a friend who's got a store that sells the kind of shirts like I used ta wear. You know the ones."

The boys most certainly did. Chow had been known for his gaudy western shirts. Many of them features outlandish colors schemes and designs. The man had been rightfully proud of his collection, but over the past couple years had lost a lot of weight so very few of them fit any more. One-by-one, they had been cleaned, folded up, and stored in plastic bags by Chow's one-time girlfriend, now his wife, Wanda.

"Wanda okay with that, Chow?" Bud asked by way of a little tease. "Will Enterprises' vision insurance cover her in case of eyestrain?"

"*Okay*? Now you lissen here, Buddy boy. Ya ask if she's okay with it? Shoot. She's the one who told me ta get out and find something spiffier than the white and blue shirts I've been wearin' lately," Chow replied. "Wanda fell fer me in my sweetest old shirts and sorta wishes she was a sewer so as ta take in some of the shirts I already got. But, next best thing is ta' have me buy somethin' new. I only ask about time 'cause I need about an hour ta taxi to this hombre's store and get back."

"Take all the time you need, Chow," Tom told him. "Our meeting should run at least an hour and the ride to and from their offices will be maybe a half hour or more each way."

Grinning from ear to ear, the cook headed back down the corridor and to his second deck kitchen.

"It may make Chow's day, but I'm just getting back my full color vision," Bud stated. He had always been the chief tease in the older man's life over everything from Chow's choice of shirts to his outlandish foods. But, it was a loving relationship between the two men and neither took serious insult in the words or actions of the other.

They landed at Los Angeles International—the only airport in the extended metropolitan area with enough ground room to park such a large jet for the duration of their visit—just three hours later.

As with many other parts of the *Queen* these days, the hangar at the rear of the fuselage that normally carried small aircraft or even one of Tom's Atomicars, work was required on the huge airtight doors. After hundreds of opening and closing cycles and a few mishaps inside that put strain on the doors, the mechanism was in need of replacement, and so they brought no transportation of their own.

The two boys took a taxi toward their destination passing through Inglewood and Culver City before reaching the offices of Monograph close to the town of Westwood.

"So much for Hollywood!" Bud said as they looked around the area. Nearby sat UCLA and the Pauley Pavilion but the offices of

Monograph were located in a small industrial area a few blocks to the south.

Their meeting was only with the director, a slight man with a pencil-thin mustache and a bored attitude as if he felt the forthcoming project beneath his notice.

"I fail to see the relevance of this meeting," he told them. "We want one thing and you are telling us you will only provide another. I think we shall go elsewhere with our little project that you are unable to produce and you can go home with nothing to show for this. How's that sound, sonny?"

Tom sensed Bud's rising anger and tapped sideways with the toe of his shoe into his friend's foot, a signal to just cool down and say nothing.

"If that is the way you feel about it, Mr. McManus, there is nothing more to do now. While I wish you nothing but good luck, I also fear that your 'my way or no way' attitude will end up getting a good stunt person injured... or worse." He stood up as did Bud, still clenching his right fist in anger.

Now, McManus looked shocked and even a little fearful as the look on Bud's face finally registered. He was used to having what he thought of as "mere contractors and underlings" quiver at the thought of losing out on a lucrative Hollywood contract and this attitude caught him off guard. It caused him to do something he'd never done before.

"Wait! What are you doing? You can't leave us like this! You're supposed to negotiate with me now and then give in!"

Tom leaned over and placed his palms flat on the table they had been sitting around. His voice was calm and even.

"Mr. McManus. I explained the impossibility of making what you want and gave you a good and workable alternative. You've insulted me, demeaned our valuable time and called me 'Sonny,' something that even my own father never utters. Let me remind you that we did not approach you to do this project; you and your partner approached Swift Enterprises. Oh, and we do *not* negotiate. We do listen to constructive input and adjust our designs and contracts accordingly, where possible, but we never allow ourselves to be bullied or threatened. Especially not over something this small. My time—my company's time—is far too valuable to waste it on people like you. We are leaving and hope to not hear another thing about this from you or your producer, Mr. Gardner." He stood back up but paused.

"Oh, and here is the script Mr. Gardner provided." He dropped the folder on the table. "I guarantee that no copies were made and that nobody other than myself, my father and our production manager have looked at it. We will say nothing to anyone about it.

Good day!"

He and Bud left the room to the gasping sounds of the director whose mouth had completely dried up and was trying to beg them to come back.

They arrived at the airport only ninety-minutes after departing, but it had been enough time for Chow to return from his shopping, now clad in an eye-hurting bright red shirt with silver threads outlining a cow and a prairie dog on the front and a man swinging a lariat astride a longhorn steer on the back.

Before takeoff he served them a meal of chicken Kiev—a rolled chicken breast with herbed butter oozing inside surrounded by a crisp breadcrumb crust—and fresh asparagus.

No sooner had Tom picked up his fork than his cell phone rang. Motioning Bud to go ahead and eat, he walked down the corridor as he answered the call.

Bud and Chow exchanged looks, rolled their eyes as if this was just what they expected, and then heard Tom speaking in low tones. When he came back five minutes later it was with a huge smile on his face.

"That was Mr. Gardner. He heard that his director had basically dismissed us and went through the roof. McManus is out of the picture, figuratively and literally, and Gardner is begging us to come back and explain what we have to him. So, let's eat a nice and leisurely lunch before we go back."

Once they had eaten, and Chow joined them part way through, they hailed another taxi and returned to the offices of the studio.

There, Tom patiently explained everything to the producer who listened, nodded at all the appropriate spots, and then asked the crucial question.

"If we update the scripts so this takes place something like today or a few years from now, can you build us a flying suit that will really work and knock people's socks right off their feet?"

Tom nodded, saying, "I need to reiterate this flying pack will not ever have visible flames coming out the back, but I see nearly nothing other than possibly funding that would get in the way, Mr. Gardner, of coming up with a real flying device a good pilot will be able to fly. I have no idea what your budget is, and I'm guessing that renting a couple old submarines and making believable miniatures and all of that aren't cheap, so my only question is will you have enough money left over?"

Gardner got a gleam in his eyes. "As long as we're not talking more than two million, the budget can cover it. Just. Are we in trouble?"

Tom shook his head. "No. Our preliminary figures point to

about three-quarters of that for R&D, and constructing the first suit will cover the remainder. If you need more suits, they will come at a price of about half-a-million each."

The look in the producer's eyes did not diminish. "I can do this with one suit so long as it can fly for up to a half hour at a time and then be reset or whatever you call it within a half hour. Are we still on the same track?"

Tom nodded.

Gardner held out a hand and the inventor shook it.

"It would appear that Monograph Studios is about to blow the movie industry right on its keaster!" he said gleefully.

CHAPTER 3 /

SIDE TRIP TO VENUS

TOM NO sooner plopped down into one of the comfortable chairs in the conference area of the shared office the following morning than the door opened and his father entered.

"Well, the prodigal son, Son," Damon Swift said with a smile as he poured himself a cup of coffee. Although he still walked with a slight limp, his recovery from his recent brain tumor and the life-saving surgery Tom had performed using nanotechnology was coming along at a remarkable pace. Mentally he was about one hundred percent, and that pleased Tom. "You've been a little difficult to reach the past two days. Care to share what's going on?"

Tom grinned but blushed a little. "Sorry, Dad. I told you about that Hollywood producer, Howard Gardner, and his director, Colin McManus, and their request for us to build a real flying suit for his movie?" Damon nodded. "Anyway, I've hit on a couple ideas only neither of them fit with what Gardner sent me in that script outline. He was asking for anachronistic and fire spewing and all I believe we can deliver is futuristic and really techno-infused."

He told his father about the trip, the issues with the now-fired director and Gardner's agreement to taking a futuristic path with his movie serial.

"Can you think of anything I need to add to my list? I've already got about fifty things on it but have a nagging feeling I'm missing a few others."

Damon shook his head as he crossed the room to take a seat behind his desk.

"Not really. I might give it a few brain cycles tonight, but as of this minute my brain is fighting with my stomach over the German probe we helped get into orbit four months ago."

"The German probe?"

"Yes. Their Venus probe. It's different from the Japanese one we did a couple years ago, by the way. While you were concentrating on my brain troubles, Red Jones, Hank Sterling and a small team of technicians took their new combination atmosphere spectrograph and MASER-based terrain mapping satellite out to high Earth orbit of about ten thousand miles. Anyway, it appears that they lost communication with it just as it rounded our planet to go into its six hundredth orbit. That was the one where the rocket booster was supposed to fire and speed it all up for its trip to Venus. They are in a real panic, and I can't say I blame them. What I can't handle is their demand that since we put the thing into the orbital launch position they insisted on, they are saying it is our duty and responsibility to go out there and find it." He made a sour face.

"Two immediate questions: one, why use MASER and not something like RADAR for the mapping; and second, why did it sit in orbit this long?"

Damon now chuckled although somewhat ruefully. "MASER because they believe the microwave technology will have better scanning results through Venus' dense and hot atmosphere. As for the delay, it was all planned so they could complete the computer programming and upload it when things were ready. That way they planned to do the finish work in orbit before sending it out. Now, something has happened and they want us to be involved in fixing it."

He raised one eyebrow and shook his head.

"But," Tom said, bothered and launching himself up from his chair, "how the heck can they put the blame on us? I mean, they insisted on that positioning. And getting it there early before they were ready. Right? What are they thinking?"

Damon shook his head. "They are thinking that they do not want to take responsibility. They are thinking that if they squawk loud enough that the world will jump to their aide. Plus, I believe they are attempting to cover up for any mistakes they know they made but hoped it would all go well if they just closed their eyes, put their fingers in their collective ears and began humming their national anthem!"

"Do they want us to bring it back to Earth?"

Damon shook his head. "Not really. I believe they want it repaired and delivered to Venus for them. So nice of them to ask us for *that* service before they make the final payment on the thing."

Tom looked at his father who seemed about ten years older than he had the evening before when he and Bashalli—Tom's wife of nearly three years—had dinner with Damon and Anne Swift.

"When do you want me to leave," the young inventor asked.

Damon chuckled. "Am I that obvious and transparent?"

Tom smiled but shook his head. "Nope, but I've known you for, oh, twenty-four years and about eight months, so I kind of know what to expect. Anyway, you were going to suggest that I take the *Challenger* out and see what might have happened. Correct?"

"I used to drive my father crazy when I second guessed him as a teenager. He hated it. I suppose that's why I left him alone to nearly drive the original Swift Company into the ground. I just want you to know how proud I am to have you watching my back."

Tom's face beamed.

"There is one more thing. Since the satellite went dark, there is little tracking data. Situated that far out it is hard to find without any radio beacon to track. It won't quite be a needle in a haystack situation, but it could take a few days to find it, secure it, and see if things can be repaired."

"What if it was hit by something? If it is damaged or even destroyed, the Germans have to understand that we can't go back in time and make it not happen!"

Of course, they both knew that Tom actually had traveled back in time, once, but that had been through his Yesterday Machine, a device based on an anomaly found in another solar system that had subsequently been returned when it was determined to only send things backward in time a few seconds shy of twenty-four hours, and the object making the trip disintegrated on returning to its proper place in time.

"Do we repair it in place if we can find it, bring it back here, or just nudge it back to the orbit they intended and let them worry about any damage?"

They discussed what a search and possible rescue mission would entail. That included a possible delivery trip to Venus. Even after he nabbed the satellite, and assuming it was in any shape to be taken to Venus, the trip was not something to be accomplished in a day.

With the *Challenger* now outfitted with a better system for overcoming the effects of inertia and the pressures of multiple-G acceleration, it would be possible to get the ship up to a constant acceleration of about 3-Gs and hold it there while those inside only felt as if they were experiencing 1.25-Gs of force.

As such, the ship could now make a trip to the Moon in about eighty-five minutes, rather than two-plus hours, and a voyage to Mars in five days—assuming proper planet-to-planet orientation. The Venus trip would be longer than that due to its relative orbital position about a third of the way retro, or backward, from Earth's current orbital position.

"So, you're sure that eight days will do it?"

"Eight there and seven-point-four on the way back, so assuming we remain there two days, that's under three weeks total."

It was decided that contact via the U.S. State Department was going to be necessary to ensure all parties knew what was requested and what was possible.

The answers came two days later.

Germany had softened its stance on the Swift's responsibilities and was asking for a retrieval mission if the probe had been damaged, or repositioning to Venusian orbit if it could be made functional. They also agreed that should it have failed to remain in orbit, was greatly damaged or was plummeting out of orbit, Tom was not to try to chase it down.

And, to Mr. Swift's relief, they agreed to pay for all expenses.

Tom and Bud left for Fearing Island the next morning, taking along Chow Winkler as well as Hank Sterling and Red Jones as their back-up pilots. Hank, with his extensive engineering knowledge, would be able to help Tom with any necessary repairs.

Germany was sending a specialist to meet them on the island. Their technician was the most senior person in the development team for their aerospace department and would be in a position to affect any electronic repairs.

That individual plus a crate of spare parts would be arriving by four that afternoon.

The boys met the German Air Force tri-engined jet as it taxied up to the control tower on Fearing. The first thing they saw coming from the side doorway was a shapely leg with a *very* mini-skirt only just avoiding a visual incident. It was followed by another leg of equally stunning appearance, and that was followed by Bud's almost inaudible whistle.

The woman attached was most likely in her early thirties, blonde, built as some would term it, "Like a brick outhouse," and was gorgeous.

"They sure build their stewardesses well," Bud exclaimed. He was about to say something more when he noticed the woman was waving at someone in their direction. He turned around, but there was nobody behind him. He turned back, eyes now wide. "Oh, geez. Sandy is going to go absolutely spare!"

The woman was rapidly approaching them, taking a small packet from her shoulder purse.

"Hello," she greeted the boys in a barely accented voice. "I am *Fraulein*, or rather Miss Giselle Ackerman. You are Tom Swift and you are Bud Barclay. I recognize you both from the many times you have appeared in the news." She held out her right hand to shake and her left with her ID.

Noting the look of confusion on both their faces, she laughed. "Ah. G Ackerman as the name provided and no indication of gender. I apologize for the oversight. It appears we are guilty of a lot of that these days."

Tom recovered first. "Should we address you as Miss Ackerman?"

"No. Giselle, please. Or, Gisi if we become very great friends." Her smile warmed both of them.

Bud piped up, "Tom's married to a Bash, but her full name is Bashalli. Kind of the same thing, huh?"

Her smile did not diminish as she answered, "Oh, yes. Except, as I have read your wife is Pakistani by birth so the diminutive of Bash is more of a deeply personal, intimate nature. Gisi is like Tom for Thomas or Bud for, I believe, it is Budworth?"

Tom nodded. Bud blushed realizing that he also called Tom's wife Bash. Was he being inappropriate? They once discussed this but Tom had laughed it off. Now, he was a little worried. He would ask Tom about it again at a later date.

They walked to the control tower building while she explained that the crate of her satellite spare parts would be unloaded from the back of her jet and placed into the care of the Fearing Island cargo handlers.

It was decided to take off within the hour so while Tom filled out the paperwork authorizing her as a crew member, Bud took Giselle on a little tour of the *Challenger* and let her know what to expect. By the time Tom arrived fifty minutes later, she was trying on one of the spacesuits down in the hangar of the ship.

Bud was standing with his back to her and Tom saw why. Ignoring suggestions that regular clothing be worn inside the suit, Giselle had opted to strip down to her underwear.

"It appears that *I* appear quite plainly through this suit, so I shall change into a jumpsuit before we depart," she said standing with hands on hips and not attempting to cover herself up.

The men went up to the control room to be joined by her, more conservatively clad, five minutes later.

In spite of Tom's suggestion that she not look out the huge view panes as they took off, she begged to be allowed to watch. Where many people became a little disoriented at the sight of a rapidly dwindling planet, she was in absolute awe.

"*Meine Sterne. Es ist so schön!*" she said before translating it to, "My stars. It is so beautiful!"

There was little to do during the voyage out so Tom and Bud agreed to show her how to fly the ship rather than join in a game of poker with Red, Hank and Chow.

"I did some flying when I was in the German Air Force," she told them, "but only supply helicopters. Though," she said considering an inner thought, "I first had to get my multi-engine license."

She proved to be an incredible student. She also, on noticing both of their discomfort at her skimpy skirt, left for a few moments to change into a standard issue Swift company jumpsuit. She wore it hanging loose from the waist up, still wearing her form-fitting blouse.

It only served to accentuate her curvy body inside.

The satellite was located on RADAR about two hours out. It had slipped into an orbit nearly a thousand miles closer to the Earth, but appeared to be in good physical shape on first inspection.

Hank and Bud left the ship to retrieve it, taking one of Tom's MultiCorders—his incredible hand-held multi-sensor device—using the Geiger counter module to check for radiation. Other than the expected background levels, the package seemed to present no dangers, so it was dragged into the hangar on the lower level.

Giselle ran it through self-diagnostics and then stood back, hands on hips and head tilted to the right.

"*Dummköpfes!*" she practically spit out and walked all around the eight-foot-wide unit. "*Für die Liebe Gottes, somepone sollten aufgehängt!*" She turned to Tom. "The idiots left out a very important safety override unit when they did the final assembly. Fortunately, I brought a replacement in that crate."

An hour later she re-ran the diagnostics and the satellite reported it was one hundred percent operational.

Back in the control room she told Tom and Bud, "I believe that the missing module was not a mistake, but possible sabotage. You see, the satellite was designed to falsely report full function status continually for the period required to finish and upload the operating software. Otherwise we would have been fielding damage reports every five minutes from it. Somebody obviously knew it would take until just before it left orbit for anything to be noted as wrong. The missing part would have shut that off letting us see the problems."

"Everything else is there?" Bud asked.

She nodded. "I will perform a series of deeper tests as we head to Venus, but I am positive this was the only... shall I call it an *oversight*?"

Tom suggested she make a report to her government while he readied the *Challenger* for the trip. They left orbit fifty minutes later. Things were uneventful all the way to the broiling-hot planet, and the launch of the satellite, accomplished by Giselle and Tom with a slight shove from the deck outside the hangar, went off without a hitch.

The ship remained in orbit while Tom took observations for a full day before heading back to Earth. The satellite was left in standby mode and would remain such for two additional days while the sensors ran tests and calibrations.

As the appropriate time came she gave Tom a special radio frequency and the unlock codes which he sent to the probe.

When the satellite failed to report anything, she blanched and began muttering words Tom believed would sear anyone's ears were they translated into English.

"We must return to fix things," she told him. The trepidation evident in her voice spoke of her being unsure if he would agree to a return and extension of their trip.

Tom shrugged and told Bud to radio back to Enterprises to tell them about a five or more day delay.

Ten minutes later he slowed the giant ship and started a wide, curved trajectory to return them to Venus.

The search for the missing probe began.

For the first full day heading back they detected nothing in orbit and feared it had crashed. Then, a brief squeak came through the speakers but disappeared a second later.

"Was that it?" Tom inquired as he sat forward and tried adjusting the radio.

Giselle shook her head. "No. I do not believe so. I have only been told about it, but I believe that might be a natural signal put out by the incredible storms going on inside the atmosphere. Not quite lightning, but similar."

Another seven hours passed with several repeats of the squeak noise. Tom cross-checked the planet's rotation to see if they were originating from a single spot. They were not. One came from what would equate to the planet's north polar region, if it actually had one. The others were spread out in different areas.

As they came to within five million miles of the planet, Red Jones, who was piloting at that time, applied the "brakes."

Chow had his headphones on listening to some old western songs from decades past and missed the announcement to strap in and brace. Perched on a stool, his rump slid off the top and ended up contacting the hard deck three feet lower. He let out an almighty howl, but was quickly back on his feet and checking his supplies.

Later in the day he was serving them all an early dinner of turkey sandwiches with brie cheese melted inside. Giselle was speechless at the taste combination, one she had never experienced.

"When we get back I want to have you come to Germany and teach my personal chef how to cook. If you can do all these wonderful things in the depths of space, I can only imagine what you are capable of on the ground."

"Wahl, shucks, Miss Giselle. I'm mighty pleased ya like my vittles, and I do have a bit o' vacation comin', but my wife would absolutely skin me alive if'n I introduced you two and she saw what a beauty I was stuck in space with fer nearly a month."

She leaned over and brushed his cheek with her lips. "I promise I'll never let her see me," she whispered in his ear, which tickled and made him start to perspire.

Bud struggled to not laugh. It became easier when Tom got his attention and pointed at his ring finger. The flyer immediately stopped smiling.

Little more than an hour later, as the ship entered orbit five hundred miles above the hidden and seething atmosphere, the signal they hoped to find came from the speaker. It was a steady series of —•••, the Morse code equivalent of the English letter B, which Giselle earlier explained was for Bosch, the name of the company that supplied the electronics for the probe.

"That's it!" she sang out. "It is somewhere still in orbit. The signal would have changed to SOS had it not remained in the orbit where we placed it."

Or, disappeared completely, Tom thought.

They had to orbit five times around the planet before Tom, with Hank's assistance, was able to get a good fix on the probe. He went over to the Megascope station—his incredible electronic telescope—and zeroed in on the satellite.

"Uh, Giselle. Can you come take a look at this?" he asked.

"Oh. That most definitely is not right," she stated on seeing the lop-sided angle and wobbly rotation it was exhibiting. "How high up is it?"

Tom checked. "About three hundred-fifteen miles above the RADAR-reflective surface. What was it supposed to be?"

She bit her lip. "That is top secret, Tom. But, and you did not hear this from me, roughly two hundred and seventeen nautical miles, or three hundred fifty kilometers."

The signal stopped for a few minutes and then resumed.

"Why would it do that?" she asked, startled at the signal loss.

Tom made a humming sound for a moment. He brought the image into closer focus. "I think it is because the antenna to send data back to Earth gets pointed too far downward as the probe wobbles and spins like that."

It made sense to her and to Hank, a trained Engineer, as well.

"How close can we get to it, skipper?" he asked. "I'll go out and get a good hold on it with the *Straddler* we've got in the hangar, stabilize it, and bring it back for a check-up."

"Straddle her?" she asked.

Tom explained. "That motor scooter-looking thing under the tarp Bud pointed out in the hangar? That is a *Straddler*, one of my smaller repelatron-driven vehicles. We use them on the Moon, on Mars at our colony out there, and keep one in the hanger just in case we need to go out and grab onto anything."

He told her of its grabbing feature, the Attractatron which used a small repelatron and that device's ability to locate and identify specific elements or minerals, then use another emitter ring around that feeding out an exactly opposite wave from the shove of the repelatron.

Bud piped up, "The two sort of cancel each other out and whatever you've got in the beam sticks there. It can't come closer unless you increase power to the attracting force, and it can't get shoved farther away unless you increase the repelatron. It grabs like having a steel beam welded between you and whatever."

Tom cleared his throat and everybody turned to look at him. "To answer Hank's question, I can get to within a couple hundred feet. Take Giselle with you, if you want to go, that is," he directed to her. She nodded eagerly. "Fine. Strap her to the *Straddler* in case she forgets to hold on and let her direct you to the best spot to grab that thing."

"I can also assist in slowing that spin. I am stronger that I appear," she told them flexing her arms inside her short sleeved blouse and making Bud's legs go wobbly.

CHAPTER 4 /

WHY?

THE RETRIEVAL went smoothly and the satellite was back inside the sealed hangar an hour later. Giselle didn't wait to change and simply flung her helmet back as she started checking the device.

Three hours passed before she left to use the lavatory, finally changing out of her spacesuit and into a fresh jumpsuit before reporting to Tom who had gone up to the control room.

"It is *durcheinander*. What you would term 'all messed up,'" she said as she tucked a stray wisp of hair behind her right ear, "and I no longer believe I can repair what is wrong. It appears to be a combination of bad parts, bad programming, and what may have been a small explosive device that blew apart a series of electronic connectors and a fuel line once we left orbit." She looked very sad and a single tear appeared in her right eye, only to spill down her cheek a moment later.

She stepped forward and put her arms around Tom letting a small sob escape. He instinctively gave her a hug. A moment later she stepped back, wiped her face and tried to smile.

"Big, strong, tough German woman with the emotions of a little girl, huh?"

Tom shook his head. "You've obviously invested a lot of your time and emotions into the success of this project so it is really okay to let the frustrations out. The truth is, four or five years ago I would have felt uncomfortable with that hug, but today I've hit the age where I can return that as a comfort. If you need another one, later, and just a hug—" he hastened to add, "—then give me a moment's notice." He smiled at her.

"And, now you may call me Gisi," she said smiling back. "Let me get that *haufen schrott* strapped down and we can go home. My little bird will never fly."

On the way back to Earth Tom asked her if she was certain it had been sabotage. "The reason I ask is because I can have our Security chief, Harlan Ames, assist your investigators. He is well versed in electronics and the sorts of sabotage that happens to technology products and might prove to be an invaluable resource. Also, because we did have possession of the satellite for three days prior to lofting it into orbit I want him to make certain the damage and tampering came before we saw or touched it."

She agreed and several radio messages were sent out. By the time they touched down back at Fearing Island, two five-person teams were waiting to take charge of the satellite—one from

Germany and the other from Enterprises.

Phil Radnor headed the American contingent while a severe-looking woman in the German Army uniform of a Colonel was in charge of the German team.

Giselle seemed glad to see her and told Tom she was the best in her field.

Tom and his team said their goodbyes and returned to Shopton where they were met by family and friends, each one of them agreeing to a three-day vacation plus the weekend to "recover from the trip."

To the dismay of Bashalli, Tom spent his first day off at Enterprises in an effort to find a method of propulsion for the movie's flying pack. And, when he did come home an hour early, it was to disappear into the downstairs bedroom he used as a den and home office.

She quietly brought him a warm ham sandwich and cup of mushroom soup, giving him a kiss on the right ear before she left the room.

He absently ate the sandwich and took a few spoons of the soup but was deep in a particular tech journal detailing the used of rapid air movement technologies. It eventually proved to be somewhat of a dead-end as deep down it relied on an electrical tether to supply the one thousand volts of power necessary to move air ions in enough quantity and quickly enough to lift a small payload of under one hundred pounds.

"Would have been nice to mention the limits at the start of the article," he mumbled as he shoved that publication to one side.

He was about to pick up the next one when there was a sound at the door. Not a knock and not a scratch, it puzzled him enough to stand up to see what it was.

Pulling the door open he peered into the hall and saw nothing. But, a tug on his left pants' leg made him look down into the upturned face of his young son.

"Dadda!" little Bart squealed with delight and he threw his arms around Tom's legs.

Laughing, Tom bent down and picked Bart up, bringing the boy's face next to his.

"And, who put you up to this?" he asked in a quiet, curious voice.

Bart leaned back from his father's embrace and pointed down the hall. "Mamma!" he declared.

"You little snitch!" came Bashalli's voice as she came around the corner with a huge smile on her face. "It's Bart's bedtime and I thought it would be a good place for you to take a break and spend a few minutes with him." She looked hopefully at Tom.

"You got me," he told them both as he stepped into the hall carrying Bart to the living room.

The three spent the next ten minutes together before Bashalli took Bart from his father and went upstairs to give him a quick wash and get ready for bed. When they were ready she called down and Tom came up to help tuck Bart in.

"Dadda, momma, hugga!" Bart ordered, a serious look on his little face.

Tom and Bashalli did and the baby shouted, "No! Hugga *Bart*. Dadda, momma hugga *Bart*!"

"He's quite demanding," his mother said. "I wonder where he gets that?"

"He's spending too much time with his Auntie Sandy, I think," Tom stated with a grin.

Bart knew what he wanted and once he got his hugs he settled down and closed his eyes. Tom and Bashalli tiptoed out of the room after turning the child monitor system on.

Back downstairs, Bashalli sat on the sofa and patted it. Tom knew he was not going back to his journals so he sat next to her.

"Now, tell me all about this flying thing you have been working on. I want to know what my competition for your affection is about."

Tom tried to tell her about the things he could, but in the end she had to be happy with a general description.

"Sorry that I can't be more specific, Bash, but right now I'm a little stumped. The three different major inventions along these lines have never really lived up to people's hopes.

He told her about the early "rocket belts" that used concentrated hydrogen peroxide forced through a silver mesh screen that instantly turned it into high-pressure, super-hot steam.

"You could only fly eight hundred to a thousand feet, safely, before the fuel was exhausted. That was less than a half minute. If you weren't almost at touchdown by then, you were in trouble."

"Did I not read where someone made a different type that could fly for many minutes?"

He nodded. "You probably did. Some engineers finally got jet turbine engines down to a size where a pair of them could be mounted on either side on a fuel tank, kerosene generally, and that could lift a medium-size man and let him fly around for about nine minutes. In fact, that sort of jet pack actually was sold for a few years but it never saw much use."

Then, he told her about the units that utilized compressed water. With a hose dangling into water below it, and a powerful dock-based pump forcing the liquid down through steerable nozzles, it could fly for as long as the pump was on, but rarely allowed the flyer to go more that fifty or so feet away or up.

"So, yours need to do what?" she asked.

"According to the Hollywood folks, it needs to fly for up to a half hour, go to altitudes of five thousand feet or more, and be able to go back up after a very fast refueling."

"Okay, but isn't there that man from Europe with his flying wing. How about that?"

"Mr. Gardner was very up front about that. It is too recognizable, to the point where a lot of people know it cannot take off on its own, but needs to be launched from a helicopter a few thousand feet up. Also, Gardner says it isn't sexy enough for his movie. What they want... what they will pay for, is a flying pack or suit that can take off from the ground, fly under very accurate control, hover when needed, and even do aerobatic maneuvers. Sort of like a mechanical Superman but in a full-body suit."

"What can you do, Tom?"

He looked at her and replied, "Bash. I have no idea."

* * * * *

For more than two weeks Tom read, took notes, made sketches and sorted through what he had. A few good ideas came up but there was also what the broadcast industry would call "dead air." In other words, nothing.

He wasn't discouraged, however, as he felt each step he was taking was bringing him new levels of information and understanding of the problems he faced.

For instance, his assumption that the flyer would need to be kept rigid proved out with a simple wind tunnel test using one of Sandy's old dress-up dolls. When positioned flat out facing the airstream, arm down at its sides, it remained relatively stable. But, when he bent the waist forward and the legs even a bit further, stability went out the window and the doll broke from its mount and slammed into the far wall.

Sandy looked at the now legless doll with the crack down its front and shook her head.

"Boys should never be allowed to play with other people's nice dolls!" she stated before taking it over and dropping it into the trash.

Tom asked if he might have it so he could build several others for testing purposes. When she shrugged and pointed at the bin, he retrieved it and put it in his pocket along with the salvaged legs and head.

Hank Sterling took the parts and scanned them in a 3D unit, then had his 3D printer turn out a dozen of them. After a little bit of painting, and replacing the blank head with the one from Sandy's doll, Tom returned one of them to her.

She was amazed "But, how?"

"Hank made you a new one, just don't tell the manufacturer or they'll climb all over us!"

As the days passed, Tom began to wonder if the project was truly viable.

"It's almost as if the solution is in front of me, but I'm in a dark room, it is hanging a few inches above where I can reach, and I have no idea where to jump to try to find it!" he told his father.

"Well, then, how about giving your old man two days of your time? You can use that to reset your brain and help me out with the German satellite again. By the way, Harlan reported to me the sabotage definitely happened in Germany. Possibly by as much as five or six months before they turned it over to us."

"So, it happened during their construction?"

"We're of that belief, yes."

"Do they or Harlan know who all had access?"

"Nobody kept scrupulous logs of people coming and going, so it is supposition, but the one person who was with things from the very start is the German woman who accompanied you to Venus. Fräulein Ackerman." He looked to see how Tom took that news.

"I can't believe she would be both the saboteur as well as the person sent out to—" He stopped. "She *was* sent out to fix or call the thing junk, which is exactly what she did. That sets the Germans back by at least a full year. More, possibly. Still," he said looking very sad, "she seems like such a nice person. Just not the sort you take home and introduce to your wife or girlfriend!"

After a minute of silence, Tom asked, "Is it just Harlan with the suspicions, or are the Germans thinking along the same lines?"

"You know, I don't have that information, Why don't you go speak to him and tell him anything you can about her and how she acted or reacted on that trip."

When they met, Ames told Tom that nothing else pointed to anybody other than Giselle Ackerman.

"They even have an electronic record of her checking back into the assembly clean room three evenings in a row about the time they believe the sabotage took place and again a month or more before they wrapped everything up."

"Video?"

Harlan shook his head. "They never thought to install a surveillance system believing that access cards and an electronic reader system would safeguard everything. The issue I found with the Germans, and particularly that Colonel woman, is they don't especially want to look any farther than the surface. My bet is there is someone else behind this. We both know how many times spies and thugs snuck into Enterprises using stolen access cards years ago. Your TeleVoc pins put nearly a complete stop to that, thank heavens."

"Sure," Tom said with a rueful grin. "Now they sit outside the walls waiting to whack me with a stick or a brick or something!"

The next day, as he plotted a satellite rebuild strategy for his father, Tom was thinking over something Bashalli had said, or maybe it was something he said, but it all pointed to small jet engines. He called one of the technicians in the Propulsion department.

"Artie? It's Tom. Listen, if you have a minute I need to pick your brain regarding little jet engines."

"I'm just waiting for a housing cover to cure so I've got a couple hours, Tom. What can I tell you?"

Tom explained, in general terms, the flying suit project.

"So, my question is those two-stage mini jet turbines you build for the military ejector seat system, could a pair of them lift a man of, oh, maybe two hundred pounds?"

"Not really, skipper. They put out about sixty pounds of thrust each, but once you take fuel and their own weight into consideration, you would probably need four or five of them. Even then, that old diminishing returns law comes into effect and pretty soon, no more fly. Sorry because I know that isn't the answer you wanted."

"No, but it is the true answer. How large would they need to be and what fuel consumption rate, to lift that same man?"

"Give me a sec... okay, got the calculator out. So, figuring raw weight... and fuel weight, and some sort of frame, plus navigation and gyros, and............ nope! I think I recall we made them that size for two reasons. They fit and they were at the upper end of size versus thrust versus weight. There are some larger ones that could lift a person, but they burn something like a gallon of fuel a minute. Having failed you again on that one, got anything *else* I might assist with?"

Tom sighed. "No, Artie. Thanks for the reality check!"

When he got home he was tired and on the verge of thinking the project wasn't going to be possible. A good meal and a night in bed saw him feeling better about things in the morning.

*   *   *   *   *

Chow stepped into his small kitchen room causing the waiting Bud to fling his arms in front of his eyes and exclaim, "Oh, man! Chow, you're killing my retinas!"

The western cook only beamed at what he felt was a compliment on his latest bright shirt. This one, an almost glowing red featured a spiral design of brilliant green starting at the collar and running down almost like a coil around this entire body until it reached the bottom.

"Like it?" he asked. "I tell ya, Buddy-boy, this here shirt'll set ya back a purty penny, but it's a real hit! Gits ya noticed right off! I kin get ya one..." He looked hopefully at the flyer.

"Think I'll have to pass, Chow," Bud told him. "Sandy hates it when I look better than she does so she'd never want to go out dancing with me if I had on a peacock shirt like that. No, you go right on wearing those. As for me, perhaps a subdued Hawaiian-style print but only if Sandy's wearing something really bright."

"Ah, shucks. Nothin' like a man all spangled up ta make folks look at the filly on his arm. But, you know yer wife better'n I do, I s'pose."

"Thanks again for the offer. Oh, and speaking of dancing, Tom and Bashalli are supposed to go to dinner with us tonight. Guess I'd better remind him."

"Well, get goin' 'cause I just saw that buckaroo carryin' out a bunch o' books 'n magazines from the company library as if he was fixin' ta spend a late night at his desk."

Bud winked and left the room heading for the shared office. There, the Swift's secretary, Munford Trent, was finishing a phone call. He pointed to the door and made a "go ahead" motion. Inside, Bud stopped on seeing the tall pile of technical journals and books sitting in front of the inventor.

He groaned.

"Huh? What?" Tom asked looking up.

"The 'huh' of it is it figures you would get stuck into something an hour before we're supposed to take the wives to the dinner dance at the Yacht Club. And, the 'what' is, you need to close that publication right now and stand up and come with me."

Tom grinned, a little embarrassed. "Chalk up another near oops on that front, Bud. Thanks for saving my neck. Give me two minutes to mark something in this one and I'll go next door and

—" His face went blank and then turned pink.

"Bud! I've pulled a boneheaded one this time. I forgot to bring my suit to work. Now I'll never convince Bash that I really remembered this on my own!"

"And, if you will just set that aside and step into the apartment next to your lab you will find that somebody brought a suit bag for her husband about two hours ago and then called me to have me remind you. She already knows, skipper. Both our ladies know. We're married and still have the same old problems forgetting important dates."

Tom sighed, shoved a piece of notepaper between two pages and got up.

The dinner and dance were fun with the foursome enjoying steak and lobster tails before hitting the floor for an hour of dancing. Usually it was the men who suggested an early night, but tonight Sandy and Bashalli both begged off from the second dance set saying they wanted to get home.

Tom and Bud shook hands while the girls hugged before they got in their separate cars.

"That was fun," Tom commented as they pulled out from the parking lot. "So, tell me what's the real reason for calling it an early night."

She snuggled into his shoulder. "It is just that ever since I became a mother and stopped working full time I feel that about half my energy is gone by noon. Bart is a dynamo and it takes it out of me. Sandy was just being polite."

Tom nodded. "I see. My sister... thoughtful? We're talking about Sandra Helene Swift-Barclay? That Sandy?"

Bashalli giggled. "Yes we are. Ohh! What was that?"

A popping noise had come from the right front of the car and it swayed in that direction. Tom fought the steering wheel for a few seconds as he applied the brakes. Finally, the car pulled off the dark side road they had turned onto as a shortcut to their home.

He got out and walked around the front to examine the tire.

"A good old-fashioned blowout, Bash. Strange, though. These tires aren't supposed to do that. I wonder..."

He crouched down to get a good look at the tire.

"Bash! Lock the doors!" he commanded as a trio of men poured out from the bushes. Two pounced on Tom and the other wrenched the passenger door open before Bashalli could react to Tom's shout.

Both fought back but the attackers came prepared, and chloroform-soaked cloths were shoved over their mouths and noses. In seconds they were unconscious.

A minute later the only sign they had been there were the fragments from the explosive device that had blown the tire, and a set of tracks showing where the car had been shoved into some bushes.

CHAPTER 5

BACK ON TRACK

TOM'S HEAD snapped up, and he looked around at their surrounding as soon as he woke up and then startled Bashalli by beginning to laugh.

"What?" she demanded with an angry hiss. The effects of the knock-out fumes left them both with a bad headache. Tom had been subjected to ether and chloroform several times so he knew what to expect.

This was her first brush with the chloroform. Her only other experience with being knocked unconscious had been with a synthetic sleep-inducing gas the time she and Sandy had been kidnapped more than a year earlier. This was much worse.

"You are not going to believe this, Bash, but this very cabin is one Bud and I were taken to one time, oh… about five years ago I think, when some thugs hired by the Brungarians clobbered us and dragged us into these woods." He craned his neck trying to see all the way around them.

"Yeah, just as I thought. Nothing really much has changed. A bit more dust and that big hole in the roof above the stove is new, but this is definitely the same place. A bit more bird messes as well. So, if you will pardon a little racket I believe I can get us out of these ropes in a few minutes. Take a few deep breaths to help clear your brain."

As she watched, admiring his calmness, Tom rocked forward and straightened his knees as much as the chair and ropes would allow bringing the legs off the ground a few inches.

Using a very uncomfortable, but mostly quiet shuffle motion he moved over to the window to their right and peered outside. Seeing nobody outside standing guard, he repeated his shuffle to the opposite side of the fifteen-foot-square shack taking a look out that broken window.

Again, nobody was visible.

"Here's where I hope time and physics play into our hands," he told her as he jumped a few inches and tilted back. As he hoped, the back legs took the entire downward weight and failed to hold together. With a splintering noise and a thud, Tom sat down on the ground, shucking his now-loose ropes off his upper body.

Quickly he untied his legs and stood up, his head throbbing. As he untied Bashalli he listened for any signs the escape had been detected. There was no obvious noise but he had to hush his wife when she opened her mouth to ask what he knew would be a series of questions.

"Get out first, ask me questions later," he whispered to her. He kissed her quickly and then rechecked at both windows. Making a "come with me" motion he headed for the only door in the cabin. He tried to open it as quietly as possible and was not surprised to find it had been padlocked from the outside.

"Let's go out that side window," he whispered into her ear.

They eased the frame upward but only to clear the small amount of broken glass still clinging to it. Tom helped Bashalli climb up and out, lowering her to the ground before silently climbing out to stand beside her. He took her hand and led her to the brush about twenty feet away, and then through the first of it to a small cleared area.

Tom reached up and tapped his TeleVoc pin. Fortunately, the thugs hadn't taken it from him. A moment later he was in silent communications with Gary Bradley, the number three man in Security at Enterprises.

"We'll have a fleet of police and Sheriff's cars out there in fifteen minutes and a Whirling Duck complete with rope ladder to pick you two up by the same time. Go ahead and leave this channel open just in case."

"Right," he silently intoned. He turned to his wife, leaned closer and explained what was going to happen. They moved another fifty feet from the cabin but were coming too close to the access road and Tom believed they might be spotted if they were to try crossing it. Most likely, way out here, that could very well be their kidnappers coming back.

They sat and waited with Bashalli clinging to Tom's arm the entire time.

At about the eleven minute mark the first sounds of vehicles, both ground and air, could be heard. A minute later two Shopton Police cars skidded to a halt just yards from where they sat, five officers jumping out, drawing their guns.

"Come out with your hands up!" one officer was shouting toward the cabin through a loud hailer. "You are surrounded. Escape is impossible!"

Tom stood up, startling two officers who swung their weapons around to point at him.

"Put those down before you hurt somebody," he told them. "I'm Tom Swift. Whoever kidnapped my wife and me left us before we woke up. And, I'd suggest a little caution and tact about rushing the cabin and scuffing up all signs and footprints they may have left. Ditto grabbing things that might have fingerprints."

The Whirling Duck came to a hover fifty feet above them with the rope ladder being lowered.

"Can you and Mrs. Swift make the climb?" came the pilot's question via the TeleVoc system.

Bashalli joined him and Tom asked her.

"Of course I can climb a ladder. Just be certain to hold it still for me," she replied. She was thinking, *I hope that my stomach holds out. I really feel sick right now. I would hate to throw up on Tom!*

He asked one of the surprised officers to do the holding and they climbed up and into the lower hatch of the helicopter.

A minute later, both now wearing oxygen masks to clear their systems of the gas, they were swinging around, heading back to Enterprises.

Gary and Doc Simpson met them and while the doctor checked them over and told them to keep the masks on ten minutes longer, the Security man began asking about their experience. When Tom informed him of the cabin coincidence, he shook his head. "That's it! We'll have that place plowed into the ground tomorrow. The owner claims no desire to take care of the place, and I know we can get Judge Cadwalather to sign the order first thing in the morning. So, who do you think is behind this?"

Tom pondered it a moment before replying. "The last time Bud and I were held there, it was by some criminals for hire out of New Jersey in the employ of a Brungarian rebel scientist. *Streffan Mirov!*"

Gary groaned. "But, we know he's dead, skipper. He's died several times and the last time was pretty conclusive."

"Yes, but not absolute! Anyway, you might start checking on that angle, and—"

Tom's voice trailed off, and both Bashalli and Gary looked at him.

"I wonder," he said more to himself that to them. "I just wonder if there is some connection between the German satellite sabotage and this. And, if there is, does that point even more of a finger at Brungaria?"

Gary shook his head. "They've been pretty quiet for a couple years, Tom. A more stable government and even some transparency with the West has nearly made them friendly. I think they discovered that foreign aide and tourism pay a lot better than stealing technology and attempting world domination!"

But, he agreed to bring it up with Harlan the following

morning.

Tom and Bashalli headed home, tired but wanting to see their son. They said nothing to her mother who had been watching the baby.

The next day Tom went back into his design for the jet backpack. Or, as he was beginning to think of it more as a "lifting pack" since he knew it would contain nothing that might be thought of as an actual "jet."

Bud popped his head around the corner of the doorway to the large lab down the hall from the office Tom and Damon shared.

"Yo, skipper? What's this I hear about you and Bash—I mean you and *Bashi* getting waylaid last night?"

Tom told his friend about the tire blowing out and their waking up in the cabin.

"I see," Bud said. "Well, your car was brought in an hour ago and the blowout was not an accident. Someone stuck a small explosive pack on the inside of that tire where it wouldn't be visible, and probably set it off by radio as you got close to them."

"I hope Harlan can find—"

"He's already on it," Bud told him. "I hear he and a team of five or six scoured the road for a quarter mile from where they found your car hidden going back toward the main road. Found lots of little stuff including what I hear would have been the radio receiver."

"Bash had a very bad night last night worried that someone would try something at our house. I tried to remind her that our door and windows are made from Tomasite and Durastress and can't be broken out or down, but she is nervous for Bart's sake. Can the two of them stay with you and Sandy for a couple nights?"

Bud looked askance at Tom. "Right. And being away from you is going to make her feel so-o-o-o much better... how?"

The inventor rubbed his shin. "Oh. I didn't think about it like that. Maybe if you suggested you and Sandy take Bart and you three stay with mom and dad...?"

"I'll suggest it. Anyway, what have you discovered to make your junior bird man sky streaker backpack work?"

"*Sky Streaker* isn't a bad name, Bud. Not too punny and not too far off from what it will do. I like it. But, that doesn't answer your question. I found an article this morning while I was waiting for Bash to fall asleep by a man in Canada who tried to come up with a viable ion drive to move heavy barges across the Hudson Bay about ten years ago. His idea was that a couple or three drives units might take a little time to get the barge up to any speed, but like we do in space they would run full time speeding things up until they reached the halfway mark where the drive force would be reversed to slow them back to zero just as they reached the destination."

He showed the flyer the article he had on his computer screen. It stated that the drive was to use some of the very water the barge floated on to create the hydrogen and oxygen that would be ionized. The hydrogen would provide the propulsive force while the oxygen allowed it to ionize much hotter, amplifying the force by a factor of three times.

"Jetz!" Bud said. "A practically inexhaustible fuel supply right under your feet all the way there and back. Why didn't he ever build that?"

"Two main reasons. First, he computed the raw electrical power needed for the ionization to work and it turned out to require up to five, fifteen hundred kilowatt diesel generators to make the necessary electricity. Those would burn about three times more fuel making the electricity than a good diesel system driving a propeller in a tug that could make the trip in about two-thirds the time. The other reason is the Canadian government pulled all funding out from under him. So, makes a good technology journal piece, but never would have been practical."

Bud looked puzzled and Tom asked him why.

"Well, I can't see how that gets you any closer, skipper. Make me understand, please."

With a small chuckle, Tom said, "The limiting factor was the amount of power needed to move that large an object. And, remember that water is a very dense medium so it would take a lot just to get the barge moving. The system I'm envisioning will be centered around one of our Mighty Max power pods—probably the one that's about the size of a basketball—that will power a pair of ionization loops. Almost like we use for the EnvironOzone Revivicators down at the South Pole, the ionized air rushes between negative and positive charged vanes and that comes out the back side as thrust."

The dark-haired flyer's mouth scrunched up and he shook his head.

"I understand that, but I've sat on an OzoneNut and it could no more lift me off the ground than a squadron of mayflies could."

"And, that is why we will use both the force of the ionization of the air along with the scorching hot ionizing hydrogen and oxygen. Those would be carried in separate pressure tanks so there would be zero need for equipment to separate them from the air. The total thrust might be in the one hundred pound range per loop." He stopped and thought a moment, "In that case I might need to add a third loop."

"You do know what my next question is going to be, right?"

"Sure. But I have to disappoint you. I just do not know. It could be a month or more and it could be six months, but only if things pan out. There are more details to iron out beyond the thrust. There's the whole flying suit and how it gets controlled. The overriding thing is safety. We can't let a pilot get into trouble trying to do more things than the suit is either capable of, or is beyond its safety margins. But, rest assured and get that sad hound dog look off your face, flyboy, there will be testing aplenty to be done and you are at the top of the list."

"Tethered, or over water?"

"See there? You're getting ahead of me again. Probably some of each, but definitely over water for anything with much altitude. That, plus I'll' be adding a quick-open emergency chute."

"As Chow might say at a moment like this... much obliged!"

"Dad?" Tom asked his father. "Do you recall an old alloy I used back when I built the *Sky Queen*? The one with super high heat resistance?"

Damon Swift stroked his chin and tried to come up with the name, but his memory failed him. "I recall you were struggling to keep your original atomic lifters from burning through their nozzles, but for the life of me the alloy name won't come to the tip of my tongue. Why?"

Tom grinned sheepishly. "Because I also can't remember the darned name. I recall it had a whopping amount of magnesium— oh! Wait, I do remember it... Magnalloy. Magnesium with titanium and a bit of Wolfram to make the binding between molecules tighter. We adjusted it more for strength than for heat properties and came up with magnetanium the next year. Right. Anyway," he explained seeing the look of curiosity on his father's face, "this backpack is going to need to run pretty hot. And, while I can protect the ion drive using magnetic power rings, I'm looking at something in the neighborhood of a thousand degrees exiting right behind the *wearer's* behind."

Damon smiled. "Wouldn't want to burn someone's backside in the name of some silly movie. So, is it your thought to build a shield behind the pilot to protect their legs?"

"I think a little more than that, Dad. The thing that's been running through my mind is that the pilot will be wearing some sort of flexible, but impermeable flight suit that fits into an exoskeleton. He or she is going to need a fair degree of flexibility to turn and look around them. It's the skeleton I'm thinking of.

Mostly open in the front—except, of course, where the straps and buckles go—and then a form-fitting backplate and some sort of backward-facing chaps."

"Just how hot will the, uhh, exhaust gases be?"

"I don't have an exact figure, but at least one computation points at around eleven hundred degrees just below the ion engines."

Mr. Swift asked about the amount of air that would be moving. "And, won't that serve to cool the exhaust?"

Tom smiled. "Sure, and without that air movement the temperature would be nearly three hundred degrees higher. As I see it, the downward force of just the ion engine loops will only account for ninety percent of the thrust. Everything else comes from air movement."

He explained that his belief was the faster the suit flew the more force available as natural airflow would increase.

It would, he said, more than make up for the drag the bulky suit and backpack would provide.

"Let me know if I can do anything to help. Right now, I'm waiting for the go-ahead to leave for Germany. It seems our new Teutonic friends over there no longer believe they can protect the rebuilding of their satellite and want me to tell them how we can do it better—and maybe even cheaper—than their best folks think they can do. I'll be back in two days, so make a list of things you'll want my assistance on."

He patted Tom on the shoulder and went to his desk to make a few phone calls.

Tom drifted out of the office and down the hall to the stairs. Taking them two at a time he quickly reached the ground floor and the side door. He strode toward the small building that housed the stairs and elevator down to the *Sky Queen's* underground hangar and his small lab and private office space. On the way he TeleVoc'd Arv Hanson and asked the man to meet him down there.

"Hey, skipper," Arv greeted him as he came into the office. "What's up?"

Tom suggested he take a seat, then slid the folder with the flight suit request across the desk. "Read that and we'll talk."

Thirty minutes later Arv looked up with a broad smile on his face.

"I like it!" Now, his face became more somber. "Only thing, is it feasible?"

For the next hour they discussed the possibilities and some of

Tom's findings. When he got to the matter of recreating the magnalloy for the structural and heat shield parts, Arv whistled.

"You *do* recall we ended up having to replace those heat shields on the *Queen* after about each fifty hours of using the lifters. As good as it was for keeping things from melting around the outlet ports, it kept getting brittle. It's one of the reasons we switched to repelatrons."

Tom nodded. "I've thought a lot about that and come up with one possibility. The small levels of extremely short duration radiation that blasted from those old atomic lifters—even the three-second half-life it had—made none-too-subtle changes in the subatomic structure of the metal. I'll run extensive tests on that theory, but I believe I'm right. Since this flying suit—what Bud has dubbed the *Sky Streaker*—puts out zero radiation, just a lot of heat, I believe we will be okay. T-W-T."

"Yeah," Arv replied. "Testing Will Tell!"

Tom told him it might be at least a week before Arv could put his model making skills to use creating a testable miniature, and the model maker agreed to keep his schedule flexible so he could jump on it when the time was right.

Next, Tom phoned Dianne Duquesne, the head of the Propulsion division of Enterprises. She had been a key player in many of Tom's flying inventions. Most her people were extremely happy whenever they could work of a "Tom project." The inventor's jobs usually proved to be more exciting than most others coming their way, and more personally satisfying.

She told him she could come over in an hour.

"Great. See you in the underground office then."

She thanked him for telling her which of the many places he might be at any given time would be the one for her to visit.

As he hung up, Tom reached over and grabbed the short stack of preliminary sketches he'd made over the past few weeks, many coming from the Venus trip. Nothing was in very good shape, meaning nothing was very clear as to what it was supposed to represent. Moving to his old-style drafting board he used four tiny magnets to hold a sheet of Virtual Velum to the surface and slipped first one and then each of the other sketches under it. The special surface amplified the darker lines and diminished lighter ones so he could get a better look at each one. A couple he set aside, one he wadded up and tossed into the recycle bin, one he held in his hand and the other four he placed next to him.

He slid the first one back under the velum and carefully traced it using a special stylus. Next, he made a few adjustments to the drawing before darkening in certain parts of the outline and adding some of the details.

One of the great aspects of the Virtual Velum was that it could be attached to a cable and the design transferred to his 3-D Computer Aided Design system. He pulled that cable over and set it in the lower left corner of the sheet. With the click of a key, the design blinked momentarily from the surface and appeared on his computer monitor. A second click cleared the sheet so it could be used again.

Before Dianne arrived he managed to transfer four of the five designs he liked with two of them showing great promise.

As with Arv, after greeting her and thanking her for coming, he gave her the folder with the project details.

"You probably only need to read the top page and then pages four through seven, Dianne."

After scanning them, she looked up.

"I hate to tell you this, Tom, but not only can't this be made to fly, I know there is an injunction by an inventor on the West Coast that says *nobody* can try to build a flying suit!"

CHAPTER 6 /
LEGALESE AND OTHER PROBLEMS

TOM WAS AGAST for a moment before he narrowed his eyes. "Wait. Are you perhaps talking about the people in California who have been trying to build and patent what they call the PFP, or Personal Flight Pack?"

Dianne's eyes widened. "Why, yes. Okay. What do you know that I don't?"

He explained that the chief investor in that project was Bud's family and that the flyer had recently heard they were looking for someone to purchase their research so they might recoup some of the money already spent on a project they now feared would come to nothing.

"Hold on a few minutes, please," he asked her before picking up his phone. A moment later he was asking for Jackson Rimmer, the company's chief legal counsel.

"Yes, Tom?"

"Jackson, I need someone to contact the Daedalus Aeronautic Corporation in Pacoima, California. Mention Bud Barclay's family name and it ought to get you to their president. I don't recall the man's name. Anyway, tell them we have been approached by a company to create a personal flying system, but assure them it is nothing like the one they have been having trouble with.

"Tell them we need to know if their current status on their own project is such that they might sue us if we proceed. I'm sure you'll word things much better than that."

"I generally do," Rimmer replied and Tom could tell the man was smiling. "I already know a little about that company as I had to help draft the non-disclosure for Bud before he went out to be their test pilot. Can you assure me that he has mentioned nothing of their technology to you?"

"I've found out more from a few news items on line and their own press releases than from Bud other than his crash. He knows how to keep secrets so give them my guarantee."

After he hung up, Tom told Dianne the lawyer suggested it might take a full day or more to get an answer.

"In the meantime, let's assume they have no issues and we go forward with this. What I will need from you and your folks are the ion drive units. These will be unlike the ones you've built for spacecraft as they have to work in the air and not use any radioactive cesium or other nuclear fuels."

Once he described the process he envisioned, she asked for three days to work with some of the top people in her organization before she could give him a solid answer regarding the viability.

"I hope it will be a yes, but the final say is going to come from your design," she told him.

"I understand. Thanks!"

Two hours later Tom was straightening things up preparing to go home when his phone rang.

"Tom? Jackson in Legal. Well, we stirred up a hornet's nest. Angry doesn't half describe the attitude I got from their vice president. It turns out the president was fired just this morning and they are out for blood, accusing us of working with Bud and his family to drive them out of business. I'm afraid that until things cool down out there and I can make them see reason, you will need to sit on that project of yours. I'll keep you advised. Got to run!"

Tom immediately phoned Bud asking him to come over as quickly as possible. When the flyer arrived he was slightly out of breath and very curious.

"So, what's the panic, Tom?"

The inventor told him. As he did, Bud's face got more and more red and he pounded one fist into his other palm.

"If they want trouble, Tom, I'll give them trouble. They asked me to sign a waiver absolving them of any legal matters arising from my test flying except in the case of equipment failure, and then they changed the paperwork above my signature page. I have the original I signed plus the version they swapped out. I've been holding out hope that they would reimburse me for the hospital trip from my crash but they have steadfastly refused. Now, I'm turning this over to Legal!"

Tom nodded. "Okay. I'm not sure that trying to fight legal matters with legal matters is going to make any of us winners, but let's leave that to Jackson and his people. Where do you have those papers?"

"Locked in my safe deposit box and the Merchants & Co bank downtown. Want me to go get them? They're open for another twenty minutes," he stated looking at his watch.

"No. Tomorrow will do and only once we both go talk to Jackson Rimmer to see how he might want to move on this."

The next morning when they met in the large office, Bud looked incredibly happy. But, when Tom asked him, he simply said, "Let's go on up to Legal."

Jackson Rimmer was waiting for them.

"Bud, I could *almost* yell at you but I found out you didn't initiate that call."

Tom looked perplexed. "Umm, what call?"

Bud replied, "The more I thought about this all the angrier I got, so I was going to call my father last night but he beat me to it and called around ten. It seems the people at that Daedalus place called him to threaten to sue, but they backed down as soon as he told them he was calling in his investment. He had a nifty little clause worked into the contract that gives him the right to request some or all his money be returned at the one-year anniversary of his investment if they do not have a viable prototype. That, by the way, comes along tomorrow!"

"And, that rig that broke and crashed with you in it says they don't have a workable model, yet," Tom said looking to the lawyer for verification.

Jackson nodded and picked up the story.

"Evidently that demand shook them far deeper than else anything might have. They are just about out of money and have been keeping up a brave front to try to woo more investors, but with their failed prototype and Bud's crash in the news, money is staying far away from that place. I fielded an early morning email from their temporary president, the same one I spoke to yesterday who was hell bent on suing us. He now says he acted hastily and wonders if Swift Enterprises might like to buy them out. Your thoughts?" He was looking straight at Tom.

Tom looked over at Bud who opened his hands, palms up, as if to say, "I have no idea."

"Well, while I hate to give into pressure, I also never want any Swift company to look like we are putting the small guy out of business. So, I suppose my answer is let's go ahead and start negotiations. See what it is they want and check that against what Bud's parents invested. I think that if we do end up buying the rights I want them to close down their business, or at least any division or team dedicated to their flying pack. No use giving them money just so they can continue competing with us. Also, the standard legal stuff."

"Consider it started," Rimmer told the two young men.

As they rose, Bud said, "Dad isn't so much interested in getting the money back as he is angry with the management and their attitudes. He believes they could care less they almost killed me. This might be a negotiating point. Also, he said they once told him, point blank, that if money became an issue, they would just find someone with deep pockets to sue."

Rimmer raised an eyebrow but said nothing until they left his office. Then, he smiled and said, "Yes!" under his breath.

Bud received another call on his cell phone, this time as he and Tom sat having coffee that afternoon in the main cafeteria.

"Bud here." He listened a moment before saying, "Hey, Pop. Can I stick you on speakerphone so my buddy Tom can hear this? He's very much involved in it." Obviously getting the go-ahead, he took the phone from his ear, pressed an icon on the screen and they both could hear:

"So are you there already? My time is precious, Budworth."

"We're here, Pop. Now, go ahead and tell us both that bit of news."

"Sure. Right. Well, as I as saying I have had no fewer than five phone calls from those crooks at Dead-Alas today. First came the threat. Then the apology. Then the, 'Oh, please, can't you spare us another half million dollars to fight the evil Empire,' and when I hung up on them, they called back with a 'That wasn't one of us. It was some crank; pay no attention.' Now comes the latest one. They want me to come a-begging to the Swifts for some funding along the lines of fifty million dollars. Promised to pay me back everything I've invested if I can get you and your dad, Tom, to pay up."

"Well, our Legal folks would advise against anything along those lines. I guess Bud has filled you in on what seems to be the basis of this standoff?"

"Yeah. Big shots from Hollywood want what you can give them and the Dead folks cannot. Dead is seeing this as a way to get money for nothing. I called Budworth to ask him to tell you to hang up on the rascals. My money might have been nice to recover, even get some gain on it, but do not in any way give them money. I own the rights to the stupid machine that nearly killed Bud and they absolutely do not. They had to sign it over to get my investment. Give me your legal eagle's email and I'll send him a copy of the contract."

Tom provided the information, thanked the man and left Bud alone to talk to his father.

Now feeling mostly free to proceed, Tom went back to the underground office and pulled out some notes. As he scanned them, one fact—the rig was far too wide—became obvious as did the solution. He pounded a fist onto the desk.

"That's it!" he exclaimed. "That's the secret. Now all I need to do is make it work."

That thought made him give off a small snort. "Yeah, just as simple as that, Tom," he muttered to himself, sarcastically.

He called Arv again asking for some help with a special mini mock-up of the flying pack.

Arv promised to bring what he wanted over within the next five hours.

"It just so happens that I have everything I need for the workings; all I need to do is 3D print the frame. See you this afternoon."

When he finally arrived he held an old shoebox under his arm. He set it on Tom's desk and opened the top.

Inside was a very strange-looking arrangement. As Tom lifted it from the box, he whistled. "Just what I was thinking of, Arv. Great job."

"Thank you. After all these years I've reached the point where I can kind of read your mind. Want the rundown?"

"Sure."

Arv took the ten-inch-tall, four-inch-wide piece. It featured a pair of circular fan ducts, barely taller that the three-blade mini-propellers inside, both set at the top. Those props were attached into the backpack via thin rubberized belts that ended at the top of two small electrical motors.

Deeper down sat a single 9-volt battery to power them.

It also powered the small servos that could change the speed of each motor and swivel them slightly to give forward and backward motion.

He also handed Tom the small remote controller.

"It'll only work within about fifty feet, skipper, but I didn't think you wanted to take this outside, at least not just yet."

Smiling, Tom replied, "Exactly right, Arv. Can I give it a try?"

"Be my guest." Arv reached under the pack and showed Tom the ON/OFF switch. "You may notice that I built this to scale to work with Hank's little dolls. Go ahead and slip one into the harness—well, the elastic straps—so the balance is more realistic.

Tom did and as soon as he advanced the controller to start, then speed up, the propellers, he realized he had a problem to contend with. The weight of the doll was sufficient to tilt the entire set-up forward sending it into a looping dive where it crashed to the floor.

"Well, that isn't good," he said while Arv retrieved the doll and backpack.

There was some damage but it was still flyable, so Tom made a small adjustment to the "normal" setting on the tilt control and tried again. This time it lifted off from the table and he managed to get it to climb a few feet, but not very quickly.

The maneuvering was stiff and he found it difficult to get the model to fly sideways or to turn around.

"Looks like we both have some more experimenting to do," Arv commented.

"Me more than you, at least for now. The set and spin of those props is just about to scale with what I expect the actual ion drives to provide. And that," he pointed at the model, "isn't anywhere close to enough. Anyway, thanks for the work. Can you leave this with me?"

"That's what I planned," the model maker replied. "Have fun!"

After a couple more tries, Tom sat down to make a few more notes. Primarily, he had decided the thrusters needed to be set farther apart for slow flight and brought in for faster maneuvers. His notes now listed:

√ Computer control of swing and set of ionic thrusters

He also noted the lack of thrust but added:

...upsizing is not the answer. If anything the thrusters need to be downsized by 15-25%

Late that afternoon Bud came by.

"Care for a walk to your house?" he inquired.

"Well, sure, but why not drive?"

Pointing at his legs, the flyer said, "Nervous energy. I even walked double-time over here from my office, but I need to stretch these things out. Sandy will come pick me up and we'll drop by tomorrow morning to bring you in."

Ten minutes later they were walking out the private entrance and down the road.

Just before the old intersection at the north corner of the property wall a new road, designed for fast access by emergency vehicles and small automobiles, turned off to the left. It shortened the walk to Tom and Bashalli's house by a couple miles and was not only paved, it featured a sidewalk. Even Tom considered it much safer than the old dirt lane he used to take to his folks house... the lane where he had been waylaid at least a half dozen times.

They were about half a mile along the mile-and-a-half street and passing a pile of large rocks that had been dug up to make for a smooth surface when there was some sort of disturbance ahead of them.

"Listen!" Bud hissed. The two young men stopped and Tom's

head swiveled around in the now darkening gloom to their right and toward the source of the slight noise. "Get behind me, skipper," the flyer insisted.

Tom, having nothing to do with that muttered, "No way. We're in this together." He pointed to the left at the closest large rock. "Up on that, flyboy, and flatten down."

As Bud climbed and Tom stood watch the noises increased to be recognizable as at least three sets of footsteps making no effort to not snap twigs as they came forward. Tom clambered up the rock and he and Bud lay flat on their stomachs now some dozen feet above the road.

Suddenly, three men, two with nasty-looking pistols, came out from the bushes across the road and looked around, seemingly confused.

"Where'd they go?" the shortest one of them, the only one not visible armed, asked. The trio turned around and around trying to find their quarry.

Meanwhile, the boys lay as flat and quiet as possible keeping their faces hidden behind their forearms in case any light reflected on them.

Tom pulled something out from his pants pocket and brought it up near his face. Bud, a grin spreading on his face at seeing what the inventor held, waited.

Tom pressed a button on the face of the one-inch square item, then returned it to his pocket. Both knew it would only be a matter of a few minutes before the area was completely surrounded with Enterprises Security men and local police.

One of the men holding a gun now pulled a flashlight from his jacket pocket and shown it all around them.

What's dat?" he asked as the beam stabbed into a bush back near where they had come from the woods.

"Idiot! It's just some stupid animal. No human has yellow eyes like that. Come on. Let's move down the road a little. They should be along here any minute."

As the trio began to walk down the sidewalk they passed within a few feet of the tall rock. Tapping Bud on his shoulder, Tom rose to a crouch and held out three fingers. Bud nodded knowing what his friend expected. As the fingers became two and finally one, both of them tensed. And, when Tom tucked the final finger into his palm they stood up and jumped straight out and down onto the three men.

The element of surprise was with them and the two armed men lost their guns, with Tom and Bud kicking them to the side at the start of the struggle.

The short man, seeing that his compatriots were being overpowered, panicked and ran. He chose to go straight back to the point they came from the forest and ran right into the path of the prowling mountain lion they'd heard.

His horrifying screams froze the other four for a moment and then everything was silent in the bushes. Tom scooped up the two guns and handed one to Bud, both of them soon pointed at the two would-be attackers.

"Not this time," Tom told them. "On the ground, you two!"

There was no further sound from the vicinity of the cat and its prey.

Seconds later five Enterprises vehicles screeched to a halt nearby, a dozen armed Security men pouring out. While four of them took charge of the two thugs, Gary Bradley came over to talk to Tom and Bud.

They recounted the brief story before asking if someone with a strong stomach might check on the short man who had obviously been attacked in the bushes.

Gary placed a hand on Tom's shoulder and nodded. "I'll do it, skipper. You two go ahead and climb into the lead truck and we'll take you home in a few minutes."

Once seated they looked over to the bushes where Gary was checking out the situation. Seeing him sadly shake his head they looked away.

"I kinda hate to say this, Tom, but it seems we are actually safer up in space or under the ocean than we are right here around Shopton these days. Why is it that every crook, thug, spy and would-be assassin seems to come here?"

Tom snorted. "No idea, Bud." He sighed and sat back in the seat. "But, you're right. Ever since Brungaria and Kranjov got the ultimatums to cease and desist in their world takeover plans or face a cut off from international funds, they haven't been able to mount any rockets to inconvenience us up there. Let's just hope it remains that way. The problem is they haven't ceased domestic espionage and these attacks."

Gary came over to the truck.

"The man's badly slashed but alive. Whatever big cat he ran into, it must have lashed out in surprise and anger but then fled. I've got an ambulance coming for him. Any idea who these jokers are?"

"Might be the same ones who took Bash and me the other night," Tom said. "I never saw a face so I can't be certain, but they wore black clothes and it was the same number of them."

"Well, that one's face is so slashed up you probably won't be able to see it for a few weeks, not until the bandages come off. Let's get you back home."

"I need to go back to work for an hour or so," Tom told him. "Something just came to my mind about this flying rig."

"Well then, it's back to Enterprises and then home."

CHAPTER 7 /

FANTASY VS. REALITY

TOM'S EYES fluttered open and he stifled a groan as the harsh light from an old fashioned bare bulb just over his head flooded into his retinas. A few seconds later he dared to take a second peek around and found he was getting use to the glare.

Next to him Bud sat, slumped in a chair similar to the one Tom now found he was tightly tied to. A trickle of blood was coming from the flyer's forehead.

"Are you awake, Bud?" he whispered, unsure if there was anyone nearby.

In a weak voice, his friend answered. "Been up and at 'em for a couple minutes, but my head hurts something awful! What happened? Get us out of here, Tom. You're our only hope!"

He tried to think. What *had* happened to them? Then, he remembered. *Nothing* had happened. Well, something had nearly happened, but they had come through it and he and Bud had gone home.

It was a dream.

I have to wake up, he thought opening his left eye and staring into the back of Bashalli's head. It was reassuring and it helped him wake the rest of the way up. He closed his eye again and tried to relax.

There was no Bud, no straight-back chairs and no chaffing ropes. Most important, no attack and no blood.

It was a dream and he knew it had been caused by the near attack by the trio of men along the road the evening before.

Probably the shock of that one man being attacked and then dying at the hospital, he thought as he eased from the bed.

"G'morning, Tom," Bashalli said, her mouth not quite forming things correctly. She tried clearing her throat and licking her lips before speaking again. "And, I spy with my little eye, something that begins with it's too darned early for you to be out of bed. Come back. Hold me and let's sleep another two hours. Please? It's only five-twenty!"

Her request was more than he could ignore and so he climbed back under the covers, took her in his arms and fell asleep almost immediately.

They woke to the shouting of Bart over the child monitor.

"Momma! Dadda! Come-a. Got potty. Momma!!!"

"Is the boy secretly Italian?" Tom asked as he got up and headed to the next room. Over the speaker Bashalli heard him say, "Daddy's here, Bart. Let's take care of that diaper and then get you some breakfast."

Bart giggled with delight both at the sight of his "dadda" and at the thought of food. First thing many mornings Tom would feed him, which worked out nicely as Bart enjoyed being fed his jars of strained string beans, carrots and applesauce by his father.

Then, as Tom went to get ready for work, Bart also enjoyed being burped by his momma, and especially liked it when a little food came up and went down her back.

That also made him giggle.

"One day, my lovely son, you will stop that and mommy will be able to wear something new when you eat," she chided him in a playful voice. The truth was, her son could do no wrong in his mother's eyes.

Tom headed for Enterprises and drove through the private gate aiming for the Dispensary. He had long ago promised Doc he would check in as soon as possible after each and every scrape, attack, fight or hint of physical danger. It kept Doc happy and it kept the health insurance people off Doc's back and that made Doc doubly happy!

He didn't get an absolutely clean bill of health, but the physician said he could go to work.

Shortly after lunch Trent buzzed Tom to say he had a visitor. "An old acquaintance who says it is very important."

"Well, as long as he or she passes your muster, Trent, send them in."

"Wes!" Tom cried shooting to his feet a moment later. "What's it been? Five years?"

Wes Norris, an FBI agent who had dealt with a number of incidents in the Shopton area years earlier grinned and nodded his head. "About that, Tom. Still getting yourself conked on the noggin by the bad guys I hear. I kind of thought after getting transferred to Cleveland all this was behind me, and it ought to be."

With a curious squint, Tom asked, "So, what brought you back to Shopton?" He pointed to two chairs and they sat down.

"I'm fairly certain it is the same people who nabbed you and your wife and then tried to attack you and Barclay last night. One we know is deceased and two were bailed out by the Brungarian Embassy in Manhattan this morning Just in time, it would appear, to avoid more charges. We didn't have enough time to fully ID them, but it turns out they are two members of a subversive gang of what used to be known as 'Patent Thieves,' in the old days. They find out about some technology or discovery, then swoop in and steal the plans and get it submitted to the U.S. Patent Office within hours. We're certain they have inside help every time. This go-around has led us to following Karl Branski and Miccos Thule, formerly of the old Soviet Union and currently with no fixed address. If for no other reason, they've overstayed their visitor visas and need to be escorted from the country."

"But, you believe they are doing these attacks?"

"I do, and so do about fifteen agents and analysts in the Bureau. I haven't spoken to Ames, yet, but I have a list of names and aliases he needs to check against any employees hired in the past twelve months. And, yes, they do tend to work that far ahead of a theft!"

Tom whistled and shook his head sadly. He really hoped there wasn't another bad egg in the Enterprises' family of employees.

"But, hey, enough about me... tell me all about how you got that goose egg on your head and Bud got the black eye I saw him sporting."

Tom spent the next ten minutes going over the entire late afternoon up to the moment they fought with the would-be attackers.

"Thank you, Tom. Your Doc Simpson tells me you have a mild concussion from a nasty roundhouse punch you took during that scuffle you had, and I'm supposed to not bug you for too many more minutes, so I'll just ask you to keep me informed about anything else you recall, anything new that happens, or if you sight anyone suspicious in or outside these company walls." He handed Tom a card with a local number, patted the inventor on the shoulder and slipped out of the office as Tom's mind switched back to the flying backpack.

When Gary brought them back to work the previous evening, Bud had opted to forget his restless legs and drove home. Tom had headed for his underground office to make some notes, but a headache—probably from the mild concussion—had him leaving for his own house ten minutes later.

Now, he looked at the notes and smiled.

The secret wasn't going to be in having just two of the ion thrust units. And, three was completely out of the question as his experiments with Arv's model showed the entire pack needed to be only thirty inches from front to back.

He pulled out a sketch and erased some of the thrust curves, now arcing them in to make a sort of lazy crescent moon shape. Propellers needed the roundness, but the ionic thruster didn't care or even benefit from that shape. The truth was, it could be a square, pentagon or this crescent.

To provide even more thrust he added a second set of crescents about a foot below the existing ones. After cleaning up the sketch he called Dianne again. She came to the office five minutes later.

"So, do we have Legal's permission to continue?"

"Almost, but we are going ahead anyway with design, just not the actual build. Take a look at this."

The sketch was handed across the desk and she sat back to study it. When she finished, she set it on the desk and looked directly at him.

"You do realize you've hit on a solution that not even my best and brightest have considered? That doubling of the thrusters is genius! As long as the lower units can handle the heat from the upper ones, you don't just double the thrust, you quite possibly triple it. In fact, you may be able to downsize the... let's call them the thrust rings for now... but they may be able to be made about fifteen percent smaller and still be more than adequate to lift a two hundred pound pilot plus what is probably going to be seventy-five pounds of suit and equipment."

She sat back again and grinned at him.

With Dianne still there, Tom called two structural engineers to come meet with them. When they arrived he described the basic project and showed them the sketch.

Immediately able to appreciate what they were seeing, both Engineers began chattering away about the basic structural elements needed, relative strengths required at movable points, materials and even what the flight suit ought to look like. An hour later everyone had plenty of notes and all were getting excited about the possibilities.

Now Tom's design had the top, or first-stage, thrusters shooting their hot ionized gases straight down and through the second stage thrusters. Those added their own hot gases to the already roasting ones and the results looked to be like running already loud music through a powerful amplifier.

After the new team left Tom tried to concentrate on the protective aspects of both the framework and the flight suit worn by the pilot.

For starters, like a fighter pilot's suit, he believed that inflatable air bladders over the wearer's vital pressure points were necessary to keep the flow of blood to his or her brain during acceleration and rapid maneuvers. Rather than rely on compressed air for this, he added a two-stage compressor to the backpack. The one he was thinking of could supply more than adequate pressure over an extended period of time.

Next, he added an oxygen extraction component to take some of the O2 from the compressed air for the use by the flyer. That also meant in a partially closed breathing system—mandatory for safety, he felt, if the suit were to fly over ten thousand feet—he needed a way to scrub out carbon dioxide.

He pulled up circuit details for his electronic hydrolung and decided an adaptation of that technology was just what he needed.

After studying photos of all the older flying suits, he realized that the simple twist-and-point controllers on thin arms from the past were not entirely adequate. For one, at any appreciable speeds the user's hand and arm would be yanked away making control impossible.

Computers were a part of the answer, but he wrote down that the backpack needed to have built-in arm rests/restraints that still allowed movement from the wrists out, but kept the hands in contact with the controls at all times.

Even small details like position of the wearer's legs and feet would reflect heavily on the suit's overall flight characteristics. His one-time idea of simply having the wearer slip their lower legs into braces disappeared in favor of a boot-like arrangement where the flyer's feet would be inserted into a knee-to-toe solid legging. When not flying, the foot would be swiveled out to a normal standing position, but in flight it would be pivoted backward to form a point, making it more aerodynamic.

Until he heard otherwise from the structural engineers, he planned to use both force-molded Durastress—an incredible polymer he'd come up with years earlier—along with high-density carbon fiber. Not only would it hold up to the dynamic pressures, if necessary an elephant could be balanced on one foot on a side and still not deflect or bend it.

Word came the following day that the Daedalus Company had decided to not pursue a lawsuit and they were closing their doors. The official letter would follow from their temporary president, but he admitted to Jackson Rimmer the former president had managed to steal about half of the funding provided by the Barclays and a few others before disappearing.

In fact, funding for the other three viable products from the company had been diverted and now they were in danger of being sued by customers who wanted the products they had paid for.

Tom and Damon discussed the situation over lunch and both came to the conclusion that a small "bridging" loan could be made so the company could at least fulfill their orders and try to generate enough others to pay back the investment money.

When contacted, the new president of Daedalus, Norman Berry, nearly wept.

"It was never the company's nor the Board of Director's intent to do anything wrong. It was that crook. Good riddance to him, but now we have to contend with the theft of many of our trade secrets. Turns out, he disappeared with plans for just about everything we make, including the jet pack. I hate how this might sound, but I'll find it difficult to trust anyone with an Eastern European accent again."

"What sort of accent?" Tom asked, suddenly feeling a pang of anxiety.

"Not sure... it wasn't Russian, but something like that. Harsh and guttural."

Brungarian! came to both Tom and Damon.

"Mr. Berry, if we are going to invest in your company I would like our Security people to be in on the investigation over those thefts, especially the flying pack design," Damon stated.

"Okay-y-y-y," the man on the phone replied, "but now I have to ask why I detect a hint something is very wrong in your voice, Mr. Swift?"

"How long ago did this past president of your company take over?"

"Well, let me see. I believe about five months ago. Why?"

"In a moment. Can you describe him, please?"

"This is not sounding good, but he was a man of about forty years age, athletic but heavy-set, dark hair and what in days past might be called a dueling scar under his left eye."

Tom looked at his father as they both mouthed, "Streffan Mirov!"

"I suppose I need to be up front with you, Mr. Berry. The man you describe may well be a renegade scientist from the nation of Brungaria. Now, please do not go talking about this with anyone until after my Security man, Harlan Ames, gets there tomorrow. Please lock up everything you still have, ensure that this man is not allowed on premises, and have photos and any surveillance footage that might show this man's face available. Thank you for your cooperation. If this is Mirov, then all I can think is he positioned himself in your organization somehow with the intent of industrial espionage."

A moment later Damon ended the call. He immediately phoned Harlan and told him of his suspicions. Ames agreed to take a Swift jet out to the Los Angeles area that evening to investigate.

"I'll take Phil Radnor and a couple of my best men and women, and leave Gary in charge. I'll give you a report as quickly as possible tomorrow!"

The report, when it came just after four in Shopton, was not encouraging.

"There is every sign of some cosmetic surgery, but if this isn't Streffan Mirov, it is a near-twin brother. I've contacted the FBI and CIA and even Interpol about this and sent his latest photo to them. If he is still in the country, they ought to get on his trail quickly."

Eleven days later there had been no movement in catching up with Mirov. He had vanished like a puff of smoke in a windstorm.

But, Tom had not been idle. He and his team had constructed a basic framework for the flying pack along with many of the control systems. Enough progress had been made to assemble a test rig.

The first ten short flights were made using a life-like dummy in the harness with remote control. Beginning at just a few feet off the ground, stability issues and fine control deficiencies were worked out.

Now, two weeks after Harlan had come back with nothing to show for his trip to California but warnings for everyone to be on their toes for more troubles, the ladies in the Uniforms department had completed the flight suit test pilot Bud Barclay would wear for his manned tests.

Marjorie Morning-Eagle and her team outdid themselves using special fabrics and coatings that would serve to make the entire suit nearly invisible to RADAR, be airtight enough to act as a sort of spacesuit for the very high altitude tests Tom hoped to get to soon, and had the property of stiffening for added protection when subjected to strong wind forces.

It would, in Tom's estimation, help the pilot from feeling buffeted and smashed about by the air forces he would be subjected to in flight.

"That is about the neatest flight suit I've seen, skipper," Bud complimented the inventor. "Not too sure about the bright orange color, but what the heck, huh?"

"I had Uniforms add that orange overcoat for visibility since everything else is going to be difficult to track electronically. The final suit, from what I've read in the movie script, is supposed to be either deep blue or a dark purple."

Like early tests using a dummy, Bud started with short-distance trips barely rising a foot above the ground. To aid in landings the backpack was outfitted with an extendible tripod of thin landing legs only a half-inch shorter than Bud's own legs when clamped in the outer boots. They could extend or retract at the press of a small button on the right joystick.

"It flies almost like a dream, Tom," he reported after flight one. "Even with all the heat shielding I could feel the hot exhaust gases behind me. Made the old tushie a bit warm."

"That will go away when we let you fly faster than a snail's pace. You've just been hanging around in the hot exhaust gases. Later, you'll leave those behind you."

The pilot described several of the control features he felt might need attention and asked if Tom might work in a water bladder. "The suit is nice but a bit hot, so I got a little dry after just the ten minutes I was scudding across the tarmac."

"I can do you one better. How about a water tube as well as cooling tubes throughout the suit to take heat away?"

"Now you're talking!"

Test two an hour later was at a height of three feet but included several tight turns and starts and stops. Again, Bud debriefed with Tom, this time having nothing new to report but agreeing with his previous suggestions.

"Tomorrow, we take the suit over to Lake Carlopa and let you try it up to perhaps thirty feet. If things go haywire, the suit and exo-frame will protect you and the recirc system will make certain you have ample air to breath. I'm going to add an emergency floatation pack tonight."

Five more tests all went without a hitch. Everything Bud suggested was available one or two flights later so he still had things to test and report on, but overall he had enjoyed every flight.

"You were right about the heat thing. Once I got above five feet the exhaust gases dissipated before they could curl back up and surround me." Bud grinned. "When do I go for real altitude?"

"First I install the parachute system and its sensors. That is going to take all day tomorrow, and I feel the need to increase the hydrogen storage. As it is, your flights have been five to ten minutes long and we've refueled after each one, but what I'm seeing points to only about twenty-six minutes of continuous flight. The target is thirty and I want a twenty percent margin of error. So, this is Thursday, we'll do the work tomorrow and you can go up on Saturday or it can wait until Monday."

Bud got a sly look on his face. "Arrange for a Saturday picnic at the lake for you, Bashi, and Sandy and I'll provide the entertainment!"

Sandy talked their mother into supplying the food and invited her and Damon along. She was immediately suspicious when Bud said he'd meet them there and arrived in an Enterprises' van, but they all enjoyed a nice cold fried chicken and potato salad lunch before Bud stood up, stretched, and said in an overly corny voice, "I think I need to stretch everything. Give me a minute; I'll be right back."

All eyes swiveled to Tom who shrugged and made a zipping motion across his lips.

Five minutes later the reappearance of Bud caused everyone to laugh. In his orange suit and the large *Sky Streaker* prototype on his back he did look rather odd. But, everyone stopped laughing when he pressed a button, gave them a thumbs-up sign and then quickly rose from the ground, heading out over the lake.

Tom pulled out a radio and set it on the ground so everyone could hear.

"Flying like a dream, skipper. With all your add-ons I'm going for that five thousand foot climb. Then, assuming all goes well I want to check her out for speed."

The inventor radioed his go-ahead.

The climb was made in just under a minute surprising even Tom; his computations said it ought to have a climb rate of under four thousand feet a minute.

Bud reported he was heading south for a run to Albany and back. "It ought to only take about twenty-eight minutes. Call you in a few."

But, fourteen minutes later his voice, now sounding very nervous, came back.

"Somebody is shooting at me! I just cleared a thick cloud layer and a line of tracer shells whizzed past me by only a hundred feet or so. *I'm getting out of here!*"

CHAPTER 8 /
"WHERE'S MY FLYING PACK?"

SANDY, in a panic, shouted at the radio, "Bud!! Get out of there!" Then, to Tom, "You have to go do something!"

Damon took her hand as she rose. He knew his daughter. She could be cool as an icicle if she was flying and ran into trouble, but would run around like a headless chicken if someone else were in that same situation.

"Sandra! Sit! Tom will try to find out what is happening. In the meantime, trust Bud to get himself to a safe location."

Tom tried the radio but only received, "Wait!" from his friend and brother-in-law. Finally, three long minutes later he came back on.

"It's okay. I'm fine. I guess I strayed into the Air National Guard airspace down here in Schenectady. Good old A-N-G scrambled five fighters and they couldn't ID me so they let loose with a warning salvo."

"Did you outpace them, or what?" Tom demanded.

"Nope. I decided to stop in mid air. That confused them so much they all started to circle around me and I slowly dropped below the clouds. It was only then I tried the emergency radio frequency. They had a laugh, but I was told to expect an FAA report and an investigation and a fine. Sorry, Tom. Sorry, Mr. Swift."

Damon took the radio. "Never mind that, Bud, Just come back and we'll see what needs to be done. Now, if I don't give this radio to your wife she'll rip my arm off."

While Sandy stalked off telling Bud how much she loved him and how she would skin him alive if he ever did something boneheaded like this again, Tom and Damon talked about the possible trouble.

"It's my oversight, Dad. I completely forgot to include an IFF transmitter. Without that is isn't a wonder they came after an unknown flying intruder."

When Bud landed, he climbed out of the *Sky Streaker* pack and then changed in the van into his street clothes. As he stepped forward his head was hanging low.

"I'm so sorry, Mr. Swift. Tom. I thought I'd skirted the flight corridors down there and stayed above the minimum clearance—"

Damon interrupted him. "It wasn't your fault, Bud. The suit is not quite—but nearly—RADAR invisible so what they did see was moving so quickly it might have been confused as a missile. But, as I said, it wasn't your fault. In fact, as long as you remained under ten thousand feet, we are all in the clear."

Looking curious, Bud told him, "I never went above eighty-nine hundred feet. So, why am I not in trouble?"

Tom answered. "While we waited for you to come back, Dad called a friend who is with the FAA. He told us the suit is classified as an Experimental aircraft, so you didn't need a flight plan or an IFF squawker as long as you didn't exceed ten thousand feet."

"That doesn't mean, however," Damon stated, "that Tom isn't going to install that identification system first thing Monday and before the suit flies again. Right?"

Nodding, Tom said, "Right."

With the *Sky Streaker* securely locked in the van, the six of them finished their picnic with big slices of a strawberry and rhubarb pie provided by Anne.

Early Monday morning Tom was sitting at his desk doodling some possible improvements to the flying suit when the door to the shared office opened and a man looking like he hadn't slept for three days stepped in.

"Come on in, Harlan. Coffee? You look like you could use some."

Ames nodded and moved his hands apart to indicate he wanted a large one. He took a seat in the conference area and motioned for Tom to join him. The inventor brought the largest mug he had full of steaming coffee which Harlan sipped with a sigh.

"Big news, skipper," he stated after drinking about a third of the mug.

Sitting next to the Security man, Tom stated, "As long as it is *good* big news. What have you got?"

"Good, big news. Or rather, big news, some good and some not so good. First, the bit of good news. Giselle Ackerman, the German woman you took to Venus has been cleared. Her former boyfriend has been implicated in a plot to sabotage the entire German space industry."

"How?"

"As it turns out, he is, or was, a plant by the Brungarians. Been there as sort of a sleeper for several years to build up trust. Now that Brungaria is supposed to be friendlier, he took it on himself to steal her ID access card on several occasions, letting himself into the secure areas and doing his dirty work. He's admitted to working on his own, not under specific orders, but with a sense of misplaced loyalty to a regime no longer in power. He once worked for Streffan Mirov so there is that angle to consider as well. Oh, and he did the real sabotage weeks or more than a month before the satellite was packaged up and brought to us."

"That's good news, indeed. But, there's more?"

Harlan sadly nodded. "Yes, there is. The Germans have three other satellites in the works and he won't say how he has sabotaged those, only that they will fail after being sent into orbit, and not the same way the Venus probe did."

With a disappointed shake of his head, Tom asked, "Do they want any of our help?"

"Unknown," Harlan said standing up. "My suspicion is they *will* come to us, but we have to wait. The Germans are very proud and stubborn about asking for assistance. If and when the time is right, I assume you'll be ready to aid them."

Tom agreed he would be ready if that should be the case.

"Finally, our good old news agencies are circulating another 'What is Tom Swift up to now' story about your flying backpack. I checked with our local nemesis and Dan Perkins swears it came from a press release."

Barely another day went past before Tom received a phone call from Howard Gardner in Hollywood. The man didn't even say 'hello' before launching into:

"Swift? Where the heck is my flying suit?"

Tom was stunned into silence for a moment. Finally, he took a deep breath and replied, "Hello, Mr. Gardner and how are you today? To answer your rather rudely put question let me remind you that just three months ago when we signed up to create the flying pack for you I told you it might be as much as five months before we had a working prototype, and then one or two more months to perfect and deliver what you want. You agreed at that time it was going to be at least eight months before you went into production and that you had no problems with our proposed schedule. Before I ask you what has changed to make you take this apparent attitude, let me ask you about your leaking information to the press about what we are building."

Now it was Gardner's turn to remain silent for more than a few seconds.

"Not sure what you want me to say, Swift. It's my right to advertise a forthcoming project to drum up publicity ahead of time. What's your problem?"

"I will tell you what my problem is. Your blabbing about the suit and talking about some capabilities it may or may not have puts us in a very bad position. There is an active spy group wanting to get their hands on such a device, and the U.S. Government is most likely going to be rather angry they were not notified about such possibilities before your press releases. I have to speak with my Legal department, but I believe your pre-announcing without clearing it with us goes against the contract we have, and we might need to halt development."

Gardner sputtered and tried to form a sentence, but Tom beat him to it.

"Also, my wife, my chief test pilot and even myself have been attacked by persons trying to get their hands on my flying system. My belief is that your announcing things about it has put all of us in some jeopardy. Unless you give your ironclad guarantee that nothing, and *I mean absolutely nothing* more is spoken, written or mentioned about the flying device, I believe Swift Enterprises will terminate our contract."

There was a moment of silence. Tom had had enough. "Goodbye, Mr. Gardner and good luck with your movie."

Tom hung up, allowing himself to remain angry for another five-seconds before he shook his upper body to release the stress that had built up.

He called Jackson Rimmer and told him about the conversation.

"Not exactly the way I'd handle it, Tom, but I agree in principle. Let me give him a call to discuss things. I may go ahead and tell him we will continue on, but will require his full cooperation on putting a blanket of secrecy around things."

Tom told him to do what he thought best. "Besides, we already have the *Streaker* working; I just need to give it more testing and then finalize the design. Only, please don't tell him we're that far along."

"As if I would," Rimmer said before thanking the inventor and hanging up.

Tom attempted to put the matter from his mind, but the fact that Enterprises was on the hook for more than half-a-million dollars in development and materials costs so far weighed heavily on his mind.

To get his head straight, Tom decided to build a simulation of the flying rig and see what the computers could tell him about the aeronautic stability, potential speed, and maneuverability might be based on a few more changes he might like to make.

It took the rest of the afternoon and into the evening, but

before heading home he had a fifteen-minute simulation scenario running.

The results staggered him.

Bud weighed one-eighty-seven, so with the entire suit and backpack, he would be flying with two hundred sixty-three pounds or thereabouts.

It seemed to be a perfect weight. Much lighter and a flyer would be subjected to too much turbulence, getting tossed around in any wind stream greater than about fifteen miles per hour.

Much heavier and the flyer would find reaction sluggish and the entire apparatus would come shy of the thirty-minute flight time target.

The combination of Bud's weight and overall height played so nicely into the simulation Tom thought anyone might believe it was a set-up. Not so, but it looked awfully convenient.

At the end of the computerized run he believed there was little to do with the actual equipment; everything from this point on would include the computerization and programming.

Patting his monitor, Tom shut things down and locked up his underground office. At ground level he noticed the fall air was beginning to get a bit of a chill and was glad he had parked just a few hundred feet away.

The main gate was closest so he headed there, only to be stopped by the night guard.

"Hey, Mr. Swift. We got word some crazy guy is blocking the main road into Shopton with sawhorses and some signs. Typical, 'The end is near' and that hogwash, but Mr. Ames called down to tell you to take the fire truck road home and avoid all that."

Tom nodded. "Thanks, Jeffrey. I'll do that. Have a nice evening."

"Good night to you!"

Tom took the indicated turn and was soon speeding along the short road, but as he neared its one fairly tight corner he slammed his foot down on the brakes.

The first thought he had as the car stopped was, *This looks like a set-up with me as a target!*

Next, he looked all around, but the cleared trees for at least fifty feet on either side of the lane showed nobody else other than the disheveled man standing thirty feet in front of him.

He was dressed all in white—very dirty and ragged from what Tom could see—and held a large, round paper sign:

MAN SHOULD NOT FLY!

Tom had a very bad feeling about things so he put the car in reverse and backed up a couple hundred feet. Next, he tapped the TeleVoc pin under his collar and silently intoned, "Security." The *ping* told him the call was being routed.

Gary Bradley answered and Tom gave him a quick rundown on what was in front of him.

"Harlan called the front gate to tell them I ought to take this route because of a disturbance on Charley Hill Road."

"Tom? Take a very good look around you and if you spot anybody other than that man, or if he is moving, get the heck out of there. Harlan did *not* call the gate. I know because he and I have been sitting here talking for the past hour."

More nervous than ever, Tom looked wildly around. There was still nobody to be seen and the crazy-looking man was still holding up his sign but staying put.

He was about to back up to the closest turning point when the TeleVoc *pinged* him. "Gary Bradley," the computer said.

"Answer." *ping* "Yes, Gary?"

"Harlan and I are running to the car and we'll be with you in four minutes. Stay put if you can. If not we'll pass you coming back this direction."

Tom decided to wait. When early evening headlights came around the previous bend in the road, he tensed at the idea it might be someone out to attack him. He put the car back into gear and got ready to race forward.

It wasn't necessary.

"We're here," came the voice inside his head. The car, one of Enterprises' all-terrain vehicles, pulled along side Tom's car.

"I'm going to go talk to that man, skipper. You and Harlan stay put."

Gary got out and walked briskly forward. The man shrank away and dropped his sign as Gary got within ten feet. Everyone could see him raising his hands in the air even though Gary had not told him to do it.

Two minutes later they saw the old man nod and come along with Gary. They reached the two vehicles.

"Tom, I'd like you to meet Cyrus Abernathy. Cyrus is a recent import to Shopton and I guess you could call him the town crazy."

Both Gary and Cyrus smiled and the old man nodded his head up and down.

Gary had the circular sign and now Tom could see it was just an old taped-together hula-hoop with a piece of paper taped around it.

"Cyrus tells me he was paid to come out here to protest. Said a man called him this afternoon, offered him twenty dollars and told him to be here by five."

"Got here at four-fifty," Cyrus almost boasted. "Ain't nobody gonna say old Cyrus is late fer nuthin'!"

Tom got out of his car and approached the man. "Can you tell me exactly what this man said. And, how were you paid?"

Abernathy had to think a bit before answering. "Had him one of them furrin' accents. Sort of like that short feller in the moose and squirrel cartoonies. And, he promised I'd get my money by six when he came along. Wanted me to stop anyone comin' along the road and see if they was, uhh, well, I forget who, but if I spotted the feller I was ta throw this at him."

Abernathy reached into his ragged pants pocket and withdrew a nasty-looking sort of grenade.

Gary snatched it from his grasp and hurled it far off the road.

A popping explosion and a lot of smoke or gas wafted out of the trees. Lucking, the breeze took it far from the waiting men.

"Holy smokes!" Cyrus Abernathy muttered. "I coulda got hurt or kill't or something. Good thing you gents come along."

"Where did you get that?

Cyrus turned and pointed. "Got left in that box over there for me."

Gary took Cyrus by the elbow and led him to the security vehicle.

"We'll take him down to the Shopton PD for a statement and then get him home. I'm guessing whoever called him also called the gate to set all this up."

Tom nodded. "Do you think this foreign man will show up at six?"

Both Security men shook their heads. "No," Harlan said, "but I'm calling for one of our men about the same build out here in ragged clothes to wait. You head home, Tom."

The inventor smiled, got into the car and put it into gear.

By the next morning, Jackson Rimmer reported that Howard Gardner was under pressure by his studio to get started on the project that was going to run over the budget they had agreed to finance. He'd allowed his anxiety to take over and understood

Tom's position.

"Mr. Gardner apologized to me and asked that I pass it on to you, Tom. He has already begun filming and will arrange things so any scenes needing the suit will come at the end of the shooting schedule. He did ask if there is some way to get a non-working version for some of the earthbound and close-up scenes."

"If you could call him back and tell him it is possible, but not within the original bid. Even a non-working model will run him around thirty thousand dollars and will be completely nonworking. Not even the air circulation system will be there, so anyone wearing the thing will need to open the visor about every minute to get fresh air in there."

By the time the word came to go ahead and build the extra unit, Tom had spoken with his father who suggested a simple fan should be built in to supply clear air to whoever was wearing the suit, and Tom agreed to make that happen.

Dianne and her Propulsion team had been working on new ionic thrusters for the suit and had come up with a refinement allowing for nearly the same thrust results from almost ten percent less hydrogen and seven percent less oxygen. This would bring the total flying time to just over thirty-five minutes and let Tom scale back on his planned upsizing of the gas storage tanks.

They would still be slightly larger than the originals, but as there was already a bit of extra space within the current frame, that would not require resizing.

It was good news all around. The larger tanks would have required even thicker walls and that would have also increased the overall size of the *Sky Streaker*, affected the balance, and meant some reprogramming of the flight and balance programs.

"I do have to tell you the new thrusters weigh about three pounds more each, Tom. I hope that can be accommodated."

Well, he thought, *there goes not having to do more programming*. To her he said, "It'll all work out fine, Dianne. Thank you to you and the team for their hard work. Go ahead and send the plans over to Hank so he can work up the housings for them."

It took considerably less code work than he anticipated as the design—earlier placed into the company's 3D CAD system by Hank—featured an auto-balance algorithm to compute the exact balance center for everything. That set of numbers easily were inserted into the program and it was compiled into the end programs before the end of the day.

Soon after he arrived home he got a phone call from Harlan.

"Skipper? Thought you'd like to hear the results of the old

crazy Cyrus thing."

"I'm guessing that nobody showed up to pay him last night."

Harlan laughed. It sounded very reserved. "Your guess would be nearly wrong. When we got him out of the police department and took him to the low-rent boarding house where he's living, there was a note on his door with his twenty dollar bill under it. Both held there with a nasty stiletto knife. The note was to you. I'll read it:

"Tom Swift, that smoke bomb could just as easily been a real grenade or even a sharpshooter in the forest. Either turn over the plans for your flying pack or the next time you will die!

"That's all it says and of course there are no fingerprints on the note or the knife and dozens of them all over the money."

"Any idea who sent it?"

"Not the specific sender, although we got several sets of prints from the door frame we're in the process of checking, but I think we both know who this all points back to."

CHAPTER 9

OUT OF THIS WORLD TEST TRACK

DAMON SWIFT looked at his son, a small smile playing on his lips.

"What is that Cheshire Cat grin all about?" Tom asked seeing his father's face.

"Nothing much, really. Just a father's pride in the accomplishments of his first born son. Plus," he said picking up a printout of an email that had come in that morning, "I have an inquiry from our favorite Senator, the Right Honorable Peter Quintana."

Now, Tom smiled. "What's he got to say?"

Rather than answer directly, Mr. Swift handed the page to Tom who read it quickly, then re-read it.

"Wow. What do you suppose he means by 'Special Forces Missions'?"

"Well, I suppose he means that some small group of special military men and women might be trained to use your flying apparatus for purposes like reconnaissance or secret operations behind enemy lines. I'm assuming that last one based on his question about durability under small arms fire."

"Yeah. And the part about stealth and silent operation." Tom's face frowned as he became puzzled about something. "How do you suppose he heard so much about this *Sky Streaker*? We haven't been exactly top secret about it, but we also have not spread the word around."

"For that, you may need to contact your Mr. Gardner out in Hollywood for a complete set of his releases before you put an end to them. My guess is it's his earlier touting his upcoming movie serial and spouting off about the flying rig."

Tom groaned. "Great! All I need is for him to be back with telling the world, getting some of the details wrong, and then everyone grouses when we turn over something else. I'll give him a call in a few minutes."

First, however, Tom called the office of Senator Quintana. He immediately recognized the voice of his secretary as the Senator's daughter.

"Hi. It's Tom Swift. Is your dad... is the Senator available?"

"Oh, hello, Tom. Dad's due back in a few minutes. He had to scoot over to the Senate chamber for a vote on something having to do with saving the wild pigeons in Central Park, or one of the other fifteen bills that take up valuable time and do absolutely nothing for our constituents. Wait, I hear his grumbling coming down the hall... and... yes! Hang on, Tom."

He heard the phone *click* into Hold and sat back, waiting. There was soon another *click*.

"Tom? Thanks for calling. I didn't add that to the email but hoped you'd get back to me. So, is anything I listed true or is it all marketing hooey?"

Tom cleared his throat. "Well, if everything you've heard comes from out in Hollywood, then there is a probability it is substantially wrong. How did you hear about what we're doing, or hope to do?"

Pete Quintana confirmed Tom's suspicions.

"A friend who works in television got a press release the other week and sent me an electronic version of it. Then there is a report from one of the Air National Guard stations up around you regarding a mystery jetpack flyer. I guess I need to ask if it is an outright lie."

"No, not a lie, but also not something I wanted spread around." He told the politician about the Daedalus company and their possible association—unwilling and unknowingly—with the Brungarian scientist, Streffan Mirov.

Pete Quintana, a man given to use of some colorful language at times, let fly with a few choice words.

"Okay, I'm better, now," he told the young inventor. "Unless you tell me otherwise, I am going to put a little pressure on that studio to keep things under wraps. Might be a 'barn door is already open' situation, but quashing anything else will be in all our favors. Now then, tell me what your rig *will* do."

Ten minutes later Senator Quintana thanked Tom, telling him if it were possible, the version of the flying suit delivered to Hollywood needed to be on a loan basis and recovered at the end of filming. He suggested some of the funding might be covered by the Government. He also offered to have an FBI agent stationed on the set to protect the equipment.

"I know you didn't have that on speakerphone," Damon said when Tom hung up, "but I'm pretty certain I know what all Pete had to say. What's your next step?"

Tom thought a moment before replying.

"I think after a few more flights around here, and *not* down around Albany and Schenectady, I'd like to give the *Sky Streaker* a real shakedown by taking it up to the space station and trying it out in both a vacuum as well as the microgravity of the central space in the station tube."

Seeing his father's unspoken questions, Tom added, "Someday, I think I'd like to investigate using a variation of it for maneuvering around up there. Replace the current backpacks workers use outside and also for when we add on to the station."

He grinned. Already huge, the first tube of the station had been planned to only be half or a third of the eventual station. As time, need and funding made it advisable, a second tube could be constructed in space and sealed to one end. Then, the new tube would be pressurized and populated with access between the two parts via the existing airlocks.

"When do you go?"

Tom replied, "I think on Friday. That gives me the next three days, plus the rest of today to add a few things and have Bud run some more test flights."

On Thursday, Tom was sitting in the main dining room having a cup of tea and looking over a checklist for the trip when he sensed someone standing in front if him. He looked up and smiled.

"Well, hello, Doc."

"Hi, Tom. Got a minute? I overheard that last part of the conversation with your dad the other day. I was talking to Trent and couldn't help but hear."

"Sure. What's up?"

The doctor looked sheepishly at his young friend and boss as he sat down. "You remember how I used to come along on some of your adventures? Sort of medic-on-demand?"

Tom recalled many such times the physician, only about seven years his senior, had come along. Most times there had been more than anyone wanted him to become involved in, but his presence had saved Tom's and others' lives on more than a dozen occasions.

"Sure. Do I sense a 'can I come along' request?"

Greg Simpson nodded. The truth was he was getting a little antsy lately. After the months-long stress of dealing with Damon Swift's brain tumor and the subsequent storm of inquiries he had to field once Tom's nanosurgery robots had proven to do the trick, things had quieted down at Enterprises to the point where he often sat in his office all day long with little or nothing to do.

He was, in a word, bored!

"Yes. Things are uncannily quiet in the world of Swift medical needs, and I've been spending a lot of time wondering if I ought to take your dad up on his suggestion of a month's vacation. The thing is, I just can't bring myself to terms with the idea you all could do without me being here for that long. Makes a fellow think he isn't mandatory!" He grinned slightly but his eyes told Tom he was feeling a little underused.

"Doc, you are welcome to come on anything I get involved in as long as there is room. I can't promise that's going to include too many long-distance space jaunts like the one out to the planet Eris, but anything where I can be mostly certain we can get you back here in no more than a day if you are needed sounds absolutely do-able."

Doc let out a deep sigh. "Thanks, skipper. And, this trip up to the station isn't just a lark. I want to try out a new low-gravity serum mixer I had Arv work up for me."

Now it was Tom's turn to sigh.

"There was a time, you know, when you came to me for all your gizmos and thing-a-ma-bobs, Doc. Have things changed that much?"

Doc patted the inventor on the shoulder. "Nope, it's just that I wanted to see if my rudimentary understanding of engineering and design was a pipe dream, or if something might come from one of several medical device ideas that have been rattling around my head this past year or so. Guess your nanobots got me thinking along new lines."

Tom thought a moment before asking, "So, what is the purpose of this mixer of yours?"

"Pretty simple for a start. Up to now nearly all medicines we have stocked at the old Outpost and now Station Beta have been brought up from Earth and stored for future use. In and by itself that wasn't the real issue. But anything developed up there," and he pointed to the ceiling, "that required liquid compounding at very slow speeds—and surprisingly that includes a lot of things—all had to be brought down here to be mixed before heading back up. Low and zero-G conditions don't let things mix at the speeds necessary to not damage the ingredients, especially when that includes living cells like blood."

He explained how his new device was a combination adjustable mixer using a trio of soft paddles at the top, middle and bottom of the chamber rotating in alternating directions along with an outer device that slowly tumbled the entire inner mixing chamber.

Tom could picture everything and congratulated Doc on an excellent idea.

"Maybe we can spend a little time sitting up there and you can tell me some of the other things you want to try. And, don't worry. If you and Arv want to work on these things alone, I'll keep out with no hurt feeling at all. Promise!"

The following morning Tom, Bud, Doc, Chow and Dianne Duquesne—very curious about how her team's ionic drive units would react in space—left in a small cargo jet for Fearing Island. Strapped in the cargo compartment was the *Sky Streaker* along with a small case of spare components.

Although Tom had thought to take one of his space saucer ships up the truth was the flying equipment was just a shade too large to fit through the access hatch. So, with it now in the hangar of the *Challenger*, the group, plus a third pilot, Scott, from the base, lifted off heading for the giant station.

"Well, that's new!" Bud exclaimed as they approached the station, slipping close into position.

Where previously the *Challenger* crew would need to suit up for a transfer through the vacuum of space, a flexible rectangular tube came snaking out from around the closest docking point and soon contacted and sealed against the lower access airlock next to the larger hangar door.

"Yes. That went in a couple weeks ago. Dad figured that not only is it impossible to normally dock this ship to the station, but there are a few nations who want to send up people in their own spacecraft that also would not be accommodated by the standard docks. For now it is just this one dock, but at least two others will be similarly outfitted in the coming months."

The group transferred to the station taking the *Sky Streaker* suit with them. Luckily, it did fit into the large airlock of this docking point. Five minutes after entering the station, Tom walked up to the man coming to greet them down on the "floor" of the station.

"Art!" he called out.

"Well, hey there, skipper and friends," the man returned. He shook hands with everyone.

Art Wiltessa, a pilot, astronaut and submariner who had worked for the Swifts since the time Tom was about seventeen, was the duty commander of the large station, dubbed Space Station Beta by most. He was in month two of his four-month rotation. He and two others divided the year into thirds allowing them to spend eight months back on Earth performing their normal duties.

"I got your itinerary and have tried to let folks know to not be surprised by what they may see zipping around in here. But, what's this I hear about wanting to fly it outside?" He looked concerned.

"It's a totally sealed suit and the normal air compressor can be swapped out with auxiliary tanks of compressed air to use in the suit and for the pilot to breath. It should provide enough air for about an hour in vacuum."

Looking to the side, Art asked, "And is Barclay the only one who will be given the chance to fly it?"

"Why, Art," Bud said with a smile. "Jealous? Let me tell you the story about being fired on by fighter jets while testing that thing. Not quite enough to put me off flying it again, but it's a good cautionary tale."

"My guess is you deserved it," Art said, teasingly. "What did you do? Buzz a formation and knock on their canopies?"

"Something like that, yeah. Anyway, if the skipper okays it I can check you out on the controls in a half hour."

"And, I hereby give that permission, but only once your tests are complete, flyboy."

While their Fearing Island team member assisted Doc in hauling his equipment to one of the two station infirmaries, Tom, Bud, Dianne and Chow accompanied Art to his offices. There they accepted drinks. With the station slowly rotating around its axis, anyone standing on the ground—actually the inside of the tube— felt nearly three-quarters Earth gravity. Food and drinks needed no special containers, only the understanding by the person consuming them that the slightly lower gravity could allow things to fly up and make a mess if they were not careful.

"Tell me about this flying machine," Art requested.

Half an hour later Art was both stunned and excited. He had been briefed before Tom left the ground on what was being transported up, but had no real appreciating for what it could mean until Tom finished talking.

Looking around the room, he asked Bud, "Mind if I use your catchphrase?" When the flyer grinned and shook his head, Art muttered, with notable awe in his tone, "Jetz!"

Tom decided to put off the flights until the following day.

"Why, Tom?" Bud asked. "I got a good night's sleep last night and feel top of the world."

"Something tells me it might be best to get acclimated to the lower gravity and let your mind accept that before you go scooting off."

Nodding, Bud agreed he could see the sense in that.

"Are we going to do the inside and outside flights in one day?"

"I think so. Short of running into a problem inside we do those two flight before lunch, I add the air supply after we eat and then you go outside for an all around flight of roughly half an hour. I've added some extra sensors to monitor all the flights so we'll have a lot of data to use in case we go into production with these."

That evening Tom sat down with Doc to see what news the medico might have from his own experiments.

"See this face, Tom?" The inventor nodded. "See how it is smiling?" Another nod. "Then I shall tell you that it is so doing because my initial experiments came out better than I could have hoped for. Well, that's not true. I could have hoped that by simply turning on my new low-G mixer that I could instantly cure the common cold, though that just isn't likely."

"But, you do have access to that new injection that makes colds go away in just two days." Tom reminded him.

"Still have to find the patient and jab them." Doc said he would be finished by late afternoon the following day and would be ready to head back to Fearing about the time Tom said the flights would conclude.

Next, he met with Dianne and Bud to go over everything they each knew about the flight suit.

Dianne held up a hand. "If I may? Fine. I would like to propose shutting down the top pair of thrusters for the inside tests. Once Bud gets about fifty feet up he will be in such low gravity I don't want him shooting to the other side and crashing."

"Good idea. How about outside?"

She shook her head. "Can't say until we review the inside flights. It could be that even the output of one thruster is too much. Besides, it occurred to me that Bud won't exactly have a good set of brakes. He'll have to go slow."

Tom shook his head. "Not so. I didn't tell you but I had Hank and his crew create a swivel for the upper pair so they can twist one-eighty and point straight up if needed for slowing and stopping. The computer will take care of that once Bud turns the throttle backward, sort of like slowing a jetliner by reversing the thrusters."

It was a concept Bud understood very well.

The first test was an eye-opener. Even with the reduced thrust capability, he barely had time to reverse thrust as he passed the half-way point to the opposite side. The computer took over after checking for the closest solid object and he landed softly. He was more careful on the next flight.

Before Tom reconfigured the suit, Art got his chance to fly inside. He opted to fly to the midpoint at one end then traverse to the opposite end and back. When he touched down he had a grin on his face that threatened to not leave for a week.

The outside test flight started out well, but nearly did not end that way.

Bud stepped out onto a loading platform completely suited up, the hiss of his air supply comforting in his ears, and stepped off into nothingness.

He floated there for a moment before Tom gave the go-ahead over the radio.

"Take it slow, flyboy. I'd suggest heading up to the top of the curve and traveling along the length of the station. Then, see how long it takes to orient yourself for a trip down the opposite end and then back along the other side of the station before returning to the platform. No hurry; we're looking for good data about maneuverability in a vacuum."

Bud started "up," but soon noticed he wasn't accelerating as much as he thought he should. Tom had programmed an override for him in case things weren't working well using the computer, and he gave the small switch a nudge with this right thumb. After a good twist to the throttle, he was accelerating quickly within seconds.

"How is it going?" Tom radioed twenty seconds later.

"Uhh, not so well, skipper. It seems I don't have much steering out here. Almost as if this thing needs to run in air. In fact, I've traveled about a thousand feet past the upper rim and am only just getting this thing to turn. Only slightly at that!"

"Well, hit the brakes and see if you can limp back. Otherwise we'll come get you with a *Straddler*."

Five minutes later Bud made a call that caused him some embarrassment.

"Okay. Help, Tom. Come pick me up. I'm at least a couple miles away from the station now and can't even turn myself around."

Tom had already suited up in case of any troubles, and now he cycled through the airlock taking one of the waiting *Straddlers*—one of the large, 8-man models—and shoved it off the platform.

"Give me a radio bearing, Bud. I'm on my way."

The signal came through loud and clear and Tom turned the space cycle in that direction. Three minutes later he began slowing as he neared Bud and the almost useless *Sky Streaker*.

"It's going to be hard to sit you down on this, so I'll swing around in front of you and hand you a tow rope."

"Great," Bud said. *"I'll just tell folks I was vacuum skiing behind your space snowmobile."*

Tom had to take things slow so when they halted Bud would

not go whipping past him, but inside of twelve minutes after handing the stranded traveler the rope they were both standing on the landing platform.

"I guess this means a setback," Bud said once they were inside.

Tom shook his head. "Not so, my friend. I should have taken into account the need for an atmosphere with this type of ionic thruster. Plus, how gravity works with the flyer. After all, it is really just an air mover. Without the air to superheat, there is darned little to push out the back other than the expanding hot hydrogen, and I guess that isn't enough. Without gravity to help orient your body, you have very little control. Sorry for the foul-up."

Bud patted his friend on the shoulder. "As long as I have you to come out as my personal cavalry and rescue me from such things, I can still have fun with these tests."

"Okay. That's enough for this trip. Let's get the suit packed back into the ship, pick up Scott, Doc and Dianne and try to pry Chow out of the fancy new kitchen they have up here, and go home!"

CHAPTER 10 /
FIRST STUNT PILOT... FAIL!

TOM AND Bud packed the *Sky Streaker* into the back of Tom's Toad jet. The rear seats had been removed and the frame strapped to the normal seat hold-down points. The basic trip was to take them from Shopton across New York, over Lake Erie, and the tops of Ohio and Indiana before making a course change, heading straight for Los Angeles.

The weather was clear, and it wasn't until they had passed over the eastern border of New Mexico that the trouble began.

Without warning a pair of unmarked gray jets came abreast of them, one on each side. The pilots, hidden behind their oxygen masks, both pointed down, the signal for Tom to loose altitude.

He shook his head, rolled the Toad over and made a sharp turn under the left-side jet taking an even harder left turn and dropping several thousand feet.

Before either of the other pilots had much opportunity to coordinate what they were going to do he shoved the throttle all the way forward and pulled back on his joystick.

The two jets were starting their steep dives when the Toad shot back up gaining thousands of feet of altitude on them before they could make the necessary corrections. Five minutes later Tom had left them far behind and below a cloud layer hovering over the Rockies.

Bud, in the mean time got on the radio calling out for the Air Force base outside of Las Vegas. He gave out a conditional Mayday describing the almost attack by the unmarked pair.

"They looked a lot like old Mirage F-1s," he reported. No visible sign of weapons under the wings, but who knows what they might have inside," he responded to their request for identification information.

"Roger. We're scrambling aircraft right now. Be with you in eleven minutes. Can you evade that long?"

Bud looked all around them before saying, "I think so. No sign of them. We're squawking seven-nine-eight-two. Do you have us on RADAR? Oh, we're a Swift jet made from a special composite so all you may get is the IFF signal."

"Right. That explains a lot. Affirmative to the IFF squawk. Suggest you maintain heading and altitude and turn off IFF temporarily in case they track you. Give us a five-second signal every sixty until our aircraft reach your vicinity."

Bud tapped a virtual switch on the control panel and a red light began blinking over their IFF signal identifier. He was about to relax when a missile streaked past them about six hundred feet to their right.

"Nellis control? Swift Two again. We've just been shot at. Air-to-air missile, small so may be sidewinder or a French Matra Magic class. It's burned out and is falling. Probably going to impact somewhere around Arizona border."

"*Can you continue to evade?*"

"May not need to, Nellis. That same materials making us invisible on RADAR keeps magnetic or electronic lock-on from happening. Oops! There goes another one. Farther out. Looks like they're shooting wild. Hope your boys get here soon, though."

There was a small chuckle over the radio. "Be advised. Boys and *girls* to arrive three minutes. Suggest you go buster if not already and do roller-coaster. Copy?"

Bud acknowledged as Tom again shoved the throttles all the way forward and began to execute a random up and down altitude changes.

Bud noted the time and energized the IFF again.

"Go ahead and leave it on, Bud," Tom requested. A quick look at him showed his face was covered in sweat.

"Need me to spell you, skipper?"

"No. Just keep contact with the Air Force."

"*Swift Two... Nellis rescue squad. Can you get down to angels five soonest? We need the space,*" came the call from what would turn out to be the lead jet in the formation of six coming to their rescue.

"Heading down now," Bud responded.

"Five thousand is going to put us close to the mountains," Tom said, but he continued their steep descent.

As they maneuvered lower and Tom dodged the occasional peak, both listened to the chatter on the radio. In three minutes it was over.

"*We have bailout on one and have the other surrounded. Will take home as a souvenir. Have a better day, Swift Two. Nellis Squadron five heading home.*"

"Well," Tom said as he regained some of their altitude, "I hope they can get something from the one they didn't shoot down."

He changed radio frequencies and called back to Enterprises asking George Dilling to make the necessary reports to Harlan Ames and his father.

"Will do, skipper. Take care."

They set down at Santa Monica Airport an hour later, coming to a halt at the end of a line of private aircraft in front of the small terminal building.

A panel van had been rented and was waiting for them on the parking apron. While Tom unstrapped the flying pack Bud drove it over next to the jet. A light cover had been placed over the suit and the two young men transferred it to the van in seconds. Nobody seemed to be around to see them, which suited Tom.

They pulled out of the airport and were soon traveling north on South Bundy Drive. That got them to the 10 Freeway and finally the crowded 405. It was early in the day but the traffic was crawling along at under twenty miles per hour.

"This is where bringing a helicopter would have come in handy, skipper," Bud said jokingly, but he was right.

It took them over an hour to get to the Monograph Studios offices.

While Bud remained with the van Tom went inside to inquire where they needed to take the suit.

When he returned Bud could tell Tom was not happy.

"We have to get back on that number Ten and then to Highway One-Oh-One, up through some hills and to Universal Studios where they have rented a couple sound stages. The woman was very helpful telling me it ought to only take two or three hours to get there... if we hurry."

When they finally arrived at the service gate of the studio, they both were tired. "Looks more like a giant industrial park than a glamorous Hollywood studio," Bud said sourly.

"If you think this looks like nothing you anticipated, wait until you get a look at the amusement park part. They run thousands of people through there each and every day in what I've heard is one of the most artificial movie and television experiences around. Come on, Bud. This map the guard handed me says we've got to weave around about ten of these large buildings."

When they found the right pair of sound stages, Tom pulled up to one large door with a bored-looking rent-a-guard sitting at a table under a tatty sun umbrella.

"Can't stop here. Head on back!" he demanded, not even rising. When Tom rolled the window down but did not back up, the guard repeated his command.

"Well, then you explain to the Monograph people why you turned away their primary prop. Tell them we are tired and are going back to New York with it if they don't come out in three minutes!"

The man stood up and ambled over to Tom's side, his eyes narrowed. "What ya got?"

Tom had just about had it. "Let me see your company ID," he demanded. "And, if you don't have it with you, I'll see you're thrown off this lot!"

The man patted his back pocket and pulled out wallet that had seen many better days. It made Tom regret being mean as he could now see the man was only a low-wage earner who had been given one simple order: don't let strangers hang around.

Tom looked at the tattered card with the man's picture.

"Walter? I am Tom Swift. My friend here is Bud Barclay. And, we have, indeed, come from New York today, braved several of what I laughingly call *free*ways, and now only wish to deliver the million-dollar piece of equipment I am carrying. If you will please use that walkie-talkie I see on the table and call Howard Gardner, we can get this over. Tell him Tom Swift is here. Thank you, Walter."

The man had to think about all this for half a minute before he did as Tom requested.

A minute later the big door on the side of the building slid open a few feet and Howard Gardner—in a gaudy Hawaiian shirt —came out, his arms sweeping open.

"Tom, Tom, Tom Swift. Welcome! I trust you had a nice flight out and a good drive?" Seeing Tom's face he said, "Oh. I suppose not. Well, let me open the door a bit more and you can drive right in."

Once Tom shut the van off and he and Bud stepped out they looked around. Inside was a completely different world. In one corner was what looked like a very futuristic multi-level control center with about fifty people in some strange uniforms milling about.

Another corner had a set for the bridge of a submarine and next to that was an oversized jet aircraft cockpit set.

In all, Tom counted eight different set areas all crowded together with dozens of people wandering around moving lights, props and shepherding actors and extras.

"Hollywood," Bud muttered so only Tom could hear. "You have to love how this strips away all the magic!"

Gardner, who had walked away from them to bring back a rather beat up older man, came back all smiles.

"Tom, and... uh... friend? This is Jack Williams. One of the top stunt performers in the business and the personal stunt double for at least a dozen actors I am not allowed to mention. Don't want to spoil the image, you know."

"Personally, Mr. Gardner—and this person with me is Bud Barclay... my best friend, our top test pilot and the man who will be teaching your flyer and telling us if he cuts the mustard—personally I don't care. Nice to meet you, Mr. Williams," he shook hands with the man. "Are you the man hired to fly the suit?"

"Yeah," Williams said noncommittally. "Only one he could get with a pilot's license. So, what sort of aircraft is this?"

Tom looked at Gardner who said, "I didn't want to spoil the surprise. Thought Willie here would like to see it with a fresh eye."

Williams rolled his eyes and shook his head. "If this is a helicopter thing, I'm going to have to step out. Don't have that rating. Single, multi-engine and even single jet are fine, though."

Tom put an unnecessarily bright smile on his face, turning to Bud. "Would you please assist me in bringing out the flying machine, Bud?"

"Why, certainly, Tom. Love to," he responded.

At the back of the van, Tom looked at Gardner and Williams. "Turn around and close your eyes," he suggested to them as he and Bud hoisted the non-functioning backpack out, Tom also grabbing the purple flight suit that Uniforms had rushed through for him.

Even without the inner workings, the frame and everything weighed in at about forty pounds.

Jack Williams took one look at it, blanched, and began stammering.

"What the H-E-double hockey sticks is that?"

Smoothly, Tom replied, "It is a flying suit and backpack. This one is not working, but we will be delivering the real one in another few weeks. Flies smoothly at anything from a hover to about three hundred-ninety miles per hour in level flight."

Williams' legs buckled and he dropped to the ground.

Howard Gardner was so in awe of what he was seeing that he completely failed to notice his brave stunt man had fainted at the thought of flying in what Tom and Bud now held up.

"It's... it's... it is a thing of beauty!" he declared. "Right?" He turned to see if Jack agreed and went into hysterics seeing the man crumpled on the ground. "Very funny, Jack. Now, get up and try the thing on."

But, Williams did not get up.

"Your man fainted when he got the first look at this. It seems your decision not to tell him what he was getting into might not have been the best tactic," Tom told him.

He pressed a switch and the tripod legs slid out. They set the backpack down and draped the suit over the right control armature. Then, the boys stepped forward to help the fallen man.

Gardner was in denial that his stunt man had passed out. He stood by, almost frozen to the spot, his eyes flicking back and forth between the flying equipment and Jack Williams.

A woman dressed as a nurse came over with a first aid box.

"Are you a real nurse or an actress?" Tom asked politely.

"Vanessa Kelly, RN. I'm what they call 'Medical Services' for this movie. You are..."

Tom introduced himself and Bud.

"Oh, gee! I thought I recognized you. But, let me attend to this man. Then, I'd love to get your autograph!"

Tom rolled his eyes as she knelt down and checked Jack's pulse. Next she lifted an eyelid and shone a small light into it. She pulled a stethoscope out from her pocket and listened to his chest.

Finally, she took a small white-wrapped capsule from the first aid box, broke it between her fingers and wafted it under the stunt man's nose.

He coughed, snorted and sat up, eyes wide.

"Just a faint," she told everyone. "Come on, Jack. Let's get you to the catering truck and some ice water."

As she helped him get up and walk to the far side of the building, Gardner came over to Tom.

"Just this darned California heat, you know. He'll be right as rain in an hour. You'll see."

Tom shook his head. "I'm afraid, Mr. Gardner, you will need to locate someone else to fly the suit. Not only is Mr. Williams a little too small, I doubt he could support the actual flying rig. But of foremost concern is that faint. No pilot who faints for any reason can be allowed to fly without passing a full flight physical. Your insurance would never allow him to suit up unless they are convinced he is healthy enough."

Gardner's face soured. "That's going to be a little inconvenient. I was counting on Jack. He's a good man and been a great stunt performer for over forty years. Guess I'll just have to pay my main actor to fly it himself."

Tom sighed. "You might be able to use him for the on-ground shots, but I would rather eat the cost of this project than see a good man kill himself by not having what it takes. This isn't a difficult suit to fly once you get the hang of it, but I would never allow an unskilled pilot to even try it. Having said that it probably is a good idea to have your actor use this non-flying suit for close-ups and ground shots."

A handsome man, in a sort of generic movie way, walked over. He introduced himself to Tom and Bud.

"Brian Pemberly. I'm staring as Bradley Truemantle, the Sky Marshall. I just got word about Jack. Is he going to be okay?"

Bud spoke for them. "He's had a faint and may not be allowed to fly the suit."

Pemberly looked shocked. "What do you mean, 'fly the suit'?"

Tom explained that the final version of the *Sky Streaker* would be an actual flying backpack.

Brian shook his head. "No, that can't be right. Green screen and wires. Right, Mr. Gardner?"

Howard Gardner, looking rather pale, shook his head.

"All the close-ups will be you in the suit as will any walking around in it but I want realism for the flying scenes, so Swift here is building an actual flying rig!" He tried to look happy but was failing miserably.

Pemberly crooked a finger and asked Tom and Bud to join him to one side.

"Is that the truth? The stupid thing really flies?"

Bud's smile and Tom's nod answered his question. "The real one will."

"I'll be a son of a—"

"We get the message," Bud interrupted the man.

"Well, don't look at me to fly in that thing. A guy could get killed... or worse."

Tom, surprised at that statement, had to ask, "What could possibly be worse than getting killed, not that anyone is going to be?"

Brian Pemberly rose to his full height. "This is Hollywood and I am an actor. Being disfigured is worse. This serial is my ticket to fame and fortune and I'm not going to mess that up. Got it?" He took a step forward, menacingly, and found himself sitting on the ground a second later.

Bud smiled down at him. "Watch you manners, pretty boy. I don't know how you feel about broken noses, but that little shove could just as easily have been a poke in the nose. Do you 'got it'?"

Now looking a little ashamed, Brian put out his right hand.

"Yeah, I have it good. Sorry." Bud took his hand and pulled him into a standing position. "I sometimes get this way when a picture or TV program leans heavily on me. And, yes," he said favoring Bud with a toothy and all-too-white smile, "I would consider a poke in the snoot to be a bad thing. Friends?"

"Sure." They shook hands.

The boys were invited to watch the next scene being shot before Howard Gardner would be able to make any decision.

They sat in high canvas chairs off to one side while about thirty men and women tried to silently move around performing their duties as the five main actors and about twenty extras did their work in front of the camera.

Finally the director, a man wearing a backward-facing ball cap, shouted, "Cut and save that one as the main take. Continuity? Note how our hero moved that one lever. Have to make certain it stays there for scenes fifteen, nineteen, and......... twenty-two through twenty-seven."

He looked around without getting up from his chair at the side of the camera.

"Okay, everybody. Set up for scene thirty. Talent remain on stage unless it's potty time. We roll again in five minutes. Move it!"

Howard Gardner came up to Tom and Bud.

"Jack gave his notice. He absolutely refuses to even put on the suit for any reason. I told him this one doesn't fly but he won't hear it. What am I going to do?"

"Well," Tom said after thinking a moment, "I'm not in your business but I suggest the next stunt man you talk to you be very up front about what they are going to be doing. Assure them we will fully train them in all aspects including safety."

Bud added, "I hear good stunt people like that word, 'safety.' I'd emphasize it."

There was a commotion at the sliding door and it came open revealing a man in an inappropriately black suit, sunglasses and a briefcase. Behind him were two similarly-dressed men.

"Hey, Wes!" Tom greeted him on recognizing their FBI man. "You get assigned to this detail?"

Removing his glasses and shoving them into an inside jacket pocket, Wes nodded. "Someone get me a cold bottle of water and I'll introduce myself and set up procedures."

A young woman was quickly at his side with the requested bottle. She even twisted the top for him. Before he could thank her she had shrunk back into the gathering crowd.

Wes drank the entire bottle in a single breath and then looked around for a place to set it. The girl reappeared with bottles for the other agents, and took the empty from him, holding out a second bottle if he wanted it.

"Thanks, uhh, miss. I appreciate it. Maybe in fifteen minutes?"

She checked her watch, made a note in a small notebook, and went away again.

Tom made the necessary introductions with Howard Gardner. The director, identifying himself as Lawrence Laurent, came over to ask what was going on. He seemed angry.

Wes showed the man his credentials and then stated, "I am here to provide security on set for the equipment the Swift organization is providing. There may be a few changes in how you do things."

Laurent laughed harshly. "Oh, yeah? Over my dead body!"

He tried to turn away but Agent Norris' hand shot out grabbing him by the right sleeve and yanking him back around. He saw the glare in Norris' eyes and didn't try to pull away.

"That might end up being the case, *Larry*. You see, we have credible evidence there is an organization that is willing to do about anything, including murder, to get their hands on the working version of Tom's flying equipment. So, until we either find and stop them or this picture wraps, get used to seeing me and other men and women who look just like me. Can't miss us. Think *Men In Black* and then add the fact we carry deadly firearms, are trained to be able to hit a target two inches across at a hundred feet, and are willing to shoot to kill and I think you will be able to spot us."

He turned slightly and winked so only Tom and Bud could see it.

"Oh, and I need to speak to the following people right now." He read off a list of five names.

At the top of the list was Howard Gardner and at the bottom was Lawrence Laurent.

Both men looked very pale all of a sudden, but one of them was close to fainting.

CHAPTER 11 /
UNEXPECTED AND UNWANTED MEETING

AGENT NORRIS questioned all five of the people on his list before one of them—a sullen-looking man in coveralls who flatly refused to say anything—was taken away in a black sedan.

"Not sure who that man really is, but," he said to Howard Gardner a minute later, "I'd advise you to replace him. He will not be coming back here."

Gardner and the director, Laurent, each spent a half hour with the agent where he informed them there was one or more people in their crew who were known associates of a foreign industrial spy.

"These are the people who will kill you to get what they want, so I need to ferret them out. Once we get them I do not want to go through this again. Please do not hire anyone that has not been cleared by the Bureau from this point on. That goes for everyone from coffee girls to directors!"

Laurent had started to protest but Norris leaned forward and whispered something in the man's ear. Laurent turned sickly white, nodded weakly, and said nothing to anyone.

It wasn't until Norris reported to Ames and Tom that the nature of this sudden lack of bravado was revealed.

"I whispered his real name in his ear and made a suggestion about how that information could be used. Now, I won't tell you who he is, but the IRS would give their eye teeth to get him as would *two* wives still on his active list. He is going to tow the line until the movie wraps and is edited and then I suppose he will disappear."

"Sounds ominous," Tom said. "Did you have to make that deal with him?"

"Sound like business as usual," Bud stated.

"And, the winner is…" Norris told them, "both of you! The deal is as long as he behaves we let him work. Keep it all under your hats, please."

After showing Brian Pemberly how to smoothly get into and out of the suit and backpack, Tom and Bud headed back to Shopton.

Two more weeks would go by as Tom and the team worked to finish the deliverable unit. Bud, along with two other Swift pilots —Zimby Cox and Hank Sterling—flew the *Sky Streaker* checking out how if operated with different height and weight pilots. Zimby was a few inches shorter than Bud and Hank was definitely several inches taller. Every flight brought refinements to the programming plus minor tweaks to the equipment, and finally would come the time when Tom could say he could do no more.

Because he could not build in a weight scale he would rely on the pilot to input his body weight and height before each flight. Small changes to the orientation of the thrusters were made automatically so each pilot experienced the same flight characteristics.

Late in the first day back Agent Norris had called Harlan who brought Tom into the conversation.

"We ended up leaning on the man from the movie company explaining that he was going to be tried for espionage and possibly the attempt on your life, Tom."

"Not strictly true, Wes," Tom said, "but you sound happy with the results."

"I am. As expected, he's a low-level criminal who happens to have some experience as an electrician, which is how he got the job at the studio. Like several others he received a phone call, was promised money to simply look, note and report on whatever you delivered, and then wait for further instructions. He said the caller told him the suit you delivered is a working model and to be prepared to take photos of it."

Harlan inquired, "Did his caller, by any chance, have a foreign accent?"

"Funny you should ask that, Harlan, but as a matter of fact, yes, he says the caller did have what he termed a 'funny sort of Polish accent or something.' I think we can guess that it is Mirov or one of his people. I'm pulling a court order for the phone company to do a back trace of the three calls he got and compare them to the five report calls he made to a number that is no longer in service. Disconnected yesterday... what a surprise. It was simply a forwarding station anyway and not a location where Mirov was likely to have ever been."

"Uh, Wes?" Tom said, curiosity in his voice. "Would that caller know his man was in trouble? Is there another spy at the studio?"

"It's top of my priority list and starting tomorrow morning we do a roll call. Anyone who is supposed to be there and doesn't show up gets a visit from one or more of our agents. I'll keep you both in the loop. Why?"

"Well, if Mirov doesn't know his inside man has been arrested, could you put someone on his phone in case of another call?"

"Tom, we do that automatically, but I'm not holding out much hope. I'll let you know any future developments. Bye."

Harlan asked Tom to remain in the large office so he could come over and fill the inventor in on something. They hung up their phones.

Five minutes later Ames walked in and sat down, dropping a folder on the conference table.

"That, is a record of every employee we've hired in the past year, along with photos. I've had both my people and the computer doing facial scanning, and I have bad news."

Tom sat down and looked at the top page in the folder.

"That is Arthur Adams. He's an electronics assembly tech we hired about seven months ago. Good man, fast at his job and kept very much to himself."

Tom shook his head. He didn't recognize the man, which was strange as both he and Damon Swift prided themselves in meeting and recognizing just about every employee. "I sense that there is more to the story."

Harlan wearily nodded. "Yeah. There is and it isn't a nice story. Turns out Adams is not his name. It was a carefully groomed identification over the past four years for the man we now know was Miccos Thule!"

"The Brungarian agent!"

"Right. Take away the clipped beard and shorten the hair and you might recognize him as one of the two you and Bud tangled with. He passed our checks which went back four years, our minimum, with flying colors. Unless we see anything suspicious in that period we generally do not go back farther for low-level positions. That," Harlan declared, "changes as of today!"

"So, this Thule has been inside Enterprises for seven months doing who knows what all spying?"

"Say the word, Tom, and my resignation is on your desk. This is about the tenth time I have let you and your dad down and I'm not feeling very good about myself right at the moment."

"No, you stay but it might just be time to do another round of background checks on everyone. I know it'll take time, but it seems we need that right now."

"I've started that this morning. It will take about five weeks but we are going back to birth records. Back on Thule; he, of course, failed to show up the day after he and Karl Branski were arrested following the botched attack on you and Bud. No sign of him other than the Shopton PD stopped his car heading to the freeway soon after he was bailed out for a broken taillight. They let him off with a warning. As you might guess, he disappeared after that."

"Keep working on things, Harlan. And, check to see if anything in any department appears to have been removed, tampered with, or otherwise. I'll fill dad in on this."

"No need. I had an hour long conversation with him before we spoke to Norris." He blushed as he added, "Your dad also told me to keep my resignation letter in my desk. I guess I work for the greatest people in the business. I'll try like the devil to make this right!"

That evening Tom and Bashalli had a quiet dinner. Her mother had come to take Bart for the night, something she and Anne Swift did in rotation at least one night a week to give the young couple some alone time.

After hearing about the inside spy, Bashalli made a huffing sound. "Fine thing! Why does the world put up with those nasty Brungarians anyway?"

Taking his wife in his arms and drawing her close, Tom patted her back. "The hard thing, Bash, is it isn't all Brungarians. There are actually some very nice ones—ones who left Brungaria before all the negative political stuff started or even more recently. It's just there are some really bad people out there. The hope is they can be found and stopped some day."

"Well," she said, unconvinced by Tom's words, "some day I want to get left alone in a room with people like the ones who knocked us out and give them a good kick!"

Tom laughed gently. "You know, Bash? Some days I want to do that as well."

The morning mail, already sorted through and prioritized by Trent, was sitting on Tom's desk when he came in. Glancing through the top pieces he saw one with a red arrow sticker a bit farther down. He pulled it out and noticed it came from the office of the Vice President of the United States. It was a request for a meeting with a committee he had never heard of.

Hitting the intercom he asked the secretary to check with the V.P.'s office in Washington to ensure it was legitimate.

Five minutes later he had the answer. "Not only legitimate, Tom, but somewhat, and angrily, mandatory according to his secretary. I checked your schedule and you have this afternoon free. Shall I tell them you will be there today?"

"Go ahead," Tom replied with a sinking feeling. It was well known that the high-ranking politician had a dislike for the Swifts in general and for Tom in particular. Nobody knew why, but it was one of many personal failings of the second most powerful man in the nation. He was, at the best of times, an abrasive man to deal with. Or, he could turn into a confusingly nice person when he wanted something.

He had his Toad jet brought over to the closest parking spot to the Administration building and flew off at noon for a two o'clock meeting.

Unlike trips when his father was involved, Tom didn't expect, nor did he get, a waiting limo. He had to take a taxi to the White House where the VP's office was located in the West Wing.

There he was informed that the VP was actually in his other office in the building next door.

He was escorted over by a fully uniformed Marine complete with automatic rifle.

"Apologies for the walk, sir," the young man told him as he held open the front doors of the Eisenhower building.

Tom checked in and was shown to the VP's office ten minutes later.

"Ah, come in, Tom Swift and take a seat," the politician told him with a scowl on his face. "Do it quickly as I can only spare you a few minutes, but that ought to be enough."

As he sat down, Tom inquired, "For what, sir? Your email said this was an important meeting with a special committee and to be prepared to answer questions regarding a few of our latest projects. Did you mean U.S. Government projects?"

The man across the desk made a sour face and shook his head. "Had to tell you that to get either you or your father out of your territory and into ours. There's no committee, just me. Now, just sit there and listen, sonny!"

Tom bristled at the tone of the man's voice, but he was determined to hold his tongue.

"In the past you Swifts have had a pretty easy ride. Contracts that might have gone to other companies went to you. Your habit of undercutting the competition is sickening to me! You and your type of people don't care who you hurt so long as you get what you want! Call me a liar on that!" he said, daring Tom to speak.

Tom stood up and leaned casually over the desk, causing the Vice President to lean back, an alarmed look on his face.

In an even and falsely calm tone that spoke little of the anger Tom felt, he replied, "Sir, please listen to me. With respect to your *office*, I do not know if you are making all that up or if you have been given bad information, but I have this to say. Swift Enterprises and our family have never, *never*, underbid a project just to get it. We bid what the project will cost us plus a reasonable mark-up and never more than that. We work differently from other companies and can offer savings based on the way we do business. Never accuse us of cheating or low-balling or anything underhanded. Not unless you have indisputable proof sitting in front of you and are willing to make your accusations out in public and not behind your office's closed doors."

Tom sat back down, took a deep breath and looked at the man. "Now, suppose we talk about the real reason for this meeting, not just so you could try to bully me."

They sat in angry silence for more than three minutes before Tom stood back up again.

"Okay. If you have nothing constructive to say to me, sir, then I shall leave. At some point there will likely be a report made to the President's people about this rather abusive meeting. You really ought to check with people like Senator Quintana on their views about Swift Enterprises and what we do for this country. Part of what we are doing each and every day is at his request and on behalf of our own Government and military. Good-bye, sir."

"Wait!"

It was a single word and spoken in an almost worried tone.

Tom turned back to face his accuser.

"Okay, Swift. Okay... *Tom*. There is a small chance I over-spoke just now. But there is a national security crisis brewing and you seem to be smack dab in the middle of it, and not on the good side of things!"

The inventor sat back down, looking at the man across the desk for more information.

He explained about a new terrorist threat to large cities and military bases around the globe. A threat to bring destruction from the skies in such a manner that could not be detected until too late and could include small nuclear bombs being delivered with great accuracy.

Tom nodded several times and then asked, "Who is the source of this information?"

The V.P. looked down at his desk and took a few breaths before raising his eyes and answering.

"A man you have been working with who is more a loyal American than you, evidently! Howard Gardner. And, don't deny that you know him!"

Tom couldn't help himself and began laughing. "Howard Gardner of Monograph Studios? The man who has hired us to build him a jetpack to fly one of his stuntmen around for a series of movie shorts? *That* Howard Gardner?"

This took the Vice President by surprise and he suddenly

looked as if he felt a little ill at ease.

Tom pulled his small computer from its bag and tapped the screen a few times. He soon turned the thing around to show the man a picture.

"This is the movie stunt backpack I am designing but have not yet finished. While it will fly farther than any previous rocket or jet backpack system, and does not use traditional hydrogen peroxide jets or even jet turbines, it only will have a flight duration of about thirty minutes and a maximum distance of about one hundred sixty miles. I am building exactly two of them, one for Mr. Gardner—who may have just ended that possibility by his supposed report to your—and one for our company."

He added that the complexity of the systems was so high that it was unlikely anyone other than a high-technology company with a very large budget could reverse engineer the pack and go on to create others.

With each word the Vice President sank deeper and deeper into his seat and looked more and more uncomfortable.

Finally, he held up a hand to stop Tom. "Enough. It has become obvious that this Gardner man is either a troublemaker or seeking publicity. In either case, I am going to order the FBI to investigate this and arrest him!"

Tom shook his head. "I have a suggestion if you are willing to trust me." When he received the tiniest of nods, Tom continued, "I am going to call our Mr. Gardner and tell him I've been approached by the FBI regarding a report and see what he says. I won't mention you or this office or even the specific accusation."

When he went ahead and made the call, Gardner was flabbergasted by the thought.

"Tom! Not only did that not come from me or my office, and other than my early press release, I have only told two people any details about the backpack and they are both trusted men! Been with me for years!"

"Well, if you are certain nobody outside of you three and the people on my team, then that means there is a spy among us. You are absolutely certain you've told nobody else?"

"Nobody—" but his voice trailed off with an uncertain tone. "Except... damn! There is one other person I told. A pretty young woman who came to me wanting an acting job and ended up accepting my invitation to dinner. She was, well, let's just say that she was overly friendly, and kept steering the conversation to what wonderful new gadgets I was working on for my movie serial. I'll strangle the little—"

"Mr. Gardner," Tom warned, "I suggest that you not speak like that, and also that you give me her name and all contact information you have. Better yet, I am going to connect you to our Chief of Security, Harlan Ames, and you give him all the details. Hold on..."

He put the first call on hold, looked pointedly at the Vice President and made the second call. Moments later he signed off leaving Harlan to take care of things.

"That man on the phone is not the same Gardner I spoke with. Yours has no accent for one thing. I may owe you some sort of apology," the V.P. said. "Anyway, consider it said, but I will warn you that you have to clear what you do that could negatively impact this nation with this administration."

Tom stood. "No, actually as a private company we do not, but we always let you folks know, when we can, what we are building and for whom. That you want to ignore that and all the great things we have done saddens me. Good-bye, sir, unless you have anything else to say. Like that apology?"

The man sitting across the desk now turned to the side, ignoring Tom.

With a shrug he left the office. The secretary outside tried to get him to make a recorded verbal report of the meeting for her records, but he shook his head. "Ask you boss what he accused me of and how that turned out."

"I'm very sorry, Mr. Swift, for his abrupt nature. But, he is under incredible pressure right now. He's—"

"It isn't any of my business, madam. In the future, however, I would appreciate it if invitations were worded in a more friendly tone and contained the true nature of any meeting and not lies."

She nodded, and it was obvious she agreed with him.

Back at Enterprises he met with his father before they both went home.

Tom filled him in on the meeting and Damon agreed it had been an affront to Tom and the company to be accused of wrongdoing based only on a press release or loose lips by Howard Gardner.

"I do wonder though," the older inventor stated, "who that woman was and who she is working for." He raised one eyebrow. "Could the caller with the accent be our enemy, Mirov?"

With a groan, Tom replied, "I sure hope not. But, it makes sense. She poses as a starlet, gives Gardner all sorts of hints she is willing to... whatever, and then he blabs about the flying pack. What I don't get is why Mirov would call them with information to the Vice President about possible terrorist uses."

Damon grimaced. "What better way to try to steer public opinion against us than to get a man known for his antagonism toward our company riled up?"

He suggested that Tom speak to Harlan. "Maybe he can get a lead on this young woman."

When the younger inventor spoke with the Security man, there was a note of disappointment in Harlan's voice.

"Well, whoever she was gave Gardner a phony name and an address that does not exist. She also gave him a phone number that is disconnected, and as much as we have been able to get the phone company to cooperate, it looks as if it was for a throw-away cell phone activated a day prior to her appearance. It has been turned off since. No doubt it is in a trash can somewhere."

"Then, we have no chance of finding her?"

"Very little, but still something to keep looking for. I've notified Wes Norris out there and sent him a copy of the CCTV picture Gardner's office got of her. It's a long shot, but still a shot."

CHAPTER 12 /
STARS ALIGN, AND SPELL TROUBLE

THERE WERE no calls for Tom the next few days other than at least two a day from Howard Gardner, a man who was quickly bringing him to the opinion it might have been better to have ignored his project.

At the four day mark Harlan called to say that Agent Norris and the FBI now believed they knew who the young woman was that had wormed the information from Gardner.

"She is a known spy for hire, at least at Interpol," he told the inventor. "Been on their RADAR for several years. They list her as Anastasia Rusova, but that is undoubtedly a phony name. Arrested five times this past year alone, but released due to insufficient evidence, or lack of desire to prosecute because there would be too much to explain. Until now, nobody caught her in the act, so to speak. Looks like she was getting sloppy because Gardner's CCTV camera is fairly obvious in his office."

He suggested Tom keep a look out for her and offered to send copies of her various police photographs.

Harlan, who also received the photos, called later to tell Tom, "Looks like we ducked a nasty situation, skipper. That Anastasia woman? It turns out she applied for a temp position here three weeks ago. Couldn't provide references or much of a resume so Personnel thanked her and sent her on her way."

"Thank goodness for some small favors."

Ames agreed.

When Tom mentioned it to his father later, Mr. Swift sadly shook his head. "Somehow we have to make it more difficult for these would-be spies to even get through our gates."

"Well, Personnel had an idea a couple years ago we might want to try now. I recall that Harlan thought it might be something to look into. Enterprises sets up a separate hiring office downtown where all applicants go. It even would have a separate address for correspondence regarding job positions. Nothing comes to Enterprises or the Construction Company. Applicants get photographed, interviewed, credentials copied and then told it will take a week to verify them. Anyone trying for a quick chance at snagging something inside the gates won't even have a chance until Harlan's folks do a very complete background check. Including the newest facial recognition software here, at the FBI and Interpol."

Damon let out a small chuckle. "I was about to say that would raise the cost of hiring people, but it hit me that the cost in losses, and even attacks, is far greater. I'll call Personnel and give them the green light to start on that as soon as possible."

Tom was beginning to feel very frustrated. His meeting in Washington had put him on edge along with the attacks that had come shortly after accepting the Hollywood project. He began to think there might be more to everything than met the eye so he decided to have a serious chat with Harlan Ames.

On his walk to the Security building he was stopped three times by eager employees asking what was new or could he verify that Enterprises was going to be in a movie.

He politely parried all questions, especially the Hollywood one, by stating that nobody had contacted them about coming to the facility for any sort of video shoot.

"We got asked if our airfields could be used to stage a drag race with a jet for a TV program about a year ago, but that fell through," he told them with a grin that said, "I wish there were more to tell and that I could tell you more, but either there isn't or I can't."

Everyone who knew the young inventor knew that grin and respected it.

With well wishes, the various people drifted off leaving Tom to continue his walk.

Harlan's receptionist greeted him, saying, "The big guy is in conference with someone in Singapore about some industrial spy. He should be off in five minutes. If you want to wait, you can do it in his office because he's in the video conference room. Can I get you anything?"

"No, but I will take you up on using his office. I can make a few calls while I wait."

When the Security chief came in, Tom was just hanging up the phone.

Cryptically, he stated, "The stars are in alignment."

Tom grinned recalling an old comedy routine from TV and responded. "My hovercraft is full of eels."

They shared a chuckle for a moment.

"Really, Tom, it appears that a lot of the headaches and ducks behind the attacks are all coming into a row. I was just speaking with Chief Royal Inspector P. K. Wong of the Singapore Police. They have the brother of Karl Branski in custody and he is asking for a deal."

"Okay, what does he get and what do we get in return?"

"If the locals guarantee not to extradite him to the U.S. he says he knows all about this brother's location, who he's working for, your attacks, and what may be coming. Interested?"

"Perhaps. Can you and I head down there to be in on the interrogation? As it is I've got a few spare days and am going a little crazy. I need a change of location."

Harlan smiled. "I knew you'd want that so I asked. The answer is Yes, we can come down very soon for their tomorrow to be in on their discussions. Now, before you ask I need to tell you we have to remain silent and behind one-way glass. Can you live with that?"

"Well," Tom sighed, "I'd like to hit him with a few questions of our own, but I guess we have to take what we get. How does the FBI feel about it?"

"In on that all. It's a three-way agreement. I can be ready in two hours if you are. I guess we'll take the *Sky Queen*?"

"Sure. It'll be her last trip before she gets a complete interior and instrumental refit. I'm going to catch you-know-what from Bash over this, so I may invite her along, assuming the grandmothers can watch the baby."

"She'll have to fend for herself while we are at the police station, but that ought to be okay. I'll meet you at the takeoff pad at around one."

Tom left the office calling Bashalli on his walk back. She enthusiastically agreed and offered to make the babysitting arrangements.

"Oh, Tom. I love Singapore. When I was a little girl in Pakistan I went there with my father three times. I've only been back once and that was almost ten years ago. I'm so excited!"

Tom muttered to himself, "She must be. She didn't say goodbye before hanging up!" He laughed about it as he opened the side doors to the Administration building.

Upstairs he informed Trent of the trip and asked that all important correspondence be offered to Mr. Swift or send electronically to the Flying Lab.

"How long do you expect to be gone?"

"I think with the time differences we need to plan on my being out of the office at least three days. I want to be back by Friday, so it will be three and a half days. tops."

An hour later Tom swung by his house where Bashalli came skipping down the walkway like a young schoolgirl. Two medium-sized suitcases sat on the front porch waiting, so he got out, hugged and kissed his wife, then brought the bags out and put them in the back seat.

"Bart is inside with your mother," she told him. "She and my mother will take alternate shifts although I suspect they will both be here most of the time we are gone." She smiled, brightly. They both knew their mothers who had taken to the idea of being grandmothers with gusto.

Tom picked his son up and held him a moment before kissing the boy on the forehead.

"Daddy is going on a short trip, Bart. He and mommy will be back soon. You behave for gramma Swiff and gramma P." He knew he ought to use their real names but those were the way Bart said them. He hoped that would make it easier to understand.

The boy seemed very concerned about something. "Dadda go bye?" Tom nodded. "Momma go bye?" Now he looked sad. "Bart-a go bye?"

Now, with tears coming to his eyes, Tom had to disappoint his son. "No, Bart. This trip Bart stays with his grandmas. We'll be back soon and I promise I'll bring you a treat."

Treat was a word Bart knew. His frown turned into a sly grin. "This big?" he asked holding his hands far apart.

Now, Tom smiled. "Maybe this big," and he moved the boy's right hand half way back. Bart looked a little disappointed, but didn't make a fuss when Tom handed him to Bashalli for her goodbye kisses.

As they drove away she looked back. Tom patted her on the leg and she turned back.

"It is different going out for the evening or having Bart stay at their houses overnight. This is very different."

"Yes, but what you had me read tells me this is good for his development. Besides, he'll be fine and they will both spoil the heck out of him!"

Although Bud would generally come on a trip like this, he and Sandy had plans so he had asked Zimby Cox to stand in as second pilot. Also on the crew would be Red Jones and Hank Sterling as alternate pilots, and Harlan along with Phil Radnor from Security. Chow was unable to make the trip but sent over three large boxes of prepared meals for them to eat in flight or, as he put it, "If'n ya get a might peckish fer good old American food and not that squiggly stuff they all eat down there."

Tom didn't have the heart to tell the old cook that over the past several decades, Singaporean foods had become very westernized. You were just as likely to find a steak house or French restaurant on any city block as you were a traditional Singapore one.

Tom had requested a route to take them up over the North

Pole and then straight down the east coast of various Asian nations until the reached the top of Viet Nam. That government had given permission to traverse their airspace until they were over Thailand and then on a direct course to Singapore.

The small but bustling city/nation had one of the busiest airports in all of Asia but had been smart and built it on a huge piece of property then passed laws that nobody could build beyond it other than the smaller private aircraft airfield.

Tom and the two security men took a taxi along a busy multi-lane highway known only as PIE until they neared an interchange with Thompson Road. It was just three turns later they pulled in front of the Singapore Police headquarters on Irrawaddy Road. Harlan, who had changed some money at the airport, paid their fare and the cab zoomed off.

On entering the building and identifying themselves they were escorted down a wide hallway to a locked door. Their guide, a young man in a somewhat ornate uniform, unlocked it and showed them inside.

"Please take seats, gentlemen. It will be five minutes until the prisoner is brought to the room next door."

"But, we can't see anything," Tom lightly protested.

The young man smiled. "You will see. Once the lights in that room are turned on, you will see all and hear all, but be advised you may not speak out, shout, touch the glass or otherwise make a scene. Thank you for your cooperation."

He left them, the door clicking shut behind him.

"How will we get any questions we want asked to them?" Tom asked. "I'd like to confront him with what we know to see how he reacts."

"I sent them a list of ten questions I want answers to right before we left, and another three while we were in the air. Let's hope they do ask them. What were you thinking of?"

"For starters, I'd like to have a few names mentioned. In the past we've had interesting reactions from underlings. Names like Streffan Mirov, Karl Branski and Miccos Thule among others." He stopped because he saw the smile on both of his companions' faces. "Oh. Already thought of that?"

They nodded and Tom decided it was best to just leave things to the experts.

A few minutes later the window in front of them brightened and the room beyond was bathed in a rather harsh light. Inside were two tables. One with three seats on one side and a single, heavier one on the other, and a small one-chair table to the side. A small microphone dangled from a single wire from the ceiling that Tom assumed was going to record everything said.

Five men entered, three wearing uniforms similar to the young man who'd let them in, one man in a business suit—who took the small table—and a man in a cheap business suit, hands cuffed behind his back and his ankles in short-chain shackles.

The suit man tried moving his small table only to discover it was bolted to the floor. When he appeared ready to move the chair over, one of the police said something in what Tom assumed was Malay and he sat back down.

Questioning began immediately with one officer reading several of the questions including some provided by Harlan.

"You name."

"Gunter Branski."

"Are you working for Streffan Mirov?"

The man gave no reaction other than to ask, "Who?"

"Are you working with Karl Branski and Miccos Thule?"

The man leaned forward and snarled, "If I wasn't here to tell you what I know, and not be accused of your trumped up charges, you'd never get a thing on Karl."

The reader nodded. "And, who is Karl to you?"

"My brother," the prisoner mumbled. "My stupid brother."

Questioning went poorly with Harlan moaning several times at the clumsy way the police were asking questions and failing to follow up on most of what the man was telling them.

"Enough!" the man shouted. "Do we have a deal of not? 'Cause if we do I'll tell you about Karl and where he is and what he will be doing to that Swift guy and his family."

Another groan came from both Harlan and Phil when the officer announced to their prisoner that Tom Swift was right in the headquarters building and listening in on their conversation.

Gunter Branski looked at the two way mirror across from him. He seemed to be staring right at Tom. A very evil smile came to his face.

"Good, because that means he's in *our* territory now. His life ain't worth a plugged nickel, not that you jokers'd know what that was. You listen up good, Swift," he said as the man in the suit stood up and tried to hush him.

"We've got you now. You'll never leave Singapore and—" One of the policemen reached over the table and cuffed him in the side of the head. He shut his mouth.

Branski now said in a lower tone, "I hear Swift brought that pretty little wife of his with him. We'll get her first and then get him when he tries to rescue her."

The guards got up and pulled Branski to his feet.

Before anyone could stop him, Tom jumped up and tore the door open. He was waiting at the interrogation door when Branski was shoved out ahead of the first guard.

Tom didn't wait to make introductions. His right fist swung in a roundhouse punch catching the criminal in the face. Branski dropped like a sack of potatoes. The inventor was about to deliver a kick to his head when strong arms grabbed him from behind. He tried to twist out of the grip and swing around, but Harlan's voice penetrated the angry red haze that was in front of Tom's eyes.

"Take it easy, skipper. It me and Phil. Simmer down."

He took a step back before allowing his companions to take him back down the hall.

Behind them Branski's voice called out from the floor, "One punch won't do it, Swift. We'll get that wife of yours if we don't already have her!"

Now stunned as well as angry, the three men left the Police station and sat at a nearby bus shelter waiting for Tom to calm down.

Harlan made a call to the airport only to discover that Bashalli and Zimby Cox had left half an hour earlier to go shopping. When he tried Zimby's phone he got a disconnected signal.

Harlan felt a shudder run through his body. Every alarm and bell was going off in his brain telling him this was a very, very bad turn of events.

A moment later they all gasped when a police car with Gunter Branski sitting in the back drove past them. Branski was laughing. Phil had the presence of mind to hail a nearby cab and they were in pursuit of the police car within seconds.

"Where are they taking him?" Tom asked.

Harlan wasn't certain his next statement was going to be accepted, but he went ahead. "From what I know of Singapore law, if a prisoner is attacked while under Police protective custody, he or she must be set free. Sorry, Tom. I didn't have time to stop you."

They raced after the police car until it neared a city center area filled with far too many vehicles, motorbikes and pedestrians to move very far or very fast.

Branski opened his door, stepped out and looked around. In a flash he darted along the sidewalk.

Tom and Phil jumped from the cab. As Harlan tried to follow,

Phil shouted back, "Don't! Your heart won't take it. Get help!" and he was charging after Tom who was in hot pursuit of Branski.

By this time Tom was a half block ahead of him, and Phil's naturally heavier physique worked against him gaining on that. But, he kept at it.

In and around individuals and groups of people, Branski dodged and ran as if he knew he was being chased. He remained on the one sidewalk where someone else might run into the halted traffic to the other side of the street.

Nor did he attempt to run into any of the busy stores they were passing.

Tom was so narrowly focused that it did not occur to him Branski might be heading for a specific location.

There was no need to wait at intersections because even the cross streets were jammed with traffic and moving at a snail's pace.

Three blocks later Tom lost sight of his prey. Branski had jumped in front of and to the left of a group of five young girls and disappeared. They moved around something and for a split second Tom hoped that Branski had slipped and fallen.

The inventor raced to the spot only to find there was a low wall around a circular stairway going down below street level. He knew there were several of these around the city. They were enormous bathrooms for the general public that sometimes extended a hundred feet in either direction. As he watched, five men and two women came up and three others went down the stairs.

He didn't dare go down as Branski might jump him if he were actually down there, or worse… have accomplices down there. Tom tried to think what he knew of these places. There were typically just the one entrance/exit although he didn't know that for certain. He craned his neck looking for a similar low wall on the other side of the street or even farther down this side.

Nothing.

He looked around and spotted Phil, now a full block back but coming and decided to wait. He was jostled by a number of people and tried to move to the side to get out of people's way.

Without warning Tom felt a sharp pain as something jabbed into his neck. He tried to turn around but couldn't even though his head was spinning.

"Get him out of here," he heard the harsh command that sounded like Gunter Branski and he was grabbed by the shoulders and the feet, hoisted into a horizontal position and moved toward the curb.

"Looks like Swift fell for the trap. Now, Karl will get off my back for not carrying my weight. Ha!"

He heard the sound of brakes as a vehicle pulled up and the door being opened and he was carried closer to the waiting car.

CHAPTER 13 /
ADDED COMPLICATIONS

JUST AS Tom felt he was going to pass out his heels hit the ground. It jarred him back to reality a second before his brain registered that it had heard a familiar sound a second earlier.

ZERACKKK!

That had been it! The sound of a Swift e-gun being discharged.

It came just before my feet dropped, he told himself. *I wonder why—*

ZERACKKK! ZERACKKK!

Tom's rump, back and shoulders hit the sidewalk and his head bounced off the concrete. It hurt, but now his brain was really working.

So were his muscles and he rolled to the side before pushing himself up into a sitting position.

"You okay, skipper?" Phil panted as he skidded to a halt.

Whatever the car had been, it screeched away before Tom or his companion could get a license number.

He looked up at Phil and then at the two men who were sprawled nearby.

In a shaky voice, he said, "Thanks, Rad. Get me out of here. I have a feeling that e-gun of yours isn't exactly registered for free use around these parts."

Radnor pocketed the gun then helped him regain his feet which threatened to come right back out from under the young inventor. Together they moved to the doorway of a nearby department store and slipped inside just as the sounds of at least two sirens could be heard in the distance.

There was an unoccupied padded bench inside and around a small corner so Phil set Tom on it and went back to look outside. The two men were still unconscious and people—possibly used to this sort of thing—were simply stepping around them or over them. Nobody seemed the least bit interested in helping the two thugs.

A trio of police motorcycles pulled up to the curb, their riders getting quickly off and shoving the crowd away. One officer tried asking some bystanders if they had seen what happened, but the actual witnesses had long since moved on. Nobody wanted to be involved; no one was able to help them.

Another officer was checking the mens' pulses and looked at

his companions, nodding solemnly. They began conferring.

Farther away came a different type of siren that Phil assumed would be an ambulance. *Good luck in getting through this snarl*, he said to himself.

A minute later, casually as could be, Harlan Ames walked past the door, stopped and reversed his walk coming inside.

"Hello, Phil."

"Hey, Harl."

"I missed the action or so it looks like. Go ahead and slip that into my pocket and I'll head down the block. There is a small bistro sort of place a hundred feet father down. See you two in five minutes. *Page* me if you get waylaid."

He felt the solid object being transferred to his suit jacket pocket before turning and leaving the store. He disappeared into the crowd a few seconds later, so Phil returned to Tom.

"Feeling better?"

Tom nodded but then shook his head. "Not sure what they jabbed me with, but it is making it hard to see straight."

Now slightly alarmed, Phil asked, "They jabbed you? Where?" When Tom tapped his neck the Security man looked at the location and tutted. "Hypodermic needle mark, skipper. Must have been a powerful relaxant to get you so you wouldn't struggle but not knock you out. I don't have anything to counteract that, but let's go see Harlan and get some strong coffee into you. That may help."

With the policemen still totally occupied with the two crumpled forms on the sidewalk—and Tom was gratified to see one of them was Gunter Branski—he and Phil slipped out the doors and casually walked along with a small group of European tourists as they moved down the sidewalk.

Harlan already had a table and there were three cups sitting on it.

At the inventor eased into his chair, Ames told him to take a moment and then relate the story.

Phil told him about Tom having been given an injection and Harlan nodded before taking a small vial of pills from his inside pocket.

"Take two, skipper. They are an anti-narcotic pill and should overcome the effects. Give 'em five minutes though. They aren't *that* much of a miracle."

Tom placed the pills on his tongue and sipped his very strong but not very hot coffee to wash them down. In two minutes he said he was feeling well enough to talk.

He told the two Security men what happened from the moment he jumped out of the cab until Phil helped him get away.

Harlan said nothing until Tom finished, then he had some news to relate.

"I tried Zimby's phone earlier but he forgot to turn it on. I was worried about your wife, but Red knew where they were heading so he and Hank took off. They are all now back on board the *Queen* and all locked up nice and safe."

"Thank heavens for that!" Tom exclaimed allowing his shoulders to relax. "We need to get back and go home."

"Agreed, but let's wait here another ten minutes. You still look a little pale."

As they sat, Tom's brain began going over some details that had not made sense at the time.

"Harlan? I have to ask about Phil having that e-gun. It isn't that I'm not grateful but isn't carrying one in a foreign country a little dangerous?"

Harlan shrugged. "Sure, but necessary at times. Like this one."

"Okaaayyyy," Tom slowly countered looking first at Harlan then Phil, "but how did you find us and even to know to bring along the e-gun to police headquarters?"

"The first is an easy answer, Tom. You still have your TeleVoc pin on under your collar. Standard procedure that you and your dad have instilled in everyone. All I did was make a pin-to-pin connection and let the direction finding capabilities of the system give me slight audible tones. Low for left, higher for right and beep, beep, beep for right here."

"And, Phil's weapon?"

Ames looked around them and then suggested Tom feel under his left arm. There was something solid there but nothing to indicate it from outward appearances.

"Extremely good tailoring from Marjorie Morning-Eagle and the ladies," he explained. "We all carry these at any time there is the possibility of danger. I firmly believed from the start this trip presented a danger to you. Hence..."

The inventor patted his Security chief's hand and thanked him.

They rose, Harlan paid the bill, and they walked farther down the block before turning around a corner. Parked fifteen feet away was an atomicar.

Tom stopped short, his eyes wide. "What the heck?" He whipped around to look at Harlan, quickly wishing he had not as his head began spinning again.

As the two other men helped get him into the atomicar, Phil explained.

"The techs fixed the hangar doors in the *Sky Queen* so Harlan could bring that with us. We didn't tell you in case you were tempted to want to use it when we might need it in an emergency. Sorry, but your dad approved the plan. Oh, and after getting Bashalli and Zimby back Red brought the atomicar here and took a taxi back. Nobody was certain when or where we might need it but it seems he picked a very fortuitous spot."

With Hank sitting in the driver/pilot seat the atomicar rose into the sky. Although not an everyday occurrence, there were several dozen such cars in Singapore so people only watched with mild interest as it disappeared over the top of the buildings.

They had to weave a little between some sight seeing helicopters but reached the airport in a few minutes.

After landing inside the hangar, Tom and the others got out and headed inside. Bashalli was waiting in the lower hallway and she hugged Tom with tears streaming down her face.

"I thought you were in trouble," she explained.

"I was until Phil and Harlan came to my rescue. Now, I need to go sit down and rest, but let's get the heck out of this place and head for home."

They walked along the corridor until they arrived at the mid-plane stairs and then went along the second deck before finally going up to the top deck where the lounge was located. Bashalli and the two security men stayed with him while Hank went forward to the cockpit.

A minute later Red's voice came over the intercom.

"Skipper? We had permission for taxi and takeoff, but they pulled it a few seconds ago. Said something about a Custom's hold. Want me to ask them what the heck they mean?"

"No. We'll find out soon enough."

"I don't like this," Harlan said taking his and Phil's e-guns from his jacket and walking over to a hidden panel. A series of strategic presses had the panel open so he could stash their weapons. He closed the panel and wiped the area around it with his handkerchief.

He sat down to Tom's puzzled look.

"No use inviting scrutiny when a simple now-we-see-it-now-*you*-don't trick ought to keep us out of trouble."

Four minutes later a trio of police cars pulled along the left side of the *Sky Queen* and two more on the right. Four uniformed officers emerged from each car and moved into a surrounding formation around the jet. Except one man.

Wearing a more ornate uniform, the older man approached the lower hatch and used a riding crop to knock on it.

Tom had already moved down to the lower level so he opened the hatch and smiled at their visitor.

"May I help you, sir? I have our Customs Declarations—"

The man attempted to brush past him saying, "I must see the owner of this aircraft," but he stopped when he spotted the much larger form of Hank coming along the passage.

Tom stood to the side. "Please come in. I am Tom Swift, the owner of this jet. How may I assist?"

The officer narrowed his eyes and looked closely at Tom.

"You say you are the owner. Do you have ownership papers?" He held out a hand as if he expected the inventor to be carrying such documents on his person.

"Well, nobody ever has questioned me about that, but I believe there are registration papers from our Federal Aviation Administration in the cockpit. If you will follow me we can go look for them."

Hank stepped past them and with one motion clanged the hatch shut. He then hit the **LOCK** button. The officer saw this and suddenly looked worried.

"Come with me, sir and we can see what I might come up with. In the meantime, can you tell me what this visit is about?"

"Once I establish that you are the owner. Take me to your documents." The man's rude attitude bothered Tom.

Tom smiled at the officer. "Now, I don't want to cause an international incident, but unless you are little more civil I will have my crew start the engines and take off. When we get to the United States you will be required to provide documentation stating that you have permission from your government to barge in here without giving any reason. By the way, you may wish to have your people stand back as the lifting engines blow a lot of air around." He was still smiling as he motioned for the man to go ahead of him.

The officer's bravado disappeared. "Mr. Swift, please. Let us be civilized men. I shall take it as fact you are the owner of this very large aircraft, but you must not threaten me."

Tom shook his head. "Sir, I am giving no threat. I am giving ample warning of what is about to happen if you do not get to the point of this visit and in a pleasant tone."

They started climbing the first stairs but the officer stopped half way up.

"Yes. Why are we here? I had the controllers radio you stating this was a Custom's matter. It is not. I am with the Singapore Police and am here regarding a former prisoner of ours that we were forced to release due to an attack by you, and then found unconscious less than a half mile away twenty minutes later." His look back at the inventor told Tom the man was fishing for information or an admission of guilt but most likely had no proof.

"Interesting. Was I located anywhere near this former prisoner? And, another question. Where is that man now?"

They continued up and along the mid corridor.

"This one?" the officer asked pointing at the next stairs up.

"Yes."

"Then I will tell you that you were not discovered in the area near that man and his equally unconscious compatriot. And, both of them are in police custody."

"I see," Tom told him as they entered the lounge. He started to make introductions but had to stop when he realized the officer had not provided his name.

"M. W. Singh, Senior Chief Officer."

After he shook hands with the others, Bashalli asked permission to go back to their cabin. The man nodded, curtly, and she left them.

"Now, perhaps you will tell me what this is about."

Chief Singh took a breath and nearly started speaking, but paused and took another one before saying anything.

"In absolute truth we had very little with which to charge Gunter Branski. He made himself available to us saying he had valuable information but we had to guarantee we would not bring charges against him in exchange. Once we had the time to investigate the man we found there is an old Interpol warrant for his arrest and extradition to Germany on charges of industrial sabotage."

"I'll bet he was Giselle Ackerman's supposed boyfriend. The one who fiddled with their probe," Phil opined.

Singh pulled out a group of photographs from his jacket. "Is this the woman you have mentioned?"

"That's her!" Tom declared. "But, she was innocent. *Is* innocent! Why do you have her photo?"

"Ah. We have it because Branski provided it saying she was his willing accomplice. I now believe that may have been one in a series of lies. We shall check this. Branski also is wanted by your own FBI on a few charges. That is why we contacted them and they contacted you. We now believe that it was Branski's intent to lure you here to witness his confession about his brother. Accomplices of his were to kidnap or kill you."

Harlan snapped, "And you people just let this all happen!"

"We had no sufficient proof of anything done within Singapore so we could only hold him for about ten additional hours if no law enforcement agency provide the necessary paperwork. Plus, this young man struck our protected prisoner so we had no choice but to release that man. It is unfortunate, but *it is our law*."

"What happens now? We obviously are disappointed and would have preferred to either get the information Branski claimed to have or to take him back with us."

"It is my opinion that Branski does not have such information and that his claim was part of his design to kill Tom Swift!"

They all sat in silence. From down the hall Tom thought he could hear the faint sounds of Bashalli sobbing.

Tom broke the silence. "Why did you come to our aircraft, if I might ask?"

"I came with only the desire to see if you would immediately throw yourselves on the mercy of the Singapore Police and confess to somehow incapacitating Branski and his accomplice with some sort of technical device. As you have not, and I have no way of telling how it was performed—there are no bruises to indicate physical violence—and we have no witnesses who claim to have seen the incident, I will depart here..." he raised an eyebrow in question that Tom nodded to, "...and you will be permitted to leave Singapore. I regret the inconvenience you have been through. Good day."

He stood up and Hank offered to take him back to the hatch.

By the time he returned Tom had directed Red and Zimby to get things running and call for the earliest possible takeoff slot.

"They have us using their long runway in five minutes. Buckle in back there!"

Tom decided to climb into bed for the takeoff. When he opened the cabin door Bashalli was wiping away the last of her tears.

"I do not want to hear what happened to you, unless it will make you feel better, Tom."

He sat on the edge of the full-size bunk, kicked off his shoes and removed his socks.

"The truth is that I made a mistake at the police headquarters, they were forced to let the bad guy go, I chased him, he zonked me with some injection, but good old Phil zapped him and his friend with an e-gun. Then, we came back here." He stood up and took off his pants then changed from his usual pullover shirt into a t-shirt.

Climbing onto the bed he let her snuggle into him.

Three minutes later the *Sky Queen* roared down the runway, but it was so quiet inside they never heard a thing. Besides, Tom was already asleep.

*   *   *   *   *

Damon called Tom into the shared office the morning after the *Queen* landed back at Enterprises.

"I needed to tell you a few things, son, and also ask you about something. What would you like first?"

"Hmmm? Go ahead and tell me the things, if they are good, that is, then the question."

"Right. Well, they are mostly good. First, Gunter Branski has been talking a mile a minute from what I hear. He says he is fed up with being his brother's servant and has been providing the police back in Singapore with a ton of information. The three things they shared with the FBI all turned out to be good leads."

"That's great news. Let's hope the rest pans out as well."

"Uh-huh. We also have heard he helped the Singapore police capture the third in their group, the one driving the car they wanted to shove you into. You'll like this. Branski called him to say he was ready to be picked up, the man drove to the police station and parked in a No Parking spot and came right inside where they arrested him. The next piece is that I think I might have slowed down your Mr. Gardner in California. He was trying to get you by phone several time a day until I took his call and informed him that each and every call set you back and his delivery was going to be later and later. He apologized and has not called for over twenty-four hours."

Tom smiled. "Also very good news. What else?"

Mr. Swift now looked serious. "I received a report from the Singapore police regarding rumors, unfounded so far, that some sort of weapon was used to incapacitate Branski and his associate.Any thoughts?"

Tom shook his head. "The Chief there told me personally they had no witnesses, just the unconscious Branski and assistant, so how that rumor might have started is beyond me. I know I certainly wasn't carrying a weapon. Heck, Dad, I was the victim. Doc says the stuff they used on me has a short duration, but if you give someone too much it'll stop their heart!"

"Ah, yes. And we all doubt Branski is intelligent enough to know how much is too much. Okay. Chalk it up to the rumor mill.

How are you feeling, by the way?"

"Pretty good. I slept nearly the entire way home; twelve and a half hours straight. Bash says I did stumble out to go to the bathroom about half way home, but I don't recall that."

"It probably is best. Finally, here is something I think you will enjoy." He handed Tom a large manila envelope.

"Oh. Its from the FAA." He grinned at his father. "And, it is delightfully thick. Rejection letters come in small envelopes and are thin. Here goes..." and he tore open the flap, extracted the first sheet of several and began reading out loud:

Tom Swift,

Swift Enterprises, et cetera

Dear Mr. Swift.

It is with pleasure that the Federal Aviation Administration (Light Craft, Experimental and Uncategorized Division) announces our intent to issue an immediate Flight Worthiness Certificate for your personal self-contained back-mounted flying system, known by your nomenclature as a SKY STREAKER. Let it be known that by the attachment of the enclosed registration numbers (See attached diagram for specific mounting locations) and the carrying of this letter—or photostatically identical copy—that this aircraft is licensed for unrestricted flight within the limits set by this or any other nation's governing body up to a flight altitude of 25,000 feet above sea level and at speeds up to but not exceeding four hundred knots net airspeed (see Airspeed Calculations Chart attachment).

Congratulations.

Please complete the enclosed form including a copy of your flight log covering the initial one hundred hours of flight time starting immediately and return it to the address below when done.

He pulled out the two decal transfers that would need to be added to the *Sky Streaker* as identification.

"Now that we have these, we can take the *Streaker* anywhere!"

CHAPTER 14

GERMAN DELIVERY

WELL, thought Tom, *it's true. It never rains but it pours!*

After working overtime for five days and nights on the function and safety enhancements to the *Sky Streaker*, Tom now fielded a phone call from a very unfriendly-sounding German woman. She identified herself as Colonel Gertrude Schmidt.

"You vill remember me as one of the military investigation committee who took the satellite and Fraüline Ackerman from you when you brought them back to your small island base."

He did remember her but for some reason did not want to give her the satisfaction of admitting it.

"I'm sorry, Colonel, but I meet a lot of military people in my business. I'm certain I saw you on Fearing Island when we arrived, but there was a lot going on, it's a pretty large island, and you didn't introduce yourself."

"This is not a matter to discuss at this time," she said in a matter-of-fact manner. "My call is to inform you that the satellite your company has been repairing for us must be placed in its orbit position around the Venus planet by this time next veek."

"I see. And, I do not wish to get into an argument over this, as I am certain it is simply a language barrier, but we are doing much more than *repairing* your satellite. We are completely rebuilding it from the very ground up. It is a long process, one your own people took more than a year to perform originally, and we have only had the old satellite for two months. It seems that your people would not release it to us until then."

"Och! Zo you can *not* place it in position on our schedule?"

Tom counted quickly and silently to ten. "I did not exactly say that, but unless you or someone there is willing to absolve us of any culpability should you insist that incompletely-tested equipment be so placed, then I can take it to Venus starting in twelve days. It will, therefore, not be possible to have it in orbital position next week."

"You haff used words I do not understand. Spell them, please?"

"I will guess that you might mean 'culpability and 'absolve'. Are those the ones?"

"Ja, I mean yes. Spell them, please."

He did and then was unceremoniously place on hold for ten minutes. When she returned she only said, "We will return a call to you tomorrow. Be available." The line went dead.

With Mr. Swift out in New Mexico attending to several important matters at the Citadel, it left Tom with a decision to call for the older inventor's advice or make up his own mind how to proceed.

He chose to try to do it alone, but also knew he needed status updates. Three phone calls had the three team leaders working on the rebuild project in the large office within twenty minutes.

He explained the recent call and looked around. Nobody's face actually said it was impossible, but they also did not look particularly pleased at the news.

The status was about what Tom thought it might be.

Electronics reported that the salvageable components—sensors and the necessary mapping MASER parts—had suffered little damage and had been brought to full operational condition within days of receiving the satellite. The new and replacement electronics were five days from completion.

Propulsion team member Artie Johnson told Tom the Monomethylhydrazine propellant for the positioning and orienting motors had leaked and both the pressure storage tank and the copper-aluminum alloy tubing used to transfer it to the motors had been compromised.

"But, Tom," he added, "we replaced everything with inertite-coated carbon fiber. We'll be ready for pressure testing tomorrow if pushed."

Finally, the "packaging" team said they were waiting for delivery of the working satellite for final sterilization and packing.

"That will take us the standard three days, skipper. No way to compress it. Well, perhaps two days."

Tom smiled at everyone. "So, I'm hearing that if we all work at a good but *normal* pace we might be able to loft this in the *Challenger* in six or seven days?"

The agreement was that was a good target, giving them at least one extra day, "...just in case."

When the call came in the following day from Germany, Tom was ready. To his surprise the caller was Giselle Ackerman.

"Hello, Tom. It is Gisi. How is my absolutely favorite American man?"

"Well, surprised, but nicely so, that it is you calling. And, flattered that I am your favorite American."

She laughed. "Well, I understand that Fraü Colonel Schmidt phoned yesterday and was quite rude to you. That is no surprise to anyone who knows her. She was also shocked at the words you used and suggested that I might, well, mend a fence or two. She believes you are angry and wish her some harm."

Tom was confused. "Words like 'absolve' and 'culpability'? I wouldn't have thought they would shock the Colonel."

"You will not believe this, but she didn't believe your intended meaning could be for 'absolve' so she looked up 'dissolve.'" She laughed again as Tom now understood. "Anyway, I wanted to call to tell you that the window she described for the satellite is impossible, and I have made certain everyone knows it. It was only part of an old schedule that called for a repositioning of the satellite assumed to be in orbit already. I guess I am calling to ask when it might be possible to send it back to Venus, and to see if I might come along again. Also, to thank you and your Harlan Ames and everyone there for helping clear my name and reputation over here."

"We were happy to help. And, as far as the satellite goes, if you can be at Fearing, sans the good Colonel, please, a week from tomorrow we can take it back out. The only issue is that I am so deeply involved in another project I won't be able to go all the way to Venus. So, I propose an alternative."

He outlined a much shorter trip to take the satellite about a million miles out and getting it up to the correct speed, then letting it do what it was originally intended to do, that being to fly on its own, go into orbit and start its useful life.

"It sound very good. My new boyfriend—well investigated this time—and I would like me to not be away for almost a month. This three day voyage sounds perfect. I will arrange with your Mr. Dilling for the trip and meet you at your base next week. Bye."

Tom hung up and realized he was looking forward to the short hop into space. But, he wondered if it was because it would mean an end to the entire German Venus probe set of problems or if it had anything to do with the fact that the very pretty Giselle Ackerman would be going with him... or rather with them.

He decided he had best tell Bashalli about the trip and admit to it included a beautiful passenger coming along.

When he did that night—and he intended to suggest she come along if there were any hint of jealousy—she laughed.

"Oh, Tom. You have beautiful women around you all the time and I don't think you really notice. I know you are mine and will come home to me and Bart, so do not think I have a problem with this German woman. Besides, you did say she is ten years older than we are. That, plus I am very happy that this trip will only be a few days and not a long one."

Preparations for work the satellite probe went forward and ended up half a day ahead of schedule. Tom insisted on performing a last physical check before the package was sealed in a vacuum covering and flown to Fearing Island.

Nothing was amiss, so he gave final approval shortly after his inspection finished.

"Bundle our little friend up," he said to the technicians as he pointed to the equipment that, even in its folded position, was the size of a small car.

Back in the shared office he phoned Germany. It would be nearly eight in the evening, but Giselle was waiting for his call confirming she should travel to Fearing in two days time.

"I was planning a late evening, Tom. You left me with the impression it might be as late as my midnight before your would call. Please tell me what you call the bottom line now. I am a little anxious. If things are not going well, I need to know."

"Things are going very well, Gisi. In fact, the packaging and shipping team have just started to bundle everything. We will finish that by the morning after tomorrow and it will be transported to Fearing. So, the *bottom line* is you can come out either that evening and stay in our guest quarters, or fly over early the morning of the launch.

She chose to come early saying that she would be bringing some very special German sausages and wurst for a celebration dinner.

"Well, I'll have to get Chow to work with you to fix them the way they ought to be served. Is there anything he needs to bring?"

"I will call that dear man tomorrow and we can discuss many options. I believe I might enjoy what he can do with them Texas style."

The next day and a half sped by with word coming from Hollywood that the shooting work had moved out to the ocean where the two old Russian submarines had been set at anchor just outside of the breakwater at Marina Del Rey. The five days of shooting on and around the subs would be finished just as Tom returned and Howard Gardner sent word he would appreciate it if the flying sequences might begin shortly after that.

"The hardest thing is we have at least four shots where the Sky Marshal is supposed to take off from or land right on the deck of the sub. Looks like I have to hire a crane and lower Pemberly on some tiny wires."

"I wish we had been able to train your stunt man, but we both know how that worked out."

"Yeah. Sure."

The trip to Fearing was set for the afternoon before the launch.

Chow had spoken to Giselle Ackerman about her food needs.

"She's bringin' some sort of German hot dogs," he told Bud when the flyer dropped by the small executive kitchen for a mid-morning cup of coffee.

"The skipper tells me she's bringing some very fancy sausages, Chow. The kind you'd be proud to serve to any German dignitary. You be nice and cook them the way she says to. Wouldn't want you to shove hot peppers inside and burn people's stomachs."

Chow took a half-hearted swipe at Bud with a dishcloth, missing but making his point.

"You scoot, Buddy boy. I got work ta do hidin' some o' the hottest chilies you ever ran into *in your lunch!*"

Bud groaned but went down the hall to see if Tom had a minute to talk.

"Sit down and sip that drink," the inventor invited. "Dad'll be back in twenty minutes from his latest Washington trip. He was asked to brief the President on my little meeting with the Vice President."

"Why not you?"

"Because dad is more politically correct than I am, plus he wanted to discuss some possible uses for this *Sky Streaker* pack we're building."

"And, is the *Streaker* really ready for prime time?"

Tom shook his head. "I'm not absolutely sure, Bud. I know that you have proven it in everything we've tried—"

"...Other than the whole outer space thing—"

"Yes, other than that. But, as we both know you are a pilot of some excellence. I find we need this whole movie thing to prove that just about anybody with some basic training can master the pack. On another subject, I'm glad you're here right now. We're heading to Fearing in about four hours. I wanted to talk to you about Giselle Ackerman."

Bud's grin widened.

"Stop that, Bud! In fact, that's the reason I wanted to talk. She is a very nice woman and Bash knows about her and has no issues, so you need to put the nudge and wink away. Please. Besides, my guess is that Sandy doesn't know about her."

Bud promised to be on his best behavior.

Tom outlined the mission including the desire to have Bud assist in the launching from the hangar deck. Because of their outbound speed the actual launch would need to be at a fairly precise amount of shove.

"This short hop came too late to build a launch system, so it needs to be manual. I've had Hank and Arv set up a sort of tackling dummy in Arv's workshop with an accelerometer on it. I need you to practice on it until you have the right feel for the push off."

Bud stepped back and saluted. "I shall endeavor to shove with a level of force commensurate to the task at hand, sah!"

An hour later Hank called Tom to report the flyer's success. "Five unsuccessful but close tries followed by eighteen out of twenty at just the right level, skipper. Bud's ready.

Tom thanked his Engineer and patternmaker before hanging up to finish gathering the last of the paperwork he wanted to bring. It included all his earlier sketches for the flying pack. It was fine for the movie but he wanted to explore more pedestrian looks for any other customer.

A half hour after Hank's call Tom headed for the Barn, the open-sided hangar close to the main building cluster, where his Toad was waiting.

"She's fueled and we did a five minute warm-up, skipper. All you need do is your final checks and start her back up. The tower has been notified of your eminent departure and the flight plan has been filed."

Tom thanked the young woman making the report before tossing his shoulder bag into the second row seat behind where he would sit as pilot. His walk around the jet went as expected finding only a small rock stuck in the tread of the right-side wheel. He pried it out using his pen before making a check of the fuel.

It was clean so he poured it into a small flask, handing that to the groundsperson. She took it off to be recycled.

"There you are," he greeted Bud as the flyer came jogging over, "We're just waiting for Chow. He ought to have been here..." Tom was saying before his voice trailed off. He had just glanced back toward the main Administration building in time to see the western chef coming, another nearly glow-in-the-dark shirt broadcasting his presence. "Here he is now."

Bud looked and broke down laughing.

Chow's shirt was mostly bright blue with orange trimming. The main motif on the front were a pair of cherubs wearing little "alpine" hats, blowing into large shells.

As he got closer he turned around to show them the back. There, in at least five different colors, was a chubby man with a mustache in a loose white shirt, green-feathered hat, and lederhosen holding a string of sausages in one hand and a stein of beer in the other. But, that wasn't the best part. He sat astride a giant pig that had a disquieting smile on its face.

Puffing as he came to a halt Chow asked, "Ya don't think Miss Giselle'll think this is a bit much, do ya?"

Tom slapped him on the back.

"Heck, no, Chow. I think she'll get a big kick out of it."

He was right. On seeing Chow once she entered the *Challenger's* control room her right hand flew to her mouth smothering a smile and a laugh. But, he took it as a compliment and beamed so she removed the hand and came over to give him a hug and a kiss on the cheek.

"That, Chow, is one of the finest shirts you might have worn. I only hope my wurst and brats do that justice."

It had been decided to hold off on the celebratory meal until the probe had been launched. That would be just thirty hours after takeoff.

The giant repelatron ship rose silently an hour later with the satellite strapped down in the hangar. What nobody could see was the extra circuit board that had been installed secretly prior to the probe being finalized and a small readout counting down.

As Tom brought the ship into the appropriate orientation for the shove off and Bud and Giselle stood ready with the hangar door open and the satellite package sitting on the porch, the small timer on the hidden board reached two hundred minutes remaining before it would activate the self-contained circuits.

"Three minutes to go, Bud. Report your readiness."

"Ready and waiting, skipper. So is Giselle. Although she seems to be nervous at the moment. Just give the word to assume shoving position and then a countdown of five and we'll get this baby off."

He looked down at the temporary railing that would ensure the probe left the ship on exactly the right trajectory. His right foot nudged the locking mechanism on the launch sled and he gave the sled a small shove forward and back to see if it was loose. It was.

"One minute to go, Bud, Gisi. Everything looks good up here," Tom reported.

"Here as well. Sled's unlocked and moving freely. I hope my muscle memory overcomes the adrenaline rush I've got going."

"I have no doubts about you, flyboy. Thirty seconds to go."

With Giselle standing to his right, an expectant look on her face, Bud assumed his final position and took three cleansing breaths. Under his breath he muttered, "Here goes the hail Mary pass!"

"Ten seconds. Coming up on five... four... three... two... and... Now!"

With practiced ease Bud rolled his shoulders forward and pressed on the exact balance point necessary to move the satellite correctly.

It moved forward and off the sled as the rollers came to the end of the track. He found he was holding his breath twenty seconds later when a rush of air from Giselle's radio told him she had also been holding hers.

"How are we doing, skipper?"

"Wait one. Well, the laser ranger shows it is moving at the right speed and is pretty much on target. Maybe half a degree off but we can correct that in a day or so. Come back in, you two. Chow's about to burst he wants us to try what he came up with."

The meal was incredible. Chow truly had outdone himself with home-made sauerkraut and dill pickles, German-style potato salad, and an assortment of roasted vegetable all surrounding the sausages provided by Giselle.

She declared his handling of her sausages to be, "The best wurst I've eaten since I was a little girl!"

When Tom and Giselle went to the control board for a check a little later, Bud assisted Chow with the clearing up and dishes.The measurements to the dwindling probe were holding steady so Giselle asked if the course correction might be hurried.

"No," Tom told her. "You see, we cannot communicate with the probe."

Her look of horror spoke of how uncomfortable she suddenly felt. "Why?" she chocked out.

Tom smiled. "Because in order to keep anyone back on Earth from sending interfering signals, I had the receiver disabled and an entirely new control board placed in there. It will take over at the appropriate time and steer the probe to Venus. No radio messages will be able to get to the controls no matter how hard your enemies try."

"I–I don't understand, Tom. Is the probe not going to work?"

He explained that to the contrary, the probe would work exactly as expected, only the Germans, or people with evil intentions like Streffan Mirov, would no longer be able to interfere with it. Tom's ingenious controller board was a full computer capable of all control functions and decisions to achieve the stated mission.

"But, should you need to change programming, just come to us. I've also installed a special type of radio, my Private Ear, that can be sent instructions. You will be able to reprogram on the fly, but any would be destroyers of your dreams never will."

CHAPTER 15 /

LOST IN SPACE

"THIS IS starting to feel like old times," Bud quipped as he and Tom banked and prepared to land the Swift cargo jet at the Burbank airport. It was the closest landing facility that could handle the large jet.

In the back were three things: the finished *Sky Streaker* suit and backpack; an atomicar with the back seats removed to make transporting the suit easier; and the old *Kangaroo Kub* mini-jet.

Tom wasn't quite certain why he had asked the little jet, once standard equipment in the *Sky Queen*, be included. After all, as Bud reminded him, the atomicar could fly nearly as fast, although not as high, and was maneuverable.

"We had the extra space, Bud. Even if it never comes out into the light of day, it feels right that we have it."

Tom was requested to check in, personally, with the airport manager before they could leave the airport grounds.

"Hello, I'm James McEwen," the man with a notable Scottish accent told them as the three shook hands in his office. "Folks call me 'boss' or 'that blasted Scot' but you can call me Jim." He gave them a big grin.

"Nice to meet you, sir, but may I ask why the personal appearance request?"

"Certainly, you may. As you may well have noticed, we have precious little extra space around here. The city keeps growing and encroaching around the airport property. Right now we've got you parked down by gate A Nine, but we'll be needing that later in the day when the commute traffic comes in. I hate to ask this, but could we get you to taxi your jet over to the general aviation side? I'm having the manager over there move a couple smaller airplanes closer together to accommodate your jet." He looked hopefully at the inventor.

"Certainly, Mr.— I mean, Jim. Just show us where."

The manager walked over to a satellite photo of the grounds and pointed to a spot just to the side of their north/south runway.

"There will be great. I appreciate this. Also, that will give you more space to bring in a delivery truck for whatever it is you've brought."

"Well, Jim, we've also brought our own delivery vehicle. And, that brings up the subject of notifying your control tower about that." He told the man about the flying capability of the atomicar.

To put it bluntly, Jim McEwen was shocked.

Then to Tom and Bud's amazement, he began to laugh. "Oh, I see. Yourself would be putting me on. What a hoot you are, Tom Swift. Flying car? Of course you'd be bringing one of them. I'll be sure to let the people in the tower know. Ummm, does it need a runway?"

Not completely sure the man was talking him seriously, Tom shook his head. "No, we'll just lift off from next to the jet. Thank you, and if you can have the landing and parking fees bill ready for us, I will pay that before we leave the day after tomorrow."

"That I'll do. A pleasure to meet you, and you, too," he said looking at Bud.

Twenty minutes later they shut the jet engines back off, now parked in the correct spot.

Ten minutes later Tom radioed the tower asking for permission to depart.

"Roger, Swift Two. We've had the word you are flying out in some sort of helicopter. Take off into the winds from the southwest, two-three-zero at five knots. Barometer is two-nine point nine-five and steady. Temperature is seventy-two. Hold two minutes for incoming on runway three-three."

Tom acknowledged but decided to not correct the impression they would take off in a helo.

"Uhh, Swift Two? I'm not seeing your aircraft. Are you actually ready to take off?"

"Roger that. Swift Two is ready. Permission to go?"

"Umm, granted?"

As the atomicar rose, swung around and headed away on the directed course, the air controller standing at the window looking through binoculars let out a small oath and then laughed.

In his office overlooking the airfield, Jim McEwen was also looking through binoculars at Tom and Bud departing. He let out the same amused oath.

As soon as he received permission to vector to their destination Tom swung the atomicar to a heading of one-seven-zero. Four minutes later they crossed the golf course located in front of the studios and came down to a height of just one hundred feet.

"Are we going straight in or did you plan to check in at the gate?" Bud asked, a mischievous grin on his face telling Tom what he would like to do.

"We'll do it the right way, but we'll also have a little fun."

He steered them over to the gate area. A delivery truck was sitting there being checked through, so Tom brought the atomicar down until it hovered just ten feet above the truck. As the larger vehicle moved forward, he came down to ground level.

The startled guard nearly fell backward into his little guard shack, but rallied and came forward.

"Tom Swift and Bud Barclay expected at soundstage eleven. We should be on your list," he said with a straight face as if this were a normal way to arrive.

The nervous man checked his list, missing Tom's name the first time but finding it as he scanned back up the list.

"Uhhh, this says you're coming in with a big, important delivery. Is, uhh," he pointed at the atomicar, "is *this* it?"

Tom shook his head. "No, it's what we have under the cover in the back. I can't show it to you but I'm sure the word will get out about it. Can we go in?"

The man gulped, his Adams apple bobbing up and down, and nodded. "Yeah. Go ahead."

As they drove through, now on the car's tires, Bud couldn't hold his laughter.

"We gave that poor guy a fright, skipper."

Tom nodded but smiled. "And, we gave him a story to tell people for the rest of his life!"

Walter, the older rent-a-guard was at his little shaded table. His eyes went wide at seeing the sleek and futuristic atomicar, but he hitched his trousers up and came over. On seeing Tom and Bud, he smiled.

"Oh, it's you two, again. Guess it's okay-dokey for you to go in, but ya gotta wait for the light to go out." He pointed to a revolving red light, something like old police cars might have sported. "They're doin' a take."

They talked for a minute before a ringing sound came from the wall and the light shut off.

"You can go on in, sir and sir!" The man actually saluted so Tom gave him a small salute in return.

Howard Gardner was practically beside himself as soon as he got the word Tom and Bud were there with the real flying suit. He hustled from the small trailer along one wall he used as his office when at the soundstage.

"Tom, Tom, Tom... and friend."

"Bud," the flyer reminded him, rolling his eyes.

"Right. Bud. So," he started rubbing his hands together, "have you got it? Is that it?" he asked pointing at the shape under a light nylon cover. "IS IT?" he nearly shouted causing people all around him to stop and look at the three.

Tom smiled. "Mr. Gardner, you will be a happy man when I tell you that what I bring is, indeed, your fully-functional flying rig, the *Sky Streaker*."

Bud made a "taa-daa" sound and reached back, pulling the cover forward and off of their cargo.

Brian Pemberly came over, a curious look on his handsome face. When he saw what was in the atomicar, and once his eyes focused on something other that the atomicar, he smiled.

"Well, it looks just like the prop one. Does it actually fly?"

Tom and Bud got out of the vehicle.

"It does, or will with the proper stunt pilot in the harness and once he or she gets about a day's instruction and passes our test."

"Formality," Gardner said hastily, "merely a formality. We have a new stunt coordinator and he's a real hotshot. You'll just love the guy!"

Bud looked at his friend and ever so slightly shook his head. He and Tom detested the idea of a "hotshot," as that sort of person often pushed things to the breaking point. And, in this case, that point could lead to their injury or death.

"Safety is never a formality, Mr. Gardner," Tom stated looking the man in the eyes until Gardner blinked and looked away. "Please introduce us to your stunt pilot."

"Yeah, well you see, the thing is, he won't be here for another couple days. So, just show me what buttons to press and what to twist and shove, and I'll see that he get the rundown."

Tom could feel his face getting red. He tried to calm himself down. Years earlier he would have rolled with such a challenge, but as he approached his twenty-fifth birthday he found it harder and harder to let such ignorance pass.

"*Mr. Gardner*," he said firmly, "there is absolutely no way I am just going to let you put a human in this rig without a full rundown and training day, *from us*, on what it takes to control it. Period. If you have an issue with that, then I'll simply take the *Streaker* back to New York and that will be the end of it!"

Howard Gardner was perspiring now. His eyes darted around trying to see if he had any backing from those around him. All he could see were members of his crew stepping back and turning away, nobody wanting anything to do with this. He fingered his collar, a drop of sweat dripping from his nose and onto his shirt front.

In a whisper, he pleaded, "Listen, Swift. You can't do this to me. It's hard enough getting a daredevil to take the kind of peanuts I can afford and want to fly something untried."

In a normal tone, Tom responded with, "There is nothing untested or untried about the flying system. It has logged nearly a hundred test hours, been in space, and passed each and every test. True, it takes someone who knows what they are doing to pilot it safely, and that is why we insist on a day's training with whomever you have hired. There is no room for negotiation. That is a stipulation in the contract we both signed and one I will not back down on. The ball, or the rest of this movie, is in your hands."

Gardner looked as if he would pass out, so Tom motioned one of the movie crew to bring a chair. When the producer was seated, he nodded.

"Okay. It's gonna kill the budget I have for retakes, but I can get the guy here tomorrow morning. You get your full day with him, but by God you better have him ready to fly the next day!"

Tom knelt down so his face was close to the producer's.

His voice was calm as he stated, "You listen to me, Mr. Gardner. If your man is good and can take directions, we'll tell you if and when he is ready. If this guy is really what you termed a "hotshot,' and cannot go by the rules we set out, if he only wants to be a showoff, then we do not qualify him. So, you need to make it clear what he is going to do, and no more. Right?" Tom now stood up so he towered over the older man.

Looking up, Gardner nodded, his head then hanging down over his chest.

Tom and Bud flew off with the working equipment ten minutes later. They agreed to be back by 8:00 a.m. the next day ready to train the stunt man.

When they met him, Tom knew something was not right. The man kept looking at Gardner—who was standing to one side—as if he needed the man's permission to even speak.

Half an hour later Tom took the producer away leaving Bud to deal with the stunt man.

At lunch, the two young men ate to one side with Wes Norris and one of his fellow agents.

"Everything going to be okay?" Wes asked.

"I'm hoping so. Bud can tell you if the man is looking like a winner or..."

The flyer swallowed his latest bite before answering. "He's a bit slow on the uptake, but he is methodical and is taking a lot of notes. We'll try simple hovering after lunch and before five I ought to have him zipping around overhead."

Mentally, Tom crossed his fingers.

The next day saw the company divide into two parts. One part remained at the sound stages completing more of the "interior" shots while Bud, the associate director, the stunt man—already dressed in the flight suit, his visor only barely open at the bottom —and about ten support crew took a minibus up and over the hills to a spot Tom learned was called Nichols Canyon. It was to be the site for about a third of the flying scenes as the camera could be set in several locations and never show any of the houses surrounding them.

By nine the call for "Quiet!" came, several of the crew announced their ready status, and the director called for "Action!"

The stunt man, hands resting on hips, looked up and around himself, and with exaggerated movements attempted to raise one arm—coming up against the restraining buckles—then brought it back into contact with the control stick and soared upward. He quickly rose to about a hundred feet and tilted forward, moving off toward the hill peak in the background. He soon headed straight up again.

"Cut!" came the director's command. "Call him back; we have to do that again—he went up too fast to follow."

When the man on the radio tried to reach their stunt man, there was no answer. He reported this to the director who swore.

"Get that idiot back here. Now!!" he ordered.

Tom stepped over to the radioman. "Let me try."

When the man failed to hand him the headset, Bud came over, took it from the stunned man's hand and gave it to Tom.

"This is Tom Swift to the stunt pilot. Press the blue radio button on your left stick. The one with the letter R on it. Over."

"I can't control this thing!" came the panicked voice of the man in the suit. "Nobody told me how to stop it and come back! Help!!"

Tom looked at Bud. They both knew there was trouble, and they were powerless to help the man.

But, the inventor motioned to Bud to take the radio. "Talk to him and get him under control, Bud. I have a bad suspicion, but see it he is even the same man you trained yesterday."

Bud gulped, but took the headset. As Tom moved off he opened the channel and started to talk to the man.

Tom told the director to call for an ambulance, in case of a crash, and to notify the FAA there was an uncontrolled flying object in LA's airspace.

As the other man ordered an assistant to comply, Tom took out his phone and called Enterprises. He was transferred to his father's line in seconds.

"No time to explain, but we've got an inexperienced man in the suit and he's in the air, and heading higher and higher every second. Can you get someone on Fearing to get the *Challenger* in the air, pronto, and head this way at top speed?"

"Give me one minute," his father replied and the line went to music on hold. When Damon came back he said, "The emergency crew will take off in three minutes. ETA, twenty minutes after that. What do you want them to do?"

"Have them try to track the suit. I left the RADAR badges on it just in case. If the man has gone too high, see if they can snag him."

"Okay. Do you want me to stay on the line?"

Tom thought a second, then, "No, Dad. But ask George Dilling to transfer this call to the *Challenger*, please."

Bud came over with a shake of his head. "He's still heading skyward, skipper. Says the throttle is stuck, but I think he's just frozen in fear. And, that is definitely not the same voice of the man I trained yesterday!"

Tom went back to the radio and put the headset back on.

"This is Tom. Listen, we understand that you are not the man we trained. That isn't important right now. What is important is that you do what I tell you to do. Do you read me?"

There was a half minute pause before the man's weak voice said, "Yeah. I'm sorry. I can't make this thing work."

"Okay. First, you have to tell me if you can rotate the top of the right joystick back in a clockwise direction. You turned in counter-clockwise to make it work. Go ahead and try to turn in all the way back."

"No! I'll crash!"

"You won't. There is an emergency parachute system that will deploy if you begin to fall and get within a thousand feet of the ground. I repeat, you will not crash. Now, turn that throttle."

"No! I can't. You have to save me!" The man's voice broke down sobbing and then went silent.

Tom's phone vibrated telling him there was someone on the radio link.

"It's Tom."

"Skipper? Red here. Just happened to be on Fearing when the

call came. We are passing over Denver right now and should be overhead in five minutes. Not seeing the target yet. Do you have an altitude?"

"Hang on." Tom switched to the radio. "Listen, it's Tom again, I need you to focus your eyes on the inside of your visor and tell me what the altitude is. Can you do that?"

He had to repeat his request twice more before the man came back with, "It says eighty-nine and a bunch of zeros. Help me?"

"We are trying but you need to do some things as well. Try to turn off the throttle. Do it!"

"I—I can't. My hand is cramped and won't move."

After a moment to think of the next steps, Tom asked the man, "What does the fuel meter say? It's the two lines running above your eyebrows, one green and one red. There will be numbers on the right side and a percent sign."

"Uhhhh, the green one is at nineteen percent and the red one just turned to thirteen percent. Does that mean I'm going to die?" His voice suddenly sounded calm.

"No. What it means is that you are going to rise about another thirty thousand feet before you run out of fuel. After that, you will start to coast up to a point where you will then start to come back down. I hope to have a rescue team on site in under four minutes, so hang on."

Into his phone he said, "Red? He's got four minutes of fuel and is above ninety-K. He should be almost directly above my position which is at the south side of Universal City."

"Got it! In fact I have your position on track and... hang on... yes! Steve says he has a track on the suit. We're heading in to try to grab him about the time he coasts to a halt. I'll let you know."

With an ease that might indicate this was a normal thing to do —it most definitely was *not*—Red Jones got the *Challenger* to within a few hundred feet of the man as he was still coasting upward, now his fuel was exhausted. One of the duty technicians had the ship's Attractatron aimed at him and reported readiness.

"Go!" Red commanded, and the man energized the system, locking on to the flyer just as his speed neared zero. He managed to get a good hold on the material of the suit, drew him in toward the landing porch outside the hangar, and dropped him the final foot to the deck where the man reached out and clung to the railing.

Whoever the pilot was, he may not have had the wherewithal to work the throttle, but he did know how to hang on for dear life.

Tom, Bud and the crew on the ground let out a rousing cheer

when Red's voice came over the radio.

"Got him! Coming down. We'll head for the airport."

Tom immediately made a very angry phone call to Howard Gardner.

CHAPTER 16 /

LEGAL DISTRACTION

TOM AND DAMON Swift sat quietly at the Defendant's table in the somewhat cramped courtroom. Why, precisely, the case against Swift Enterprises and Tom had been set to take place in Connecticut and not New York or California where the two sides were located had not been made clear.

What was clear is that the unqualified man who had been hired by the producer to replace the trained stunt pilot who had come down with appendicitis had recovered from his near-tragic flight and had filed a very large lawsuit against the Swifts. There was no corresponding suit against Monograph Studios or Howard Gardner.

Jackson Rimmer sat between them going over several papers he had taken from his impressive briefcase moments earlier.

"Surely they can't have anything to hang this case on," Damon muttered to the lawyer.

Jackson set the papers down, took a breath and answered in a low tone.

"Damon, you would be mighty surprised how flimsy some cases are and even more so to find that those sort of people win more often than they do not. However, in this case we have ample paperwork and releases and even testimony and depositions to show it was Howard Gardner and his studio that ignored all safety precautions and the man flew the suit beyond its specifications and refused to follow instructions. Hell, and pardon me for swearing, but even this supposed stunt pilot told us he was ordered on penalty of dismissal and a negative report to his stunt union to fly or else!"

He stopped as the doors at the back of the room opened and a noise could be heard. It was a combination of cameras, people, and a woman's voice assuring those around her that, "This is as open and shut as I've ever tried and mark my words, this will be over in a half hour with my client prevailing. Stick around, ladies and gentlemen, and watch how an expert does this!"

Jackson Rimmer said a dirty word.

"That," he whispered to the two Swifts, "is Sylvia Alvarado Niles, one of the biggest publicity-seeking lawyers in the country. She's known for only taking on cases where she believes she can get her name in the papers above that of the client."

With disbelief in his voice, Tom asked, "Is she any good?"

Rimmer snorted. "She's averaged about eighty-five percent in the past, but this one surprises me. She goes in for the Hollywood stuff, for sure, but generally it is around the 'such-and-such evil male producer made an ill-advised pass at a young starlet and she is suing for twenty-million dollars because she is no longer able to act' sort of case where she portrays her client as a ruined person who will never be able to work again so she deserves a large compensation. And, yes, it *is* nearly always women she represents."

"Sounds like a publicity schemer to me," Damon muttered.

"More than that, Damon, it is borderline illegal what she charges for her services. Last thing I read she was forced to return some of the money she extracted from a winning case when the Judge took exception to her sixty-six percent fee!"

Tom let out a low whistle.

"I'm not certain who you are, but I am about to win big money for my poor client who your clients nearly killed," came a somewhat shrill voice from their left.

All three men turned to see Ms. Niles sporting the same sort of smile an alligator has when it is digesting its latest meal. "No offense, but you boys are way out of your league here!"

Without waiting for a response, she turned away and appeared to become busy looking at some paperwork.

A moment later the Bailiff nodded to his counterpart at the back of the room and the doors were closed.

"All rise. The Honorable Percy Archibald, U.S. District Court for the District of Connecticut, presiding," intoned the deep-voiced Bailiff.

Everyone stood as the door to the left side of the bench opened and an extremely short man clad in a black robe entered. He was clearly a dwarf and the sight of him caused Ms. Niles to snicker.

As he climbed into his seat and pumped the chair upward so he could see over the desk, he glared at her.

"I suppose you find my stature funny?"

She paled. "Oh, no, your Honor. I was chocking back a cough." She cleared her throat to demonstrate it. "I apologize unreservedly, sir if you assumed otherwise!"

To Tom she sounded glaringly sarcastic. He noticed with satisfaction the judge was bothered by her tone.

His gaze swept to the table with Tom, Damon and Jackson. "You three?"

Jackson stood up to address him.

"No, sir. None at all. In fact Swift Enterprises prides itself on caring little to nothing about a persons appearance so long as they have the qualifications for our company. We have a very highly-place employee who is a *skeletal dysplasias* dwarf. One of the top persons in her field. So, no issues with us." He sat back down.

Now Tom detected a look on the jurists face that spoke of his approval of this statement. The man appeared to have the same physical growth issues as Stefanie Bodack.

Ms. Niles suddenly had another coughing attack during which she also seemed to utter the phrase, "bull pucks."

The judge's eyes switched back to her. "That will be quite enough or the next unsolicited name calling earns you a contempt charge along with a rather nasty fine. And, yes, I have exceptional hearing. Where is your client?"

"He is suffering from extreme nervous exhaustion and cannot attend. I have a doctor's note attesting to his being unable to be here to face the men who nearly ended his life."

"Cease editorializing, Miss Niles. I do not like cases like this and your 'poor, nervous client' may be called to testify. You will have until tomorrow morning to get him here."

His scowl turned as if my magic to a smile. "Now then, if Officer Schmidt will read the basic charges we can get this trial underway."

The Bailiff stood up and looked at a sheet of paper. He read off eleven charges, each one embellished with subtle and not-so-subtle wording attempting to shed bad light on the Swifts.

At the end, the judge reached out and wiggled his fingers until the officer came over and handed him the sheet. Taking out a rather large marker he looked at the list and began crossing things out. A minute later he handed it back.

"Okay. Some editing was necessary to keep me from dismissing this case completely out of hand, so please read the revised charges."

"Uhh, the defendants are charged with gross—oh, no, you crossed that part out—hmmmm, charged with neglect in the case of all design aspects of the alleged flying suit. Further, they are charged with failure to advise, warn or otherwise instruct the test pilot in the proper use of said equipment."

As he scanned down the abbreviated list Tom took a quick sideways look at Jackson Rimmer who was now smiling.

"Well, the final charge still here is one of refusal to provide detailed engineering information to the plaintiff's attorney. That's it." He turned and sat back down.

Sylvia Alvarado Niles was red-faced and could barely speak. "This is preposterous! Those other charges are vital to the case and must be reinstated or I will call for your recusal and the case handed to another judge."

"As would be your right if it were not for the fact that you specifically requested the highest sitting—" he smiled as he looked down at his chair, "—judge in this state and District. That is me. So, you have the choice of canceling the entire case so you can try to go higher, or letting it go through with only the truly germane issues on trial. Ball is in your court, so to speak, counselor."

"Postponement!"

"Denied. There is no apparent reason for one."

"Recess," she said through clenched teeth. "I need a thirty minute recess."

The judge nodded. "You can have a ten minute one to ponder your options, but I would like to stipulate that everyone is to remain in the courtroom during that time. Oh, and you may make a phone call but it should be to your client who I now insist ought to be here for this. In fact, I am bothered that he or she is not here. I hope you have a sworn affidavit from him. Or, her. Otherwise I cannot be certain this is suit was legitimately filed in his or her best interests!"

"Approach!" she cried out as he was about to rap the small cylinder of polished wood he used in lieu of any gavel.

His eyes flickered up to her and then to Jackson, who nodded.

"Agreed. Both counsels will approach." He covered his microphone with one hand and leaned forward.

Jackson rose and stepped behind Tom to get to the aisle where he and Ms. Niles walked up to within a foot of the front of the bench. In tones too low for anyone to hear they went into a discussion for over four minutes during which it was evident to all that the prosecuting attorney was very agitated.

Jackson must have asked a question because the judge nodded and held up a warning hand to stop Ms. Niles from saying anything. The Swift's attorney came back to the table and picked up the papers he had been looking through earlier, taking a second to grin and wink at his clients.

Returning to the front he handed the papers to the judge, pointed to several parts on at least three pages and then waited for the judge to review them. Finally, he slid them over to Ms. Niles who read them, threw the papers to the floor and stalked out of the courtroom.

"I would tell the Bailiffs to stop her for contempt but I really do not want to keep her from departing the state with all due haste, so all I will say is that this case is nullified, and with prejudice. What that means for anyone who is interested is that Ms. Niles and her client are barred from speaking about the case, refiling this case, or any other one based on the same or similar charges, in any court in the United States of America. So, as the old saying goes, case dismissed!" He again rapped the block of wood on his desk.

His chair quickly lowered and he walked down the steps and out the side door only taking time to make a "come here" motion toward Tom and Damon.

"The judge wants to speak to you two as soon as the room clears out. We'll sit a minute while he gets ready for us."

"What just happened?" Tom nearly blurted out.

"Well, the judge took an immediate dislike to the prosecution and some of her wording on the charges. I agree with him. Things like 'willful and grossly negligent disregard,' 'obvious disregard for precious human life,' and 'wanton nonobservance of basic safety precautions.' That sort of thing. Then again, she neglected to tell the Court that her client had signed—with Notarized witnesses—all contracts and waivers and that the deposition from the stunt man indicated he was refused adequate training or practice time. Ah, there is our invitation." His head nodded to the side door where a young woman was motioning them to come.

"Gentlemen," the judge greeted them in his Chambers, now in a business suit with the tie loosened, "thank you for coming in now. I am sorry this case got this far but it was the only way I and my advisory panel could see of putting an end to such frivolous nonsense without opening things up to more trials elsewhere."

Damon looked at Jackson who nodded. "Go ahead."

"Okay. Well, Your honor, my son and I thank you and I suppose even understand this, but I wonder if this woman is going to persist to the point where she starts to tarnish our reputation?"

The judge chuckled. "No, and I'll tell you why. As she tried to run outside and call a press conference to decry the injustice of it all, I had officers put a stop to that. I am ordering her to not comment on the case or else face 'contempt in absentia' charges and a penalty starting at one thousand dollars per incident. After three of them, she goes to jail for up to thirty days. But, I have no doubt that Ms. Niles will want to keep this one hush-hush as it makes her look like a fool and not, in my opinion, a very good attorney. But," he sighed, "if she does say anything, or if you and Mr. Rimmer here decide your personal or company reputations have been negatively impacted, I will entertain a suit charging her with defamation and for any reasonable amount of money you should believe due."

A few minutes later they were walking to the rental car and soon driving to the airport where Tom gladly took the controls of his Toad and flew them back to Enterprises.

As they were descending for landing Jackson, sitting in the third row doing some paperwork, moved to the seat just behind Damon.

"I decided to write a press release about the trial and the trumped up charges. See what you think." He handed a single page to the older inventor.

"Well," Damon replied after he read it, "while I have a basic aversion to first strike tactics, I do like the part where you call her out for 'total disregard for the facts in evidence' and 'placing the case before the public rather than in the courtroom.' How about if you run this past that judge and see if he feels we are telling only the truth?"

"Planned on that. And, I will not even have Dilling send this out; I'll send a copy of it to Ms. Niles' office along with a reminder that the judge has placed a gag order on all details and suggest we won't say anything if she doesn't."

Three days later there had been no response from the lady lawyer.

What *had* happened was all out in Hollywood.

Wes Norris reported to Harlan and Tom that an attempt to steal the *Sky Streaker* had been made the day before. During a break for lunch the suit had been moved into one corner of the second sound stage where the hero was being filmed in several variations of getting into and climbing out of the rig.

"Everyone was supposed to be in line for food but a shout went out from the second assistant director and I raced back to that set. Two men, a couple of replacements for set carpenters, were carrying it toward a door."

"Do you know who they are?"

Norris paused. "I'm afraid they are Karl Branski and Miccos Thule, the two we've been looking for. The two that were part of the hired team that attacked you and your wife, and you and Bud. Now for the good news."

"There really needs to be some," Tom stated.

"Well, this is good and bad. First, they had no idea they were trying to make off with the mock-up. Both believe it is the fully-operational unit. We're not telling them otherwise. Next, Branski is looking at more than twenty charges and broke quickly. He wants a deal to rat out his boss."

Harlan now spoke. "Has he named the man?"

"Oh, yes. All together now, that name is... *Streffan Mirov*!"

Tom and Harlan groaned. Finally, Tom found his voice. "We all thought he was dead. How in the world does he keep popping up like this?"

Wes replied, "He is a master of illusion. He's like Moriarty in Sherlock Holmes. Just when you see him plunge over a waterfall that obviously will kill him, it turns out both he and Holmes had doubles who died, and they went underground."

"What about the other one. Thule?"

"Well, Tom, Thule is a tougher nut. True, he's facing a lot of charges, including espionage at Enterprises, but he's fiercely loyal to Mirov right now. He only smirked when we mentioned than name. We'll crack him."

"Where are these two being held?" Harlan asked.

"Bureau headquarters in Los Angeles. They're being kept in separate soundproof rooms, no outside communication, and will be transferred to our D.C. offices day after tomorrow under extremely tight security. I'll keep you both advised."

With little more to report, Norris ended the call assuring them the mock-up was now to be moved into its nighttime steel case, far too heavy to lift with anything other than a forklift, any time it was not actively in use or surrounded by crew and cast members.

Tom went back to his work on the flying version of the *Sky Streaker*. He had brought it back to triple check it in case the errant flight had been due to the equipment. He intended to have it back in California the following Monday. That would make Howard Garner a happy man as he had been making almost hourly calls to tell Tom they were about to get behind of their shooting schedule.

Bud took the checked and okayed suit out for a night flight on Friday. Tom installed temporary reflective shields on all joint points like the legs, and on the chest and the back of the frame.

These meant that the RADAR in the upper control tower—the one on the hill overlooking Enterprises—would be able to track his movements at all times.

With Tom, Hank, Arv and Dianne Duquesne standing to the side, Bud walked the rig forward, his visor still up.

"It's still a bit heavy," he said, "but kudos the whoever rebalanced things. I don't feel nearly as off-kilter as with the prototype or even this version the last time I wore it."

"We moved the two tanks forward an inch," Tom replied.

"Oh. Neat!" Bud ran through all the pre-checks while his small audience watched the thruster crescents swing in and out, the small deflector wings below the bottom thrusters that would provide turning capabilities wiggle in and out, and the computer system status lights now flashing inside the visor.

Everything looked to be green and "go" so Tom walked over and had a quick word with the pilot.

"We have FAA permission for you to take the suit to twenty thousand feet for up to ten minutes. I've downloaded the flight parameters into the computer so keep a watch on the exercise area markers." He glanced at his watch. "There will be a commercial jet passing overhead at nineteen thousand in thirty-two minutes, so get back under twelve-K with five minutes to spare."

"Right, and I will remember to keep an eye on my consumables. Thirty-five minutes and no more before I touch back down."

Tom smiled and started to turn away, but he swung back.

"And, no unnecessary testing of the emergency parachute!" He smiled and Bud nodded as he lowered his visor.

Tom gave a countdown as he looked at his watch, At exactly nine-thirty Bud nodded, twisted the throttle and rose quickly into the night sky.

"How will we see anything he does?" Dianne inquired.

Tom pulled out his tablet computer, telling her, "I've set this to tap into our RADAR so we can track him. Also, if you notice he has navigation lights on the bottoms of his feet. See them up there?"

Everyone could see the strobing white lights and soon watched as they changed direction, zooming to the north before disappearing behind a wispy cloud.

Bud's flight area stretched from a point thirty miles to the north of the top of Lake Carlopa, fifteen miles to the west and east, and down to a point five miles south of the lake. Everyone crowded around the inventor could see the area outlined over a daytime satellite photo of the area, Bud's position marked by a bright red three-ring bullseye.

Near the bottom of the screen was a set of moving numbers. Everyone guessed it was Bud's speed and height and they watched in amazement how quickly he zoomed to his maximum altitude, maneuvered in a series of spirals, and finally dropped back down to about five thousand feet.

"How's he doing, skipper?" Arv asked.

"Everything I'm seeing points to maximum results, Arv. I'm still so amazed at the rate of climb I'm going to have to ask flyboy if it is too much. My guess is that the stunt flyer is going to find it uncomfortable, plus I want to avoid another incident, so I might need to put in a restrictor program. We'll see."

A pulsating blue X moved into the screen with a series of four letters next to it.

"That, in case you haven't guessed, is the commercial jetliner coming down from Toronto to New York."

Four minutes later, at exactly ten o'clock, Bud touched back down. He hit the button to extend the tripod legs and then shut the *Streaker* off.

His suit was released and he stepped out of the foot coverings and came over to the waiting group who applauded him.

Flipping the visor up, his smile was so wide and so bright, Tom thought his face might split.

"Jetz!" he said as he removed the helmet. "That is the most fun I've had, almost ever, or at least in the air!"

As the others headed for home, Tom and Arv put the *Streaker* into the van they'd driven in and the three men headed for the secure storage building where the backpack and suit would spend the weekend.

Bud agreed that the rate of climb was a bit more than simply exhilarating.

"It probably puts the pilot under three-Gs downward pressure. If the suit didn't have the air bladders I might have gotten woozy. So, yes. I'd think cutting the maximum rate of climb is in order."

He concurred with Tom the rate needed to be set at no greater than three thousand feet per minute. It was a figure Tom already had programmed in the master computer in his office, and would download into the suit the next morning.

Everything, he thought to himself as he drove home to Bashalli and Bart, *is coming together!*

CHAPTER 17 /

"IT'S GONE!"

ONE FINAL change he made on Monday was to allow each of the four thrust rings to independently move, fractionally, to provide the most stable flying possible. This included swapping out the upper mounts so those thrusters could swing a few inches farther out to stabilize hovers.

Bud gave the suit one final test flight in the mid morning before he and Tom packed up the suit into the cargo jet.

As they entered the jet, they were greeted by two smiling women.

"Thank you, Tom, for *finally* living up to your promise to take us with you to Hollywood," Sandy told him. She punctuated it by sticking her tongue out at him, but with a smile behind it.

"I only hope the movie magic doesn't get ruined for you both. But, a promise is a promise. Strap in and we'll get out of here in ten minutes."

Bud started to ask when the in-flight beverage service would be but stopped when Sandy shook a fist under his nose and said, "Watch it!"

Tom spent five of those minutes working with Bud to perform the final flight checks and then another two on a phone call informing Howard Gardner that this was to be the man's very last chance.

"Either you have the real and trained stunt man there or you have another one who will be there for everything, and I mean everything, or I take back the prototype and do not let you have the final version. As it is I've got the U.S. Government on my back over this. Do we understand one another?"

Gardner started to try to soft soap the inventor but Tom stopped him. "Agree or I do not take off."

"Okay. I agree already. That last minute replacement was out of my control. He—"

"*Nothing* is out of your control. As producer you control everything. You tried to pull a fast one and that was your last chance. Do I take off or not?"

"Take off. The stunt man you trained said he'll be in shape to fly day after tomorrow. We'll do the last of the close-up shots with the real actor in the fake suit tomorrow."

Tom signed off, shoved the twin throttles forward a little and taxied to the end of the nearest runway. With no wind coming across the field, he took off from the west-to-east runway at the north end of Enterprises rising to about a thousand feet before turning to their course for California.

Bashalli, who had gained her pilot's license more than a year earlier plus her multi-engine rating two months after that was now going for her jet endorsement. Tom slipped from his seat and let her take the controls as they passed eighteen thousand feet. At twenty-five thousand, Bud let Sandy take his seat. The two young men retreated to the small lounge between the cockpit and the cargo area.

"You're going to have a commercial pilot on your hands pretty soon, skipper. Together, I'd say we have the best looking cockpit crew going."

Tom smiled. "I agree but let's not get their heads any bigger than they are right now. Seriously, though, I am really proud of Bash and how much she's taken to flying. I hear the Red Jones had her up for a couple hours two weeks ago and ran her through several emergency drills. Said she didn't panic and just methodically got things back to right. Maybe a little slow, but we both know that comes with time."

"Yeah, but that means we might be out of jobs someday," Bud quipped.

"Only as chauffeurs, flyboy. Anyway, and I'm telling you this as a heads up, but dad would like to have you on the ground more often and a little more involved in the running of the company. Some day, or so he tells me, I am supposed to take over and we both think you are the perfect number two for Enterprises. So, it is only logical that Bash be able to take on a few of the demo flights that Sandy can't with her regular duties for George Dilling in Communications, and you shouldn't have to do."

An hour later Sandy buzzed them.

"Boys? We have visitors on our starboard. Looks like Air Force jets, four of them, but you'd better come back up here."

Tom looked, wide-eyed, at Bud and they launched themselves from their seats.

In the cockpit, Bud looked out the right side window.

"Sure enough, gang. We've got four shiny F-99s out there. Newest thing in the air fleet. Can operate manned or by remote and use lasers and a rail gun instead of bullets and missiles. Good thing they are on our side!" He waived to the nearest pilot who tapped his helmet and held up a series of finger signals.

"Sweetie," he said to Sandy, "please switch the radio to three-five-five-two. They want to talk to us on an untappable frequency."

She complied and they soon heard, "—orce Seven Seven to what looks like a Swift cargo jet. Air Force Seven Seven to what looks like a Swift Cargo jet. Do you copy?"

"We copy," Bud answered. "Just got to the frequency. What can we do for you? Oh, we go by Swift Two."

"Be advised, Swift Two, we've had a report of unidentified aircraft wandering around this area. We're out of McConnell AFB on temp assignment to their refueling wing. We're actively searching for any bogeys. Can we escort you through the next one-K miles? It'll give us another air fueling cycle if nothing else."

Tom nodded and Bud answered. "Affirmative. You be advised we have a pilot working on her multi-jet rating at the controls. Suggest you give a little more clearance."

A short laugh came over the radio before the pilot said, "Understood. Moving out an extra thousand feet. Good luck to the lady. From what we've observed she's rock steady at the controls! If she isn't doing anything else with her life the Air Force can always use good pilots."

Bashalli was beaming from the compliment as Tom asked if she wanted to keep at the controls.

"Of course I do. This is getting exciting."

When the time came for their escorts to leave them Bashalli had turned over control to Sandy and headed to the ladies room. She came back to find Bud in the pilot's seat talking to his wife. So, she went back to the lounge and sat with Tom telling him how much fun it had been to fly in formation and to watch from below and behind as their escort jets had refueled in pairs.

They were crossing the California and Nevada border before Tom took command and contacted Burbank control.

"Roger, Swift Two. Welcome back. Mr. McEwen has given orders to put you back on general aviation pad one."

"Roger that."

They landed just after three in the afternoon, local time. Tom and Bud pulled the atomicar out and the four were scooting through the air fifteen minutes later. As a treat Tom flew them over Mount Lee several miles east of their destination so they could get a good view of the famous Hollywood sign.

Both women took photos and were as enthusiastic about that as they were about seeing the Universal Studios public tour area from the air.

It wasn't until they landed at the back gate that Sandy muttered, "It ain't all glitz and glamour, is it, Bashi?" They were most unimpressed by the plain and downright dingy appearance of the outside of all the sound stages. But both their attitudes changed when they caught sight of three young people standing outside one building as they drove past.

"Wasn't that—?" Sandy gasped.

"Yes. That was Randy Manion and Sandy Bright and that other one from that show. Ohhhh, what's it called?"

"*The Incredible Life of Undercover Cops*! Yes. Oh, Tom? Can we go back and ask for their autographs?"

Instead of answering, he swung the atomicar around retracing their last few hundred feet. But, the trio had gone inside by the time they got back.

"Rats!" Sandy declared.

Bud grinned. "Have either of you heard of some joker called Brian Pemberly?"

The ladies immediately brightened and nodded. "Of course!" they chorused.

"Well," Bud told them, "if you are very good I'll introduce you to him."

Tom soon pulled up to the sound stage. The guard came over to greet them.

"Hello, Mr. Swift and Mr. Barclay. Ladies. They're in the middle of a long scene and I think they're having troubles so it'll be a few. Go ahead and pull up to the big door."

"Thanks. Walter. These ladies, by the way," Tom told the security man, "are my wife, Bashalli and Bud's wife, Sandy. Say hello to Walter, girls."

"Hello, Walter," they said together, both smiling so brightly at the man he started to blush.

Two minutes later the light went out, the buzzer sounded and the big door slid open.

Tom let seven or eight people out who immediately lit cigarettes as if they had been deprived for days instead of minutes, and drove inside.

Wes Norris was off that day but the agent replacing him came over.

"Tom? I'm Agent Gee," the man with slight Asian features told him. "We met a couple years ago before Agent Norris got his transfer."

"Yes," Tom replied, "I do remember you. You grew up in Thessaly, didn't you?"

The man smiled, a rare occurrence for an FBI agent.

"How the heck do you remember that?"

Tom shrugged. "I just do. Plus, it isn't every day you meet someone from a small burg like Thessaly. So, how are things going around here?"

"We should talk. I'll have Agent Dale take Mr. Barclay and your companions over to craft services for a cold drink. Then we can get Mr. Gardner. He's sort of been holding up in his trailer and not coming out much."

The agent and Tom walked away as two other men in dark suits came over. One, Agent Dale who Tom remembered, spoke with Bud and the girls while the other one leaned his back against the atomicar and acted as if he were standing guard. He was.

"Things have gone fine as far as the actual movie stuff, I guess," Gee told Tom, "but we've had to put an armed guard on the fake suit the past four days. Before you ask, it is because we came in on Thursday to find that it was gone."

"Gone?" Tom said with alarm.

"Yes. Gone as in taken from the locked steel case and moved into a far corner. The one dinky security camera they keep up in the rafters," he pointed above them, "caught about twenty flashes as if someone was taking serious photos of the rig. No good look at anyone, but it appeared there were two shadowy forms involved. We can't figure out why they didn't just put it back. Chances are we'd never have noticed the difference."

Tom asked to see the suit.

When he examined it he immediately found something.

"Well, they tried to sabotage the suit. Used a super acrylic glue on the throttle to keep it stuck in the full on position. Pretty dumb of them, but I suppose they couldn't have known it was the non-working rig plus we have a safety switch on the real one that means it will not start up unless the throttle is in the off position. As for not putting it back, maybe someone is trying to send a message?"

Now, the agent shrugged.

Tom and Agent Gee joined Bud, Sandy and Bashalli and they all enjoyed an ice cold soda. As they were finishing them, the haggard form of Howard Gardner came over.

"Swift. Am I glad to see you. We've got saboteurs and spies everywhere!" he declared, looking a little crazy. "Did this guy tell you? Tell him!" he demanded without waiting for an answer.

"The agent told me about the movement and probable photos being taken. But, since this was the non-working suit it isn't much to worry about other than from an outer design point."

Gardner began waiving his arms around. "Not worry? Not worry? I come in and the first thing I hear is 'The suit is gone!' That's what I come in to. Near come to stopping my heart. So, *not to worry*? Pahh!"

Tom spotted the nurse, Vanessa Kelly, and motioned for her to come over. Without saying anything, and out of Gardner's site, he tried to get across to her the man was in some sort of distress.

She understood and knelt down next to him.

"Hello, Mr. Gardner. Been having another little spell?" She had his wrist and was checking his pulse as she asked.

"This is all too much," he said weakly to her. "I need to go to my trailer. Take me there?"

"Certainly. But, did you need to talk to Mr. Swift about anything. Like," she tried to prompt him, "how the stunt man has been grounded by the FAA?"

Gardner wailed in emotional distress. She helped him to his feet and explained, in a whisper, to Tom, "I had to report the man. He is having complications from his appendectomy surgery and I didn't want him rupturing in mid-air. Sorry."

Tom patted her in the shoulder. "Nothing to be sorry for. You did exactly the right and medically mandated thing. We'll make this work. You just get Mr. Gardner settled and, well, relaxed."

She shook a small bottle of pills she had taken from a pocket. "Can do. He wanted to do today without them but ought to be feeling pretty good in an hour."

She walked off with the producer leaving Tom to make a brief explanation to his companions. A minute later came the call for "Quiet on the set!" and they moved quickly and silently over to watch another scene being shot, this time in the submarine control room set.

When the brief scene was over the director called for a second take from a slightly different angle. During the two minutes it took to get the camera moved and refocus Brian Pemberly's main light—what Tom recalled was known as a key light—the girls conferred in hushed tones about the actor. Evidently, he was more handsome in person than on screen and both were about to burst they wanted to meet him so badly.

The chance came twenty minutes later after five takes of the scene with the new setup.

Pemberly had spotted Tom and Bud but had really homed in on the two beauties with them.

"Hello, Tom and Bud," he said in a tone that made Bud want to gag a little. "And, who are these gorgeous ladies?"

Tom introduced them.

"Wow," Brian told them all. "Why do you have two ladies who would melt a camera lens and we get these overly made-up thirty-somethings trying to still be teenagers? It isn't fair."

Then, he did something Tom never would have thought of. He offered to sign something for them if they would sign something for him.

"I want to have your first official Hollywood autographs in case you drop these two guys and come here to act. Deal?"

The girls thought it sounded like an excellent deal.

"Oh, Tom?" he said as he finished signing some discarded pages of a script sitting nearby. "Gardner wants me to be in a couple of shots where the suit is taking off, the visor up so my face is showing. I think the idea is I start things up and then dramatically drop the faceplate down before shooting off into the sky. Obviously, the stunt man, whoever that eventually turns out to be, will do the high flying, but I was wondering if I might get enough training to take the thing up to, oh, maybe twenty or thirty feet?"

"I'll have to think about it, Brian. Not because I don't believe you can handle it, but Mr. Gardner has pulled a few things on us with the suit and I have to avoid any more incidents or I take my stuff and go home."

Brian nodded. "I understand. Well, I've got to go back and get set for the next scene, but if necessary I can stay late and take a little training, or come in early or whatever." He turned back to Sandy and Bashalli. "Ladies, it has been a pleasure and I hope we can all do dinner tonight. I know of a great place twenty minutes from here. They do a biriani and mutton kabab like I hear is as great as they have in Pakistan." He smiled at Bashalli who smiled back and nodded.

He disappeared through the crowd of people and the "Quiet" call came a few minutes later. This time they had to remain still and silent for only five minutes.

When the bell rang again and the work lights came back up, the nurse walked over to Tom.

"He's much better. He's been having panic attacks and has to take three pills a day for it. As I mentioned, he wanted to try today without them, but he's admitted it was a mistake. Come on, Mr. Swift. I'm not sure if it would be a good idea for everyone to come, though." She looked over his shoulder at the other three.

"It's fine, and call me Tom. Bud, you take the ladies over to the second sound stage and show them the other sets. I think they are only shooting on this one right now. Walter will be able to tell you. See you back here in half an hour."

When they knocked on the trailer door, Howard Gardner, face reddening in embarrassment, open it and invited them both in.

"Hope you don't mind the company," he said nodding toward Vanessa. "She's my lifeline these days. I'm going to have to retire after we get this picture finished. I just can't take the pressure any more."

"Then, let's put all the cards on the table," Tom told him. "You have pulled a few fast ones on this shoot and I am about ready to pull something of my own. Namely, the entire suit, even the nonflying one. From this moment on, you have to follow the rules. We all do."

He told Gardner the entire story about Streffan Mirov, the various attacks and even the infiltration of Enterprises by one of Mirov's henchmen who had then shown up in the crew here. He did not spare the producer any details. As he finished, Gardner was pale but looking more at peace.

"Okay. Message received, understood and I will follow your lead to the letter, Tom. This is a magic and yet somehow damnable industry I am in. People see the end product but never see the injuries, the hatreds, the infighting and even the tantrums. That is why Hollywood is a magic place. For ninety-six to one hundred-fifteen minutes, on average, the real world disappears and the perfectly orchestrated world of the motion picture takes us over. What you or the FBI agents or whoever says, it goes when it comes to that flying suit."

Tom nearly had to chuckle. "Regret ever contacting me?" he asked.

Gardner laughed. "Regret it? I hate myself each and every minute but I know that this would never be possible without you. I regret not taking my pills today, or last evening for that matter— and sorry to you, Vanessa for not telling you—and I regret trying to pass off a stand-in stuntman. I, uhh, hear there was a nasty after effect."

"Speaking of which," Tom said looking curious, "why is it that he tried suing my company and not you? Or the studio?"

Gardner sadly shook his head. "It is a fact of life that if you need to take out a suit, you don't aim it at anyone who might put and end to your career. Sadly, that piranha lawyer who got her fangs into him has made it impossible for him to get any work. Now, every studio and producer is afraid she'll come with the package."

Tom told him that the flying system was now back, had been scrupulously checked and it was through no equipment fault the man headed skyward. He said the four would remain in California a few days until a new stunt man could be secured, and they would go back through the entire training with that new man.

"In the meantime, I understand from your star you might want to shoot a few scenes of him taking off, with close-ups of his face?"

Howard Gardner didn't meet Tom's gaze, but he nodded. "Yeah. Pretty stupid idea, huh? It'd look great but I know it is impossible."

"No. It's okay," the inventor told him. "We can do that!"

Now, the look on the producer's face was one of a man who had just put his hand on a life ring as he is about to go under for the third time.

"Going to kill my budget this is, but we're too far along to quit now."

What Tom told him next was almost more than he could stand.

"As it happens, creating the finished version of the *Sky Streaker* cost us less than we anticipated. About a hundred thousand dollars less. So, rather than chalk it up to extra profit, how about we split it? Half to cover our extra several trips out here and multiple training times and the rescue mission, and half to you to get a really good stunt pilot?"

Howard Gardner's eyes brimmed with tears of happiness.

CHAPTER 18 /
STUNTMAN NUMBER THREE WASHES OUT

THEIR DINNER with Brian Pemberly went well with the four from Shopton enjoying his tales of life in Hollywood, anecdotes of famous people who were a lot less in real life than their on-screen personas, and him voicing a few of the frustrations of being a working actor trying to break into the "big time."

The big time meant getting offered more "leading man" rolls rather than "best friend," or "also staring" parts.

"You seem to be doing very well in the scenes we watched," Bashalli complimented him.

"Thanks, and I guess you're right. At least it all feels like it's working. We'll see what it ends up as once it gets cut."

"Cut?" Sandy asked. "Sounds like they will chop it all to pieces."

He laughed. "It feels like that at times. Do you know that my first screen performance, all thirteen scenes and fifty lines of dialog, got left on the cutting room floor? It changed the entire movie and at least one critic asked the question why there wasn't a character like mine in the film to make it all come together. The thing bombed. El Stinko!"

"That's got to frustrate the bejesus out of you," Bud opined.

Brian nodded. "Yep. But, it is part of life in the cinema." He sighed and took his last bite of the steak he had been nursing.

He picked up the near-empty bottle of expensive wine he'd ordered. None of the others wanted a second serving so he dribbled the last into his own glass.

"Here is to my fingers-crossed career," he intoned with a little grin. "Long may it fly, along with that incredible rig you've built."

"Speaking of which," Bud told him, "I hear we have to go-ahead to show you how to get it a few feet off the ground. When can we meet tomorrow? I'd really like to have at least an hour of your time to get you up to speed."

"My call—that's when I have to be at the stage for make-up—" he explained to Sandy and Bashalli, "isn't until nine tomorrow. So, since I generally rise at five and scan my lines for an hour before heading out, how about if we meet around seven?"

It was agreed, and after draining the last of his wine, Brian excused himself and left, but not before having a small but friendly argument with Tom over who would pay for the meal. In the end Brian insisted he pay for the wine and dropped four twenty-dollar bills on the table.

"He's nice!" Sandy declared.

"He's very handsome," added Bashalli.

"He's almost a regular guy," Bud told them both. Sandy and Bashalli glared at him.

"Okay, we agree Brian's a nice man, but what has he been in? I must be too out of touch because I don't recognize him," Tom admitted.

"*Law Enforcement: Seattle, American Hospital*..." intoned the ladies and they went on and on.

Finally, after what seemed like twenty listings, Tom stopped them. "We have to go back to the airport and then to the hotel where we have reservations. Come on."

They all got up at five—eight by their internal clocks—and had breakfast at a nearby diner. Four plates of pancakes covered with granola, strawberries, bananas and whipped cream, and nothing —Tom's helping—later, they flew back to the studio.

It was a very different scene at seven a.m. Technical people slouched around moving equipment from one place to another, electricians and riggers were checking all the lights, replacing burnt or near-death bulbs, and the catering people were preparing huge vats of breakfast items.

"I guess we could have eaten here," Bud said.

"That's okay. I enjoyed my pancakes made one at a time and not by the hundreds," Sandy said to them.

A short time later Brian came in looking pretty well rested, a script in one hand as he was silently saying lines he would record in just a few hours.

After greetings, along with kisses to the girl's cheeks, he and Bud left to go though the training he would need.

Tom begged off exploring the studio telling the girls to see the young woman who brought around water and other things. "She might be able to arrange a tour or something for you. I have some work to do before Bud let's Brian head into the sky."

The errand girl, who they found out was named Emily, got on her walkie-talkie and called for someone from the studio tours group to come get the ladies.

"She'll give you a private tour before the place opens up to the public. You'll actually see a lot more than you would on the paid tour. Maybe even a few of the stars as they wander here and there. Enjoy!" and she was gone again.

Ten minutes later a young black woman named Bonnie came

over and introduced herself.

"We have about three hours before things get really hopping and we'll have to stay out of everyone's way, so let's go. I was thinking you might like to see the sets of the five situation comedies we shoot here first. By the time we get to the third one some of the actors ought to be rehearsing and I'll introduce them to you. By the way, you two are drop dead beautiful so don't be surprised if you get hit on by actors or if someone tells you to take you place for the next shot."

The three women climbed into a very fancy golf cart and silently moved off seconds later.

Tom heard little of their conversation. He had his tablet computer out and was accessing the computers at Enterprises. A thought had come to him at breakfast and he wanted to see if he might follow up on it.

As he suspected, the access was too slow so he made a phone call to Hank Sterling. "Hank? Tom. I have a really fast job for you if you can do it." He explained how Bud was training the star to fly a little into the air for some shots.

"The thing is, I don't want a repeat of the last time, so I want to limit the elevation the thing will reach. Can you go look at code lines 13,255 through 13,522 and see if you agree that we can install limits?"

"Okay, but how high?"

"Maybe just thirty feet... fifty tops. It also might be nice to make it the normal mode so if anyone tries to steal the *Streaker* it won't let them go far. And, now I think about it, how about setting things to go up, hover for no more than, umm, five seconds, before coming back down on its own?"

Hank agreed and said he would call once the software was ready for download.

"No need," Tom told the engineer. "You can remotely do that from Enterprises." He told Hank how to perform the task and hung up.

Hank phoned the inventor around eleven.

"Sorry it took so long, skipper, but there were so many new code lines I had to create new subroutines and renumber some other stuff, and you know how that messes up specific line calls."

"I sure do, Hank. The important thing is, did you get that programmed in?"

"Not only programmed but tested in a dozen simulation runs and then uploaded to the suit twenty minutes ago. Hope I didn't hold up anything."

Tom said the flights with Brian Pemberly were not scheduled until mid afternoon, so there was no issue with timing. He was just glad to have that safety override now installed in the *Sky Streaker*.

Another person glad to have it working was Wes Norris. He had had a quiet word with Tom the previous afternoon once it had been made known that the star was going to do some actual flying.

"Tom, I can't put my finger on anything, but I have a bad feeling about this. I have to trust that Pemberly guy but what if somebody takes his place and tries flying the real suit out of here?"

Tom explained about the limiter program.

"Thank heavens for that! Okay, you've read my mind and jumped far out in front of this old cynic. Thanks!"

With lunch almost over and Bud sitting with the star going over some of the instructions for about the tenth time, Tom wandered over to where they sat.

Bud was just telling Brian, "Then, I hear you are to hover for five seconds then come back down. That gives Mr. Director time to cut each up and down into separate takeoffs and landings. Just remember to turn that throttle only enough to get your feet off the ground and then a fraction more to move up. Oh, hey, skipper. What's up?"

Tom, keeping a straight face, replied, "Brian, but only to about fifty feet."

The two men sitting at the table stared up at the inventor.

"Uhhh... what?" Bud asked.

Tom sat down with them.

"We now have a limiter in the suit that will only let Brian here go up about fifty feet, stay there for five seconds, and then it brings him back for a light touchdown all automatically. All you need to do, Brian, is to turn the throttle when the director yells 'Action,' then sort of slack off on it and let the computer do the rest."

He had never seen such a look of relief on a person before. Brian nearly fell off his chair he was so overcome.

"Thank you," he whispered reaching out to grab both Tom's and Bud's hands. "I've been trying to convince myself that I can act my way through this. Just another role, Brian, I've been silently chanting. The truth is, I'm scared you-know-what of heights unless I have something solid under my feet. Please don't let that get around."

"Our lips are sealed. Why didn't you say something earlier?" Bud asked.

Brian looked to both sides before answering. "If you were supposed to be the big, brave hero in an action movie, and got that role because of a resume full of heroic action parts, would you want to admit to nearly wetting your pants at the thought of dangling over... *nothing*?"

Neither of them could answer that but they both agreed it was not something that should be made known.

Bud and Brian left to go suit up leaving the inventor with nothing much to do. He wandered around the sound stage and even went to the identical building next door. It was the first time he had been in that one and was amazed at what he saw.

On one side was an elevated area that featured a wrap-around backdrop of vibrant green and a water tank some fifty feet by fifty feet that would be about five feet deep assuming it went down to the floor. Next to it were the two miniature submarines. One looked like it was capable of floating, but the other one was open on the bottom and had eight small wheels supporting it.

Exactly opposite that was another large set, this one of the outside of a three story building, a pair of wide doors in the middle and a five-foot trampoline thirty feet out from the doors. Another ten feet from that was a very thick pad, obviously the one someone would land on after pretending to leap into the air, and likely wearing the *Sky Streaker* suit.

Above the building facade was another green wall, but this one arched overhead by perhaps forty feet.

"Well, that landing's got to hurt, even with the non-working one. It's pretty heavy to have come down on somebody's back!" he muttered.

He was about to turn when Lawrence Laurent came in.

"Oh, Swift. There you are. Are we about ready to fly our hero?"

"We are. Tell me, Mr. Laurent, how you keep someone from being injured with this?" He pointed to the trampoline and pad.

Laurent laughed.

"It's simple. The stunt guy is harnessed to that nearly invisible winch up there." He pointed to a green-painted piece of equipment attached to a green track. "The hero comes from the front doors, does something like look around or flip his visor down or even turn and call out a line back into the building. Then he activates the suit, runs forward and leaps into the air. The winch is there to lower him to the pad after we get him soaring over the camera. The green screen gets a moving sky with clouds treatment in post production."

"Oh. Now I see. More movie magic?"

"Yeah. Movie cheating is more like it but without having a stunt guy to do some actual flying. It's what we have to contend with."

They walked back to the first stage where Bud, Brian and several others in the camera crew were preparing to go out to a waiting bus and truck.

"It's back to Hollywood canyon," Bud quipped. "We'll only be there two hours or so. Want to come?"

After thinking a moment, Tom asked, "Do you need me?"

Putting on his best "Movie Agent" voice, Bud pretended to be chomping on a cigar when he replied, "No, kid. But, I like you, see? Want to see you going places. Big things in store and all that!" Then, changing back into Bud, he said, "I have this one, but you are always welcome to come."

"No. I think I'll wait here. The girls went off on a second tour with that Bonnie person. She promised them a chance to eat with the stars and to sit in the audience of a game show they shoot here. '*Make A Fortune*,' I think it's called. The other possibility is their classical music quiz, *Just a Minuet*. Anyway, they ought to be getting back here around three, and you will still be out shooing then. Go have a little fun and make sure Brian doesn't get into trouble."

The bus departed a few minutes after the truck and the soundstage went into high gear. Amazed at what was happening, Tom watched as two of the sets were taken apart, almost as if in fast-motion, and one new, larger set was erected in their place. The entire thing took less than twenty minutes. Shortly after that other actors and extras got ready for their scenes.

He sensed someone at his side and looked over to see Emily standing there.

"Well, hello, Emily," he greeted her, startling the girl a little. "Pretty interesting for an outsider to watch that, but you must be used to it."

"Not really," she admitted in a quiet voice. "This is my first movie. I've done a couple TV episodes as gopher but when this chance came up I jumped at it. Kinda hard work and not much glory."

"You're doing a swell job as far as I've seen. Keep it up and I'll bet some day you get to move up the chain."

She offered to get him something to drink, but he said he was fine, so she left him.

Bashalli and Sandy came back nearly an hour later than

expected and both were grinning from ear to ear.

"We got to be on a game show!" Bashalli told him excitedly.

"We won prizes and money!" Sandy said.

"What? How?"

Sandy now said, "That show is known for picking people from the audience to appear on camera, and the nicest young man came right over to us and said we'd look swell on camera and could we handle being on camera with all the lights and that."

"And, we said Yes!" Bashalli finished.

They were telling him about the prizes they had both won along with several thousand dollars each when the bus returned. Bud and Brian stepped out, both looking happy.

"It went very well," the flyer said. "Brian did a truly great job."

"Hi, Sandy, hi Bashalli," the actor greeted them. "I couldn't have done it without your two guys. Great, just great!" he left them to go shower and change into his Sky Marshall costume.

Mr. Gardner came over with a thirtyish-looking man in tow.

"This is the stunt man we've been waiting for!" he declared and introduced them to Derick Comstock. "Comstock's grandfather was well known back in the sixties, seventies and eighties for his incredible stunts. His dad did it for fifteen years before he ruptured his eardrums and never had the balance after that. Now, third generation and all that! So, give him the rundown on the flying rig and we'll shoot his scenes starting day after tomorrow."

Bud looked at the slightly older stunt man. He was about Brian's build, unlike any of the others, and didn't appear to be the sort you might classify as a hotshot or showoff.

"Okay," he finally sighed. "It's getting late in the day, but let me drag in the practice rig and we can do the walk-around today then I'd like to start at seven tomorrow with the instructions."

"That might not be necessary. You see, my grandpop owned one of the old Bell rocket belts and I had the chance to fly it about fifteen times before it had a nozzle blowout. I probably have more experience than anyone out here. No matter, though. I'll be here at seven. Where do you want me now?"

Bud pointed to a quiet corner close to the trailer used by Howard Gardner. "I'll bring the mock-up over there. See you in five."

Tom helped him retrieve the nonfunctional suit from its storage container and carry it over. They set in on its extendible legs and the inventor left Bud to handle things.

As time approached to call an end to the day's shooting, Bud angrily stalked over to where Tom and the girls were sitting.

"That man is impossible!" he said with more than a hint of frustration. "He's all, 'Yeah, I know all that,' and 'I can do that in my sleep,' and darned little paying attention. And, he keeps calling me Buck! I'm sorry, Tom, but I've had it up to here with these jokers. I've got to get out of here!"

Tom was attempting to calm his best friend down when the producer came walking briskly over.

"What's this I hear about you telling the stunt man to get lost?" He sounded angry.

Bud who was more angry that he should ever be glared at Gardner and grabbed the man's arm, turning him around and pulling him outside where they went into a very heated discussion.

Howard faced the furious Bud. He got an earful about how the flyer had had it with the stuntmen who all turned into duds, how he wouldn't certify "that clown" who wasn't listening to his instructions, and he was letting the producer know about it in words Tom was glad the ladies couldn't hear.

Tom decided to let him have it out with the man.

For his part, Gardner appeared to be giving Bud an earful as well. Several times he could be seen walking away a few feet only to turn around and say something, or shake his fists in the air, or throw his hands up in resignation.

Eight minutes later he walked back into the soundstage and past Tom, Bashalli and Sandy. His face was beet red but he no longer looked angry.

Bud came over to the inventor.

"Well," he said with a big sigh, "I told Gardner I was fed up with it all and that as far as I was concerned I've had it with training these idiots who should never have been hired in the first place. He tried telling me that it isn't up to us who he hires or who the stunt people send over and I told him he was an idiot."

"And..." Tom asked, not because he wanted to hear all the bad parts but because his friend didn't actually look as angry as he should be given the circumstances.

"Well, then I sort of said something that he liked and we now have come to an agreement."

"I see. Except... No, Bud, I really *don't* see. What did you say to him?"

Bud had a guilty grin on his face now. "I told him that this is all his fault for demanding there be a real flying rig and refusing to do things the safe way, so if he couldn't be trusted to find someone to fly the suit, I was going to do all the stunt flying for him!"

CHAPTER 19 /
...WITH AERIAL STUNTS BY B. BARCLAY

TOM WAS flabbergasted.

Bud had a goofy grin on his face, but he suddenly turned serious.

"Jetz! I never even thought to ask you if that was okay. Oh, man. Am I in trouble?"

Tom laughed. It was a good release of the stress and pressure he had been feeling and it came out loud and for enough of a long time Bud became concerned.

"I mean," the flyer went on, "I never wanted to overstep boundaries. So, if you say the word, I'll go tell Gardner I was overcome by the heat and can't fly for him."

"Bud? Do you realize you hit on a great solution to a very annoying problem? I'm not certain why I never suggested it to him in the first place."

Howard Gardner had an answer for that when the two men went to see him.

"Well, I just got off the phone and the Brotherhood/Sisterhood of Stunt Workers, that's their union, says no-can-do." He looked helpless.

"Why?"

Gardner looked up at Tom. "Huh?"

"Why?" Tom stood looking down at him with a look that only spoke of curiosity.

Gardner sighed and stood up. "Okay, the straight story is they are a union and they make money by placing union stunt people here in Hollywood. No union stunt man, no money for the union. They don't like that so they threaten to never work another picture for any studio or producer who doesn't use their people."

Tom nodded. "Fine, but they haven't been able to send you anyone capable of flying the suit. I say call them and tell them you need to have a qualified person with the necessary strength to lift the rig, who can take instructions and go through a full day's training. If they can't deliver, they should have no argument with you finding outside help, especially since it comes from the manufacturer of that same flying equipment."

Howard Gardner appeared to be having a silent conversation with himself. It went on for nearly three minutes before he looked back at the inventor.

"You call them."

"Fine. I'd be happy to. Dial the number and give me the handset."

Howard Gardner knew the number by heart so he dialed it and gave the phone to Tom."

A bored-sounding woman who identified herself as the Executive Union Senior Secretary answered and listened as Tom told her who he needed to speak with.

"You Union?"

"No," he replied with patience he wasn't feeling. "However, your Union has sent at least two unqualified stunt persons to a movie set and have charged the full price for them. Please suggest to your boss that there are probably laws in the State of California that say he isn't supposed to take that money for failing to supply. I'll wait."

The woman was speechless but she did a good job of sputtering and stammering that he had no right to threaten her like that.

"Ma'am, neither did I threaten nor did I even direct my words at you. It is your boss and him or her alone who needs to take my call. Thank you."

She put him on hold but it lasted only a moment. An angry man came on the line starting out by yelling that whoever was calling was looking for a Union action! Tom let him expend his breath and anger before telling him the nature of the call.

"Gardner? Gardner... hmmmm. Some sort of flying picture, right?"

"No. It is an adventure movie that includes scenes where the hero flies using what you might call a jet pack. It is not a jet-powered pack, but that is the basic idea."

"Yeah. Hang the guy from wires, move him around with winches. That stuff!"

"Again, no. I have the original request paperwork in front of me and it spells out the need for a strong flight-qualified pilot. The first man you sent fainted at the thought of flying and the second one ended up with a ruptured appendix, so you substituted a totally unqualified man that ended up nearly losing his life when he failed to control the rig. It cost my company—the one that built that rig—a hundred thousand dollars rescuing him before he might have died at high altitude. I am calling as a courtesy to say that you and your union have had your chances and failed. So, I am assigning one of my test pilots to fly the rig for this movie."

"Hah! You can't do that. We've got an ironclad Union mandate with all the studios."

"And I have a bill for our rescue services and our two full days of wasted training plus four cross-country flights to try to make all this happen to send to you and a team of lawyers who will back me up. So, I am suggesting that you back down and agree to allow this movie to continue with a trained professional that you are unable, or is it *unwilling,* to supply. No complaints. No threats. You won't even have to send back all the money the producer has paid you."

There was silence on the other end for a minute. Then, "Call me back in an hour." The line went dead.

Tom now called Jackson Rimmer telling him of the situation.

Jackson listened and then told Tom, "Let me give him that call. I happen to have researched a bit about Union stunt people when you had such trouble with the first one. The California law is plain and direct. It states that if the Union fails to provide what is asked for and paid for, it has to both stand aside allowing outside professional help to do the work as well as pay back every penny spent hiring the stuntman, training them, and the Union fees. In fact, I can quote him the appropriate laws. I'll call you back in about ten minutes."

When he did it was with the news that the Union saw the logic in allowing Bud to perform all the stunts, "...but only as long as it does not happen within the studio. One more thing. They really hate giving in like this so I assured him neither the Swift organization nor your Mr. Gardner would make any announcement that might, well, embarrass them."

"Understood. Thanks, again."

"It's what I get paid to do, Tom, And, happy to do it. Tell Bud to either break a leg or not, depending on which superstition they adhere to out there."

The second unit that had started shooting when the unskilled man had gone for his uncontrolled flight would pack up and head back to the canyon the next morning. With Bud at the controls, everyone believed the full day could be accomplished in just four hours. Following that they would pack up people along with two large trucks of set pieces and head for the desert to the east of San Diego, near the city of El Cajon. There and outside of any commercial flight paths, they would have nearly three hundred degrees of hills and sky to use.

Tom and the ladies attended the first hour of shooting in the nearby canyon. Then, before lunch, he checked in with Bud who stated he was having a great time, and the three left to go eat and sightsee.

They presented quite a sight floating along several hundred feet off the coast as they paralleled the Pacific Coast highway on their way north. Their goal was a restaurant in Malibu that had been suggested by the ladies' tour guide, Bonnie.

"This is incredible, seeing the coast and all the boats and everything without being stuck in that traffic," Bashalli said pointing out the passenger side at the totally-stopped line of cars attempting to head both directions.

They landed in the parking lot of the resort where the restaurant was located. A young man in a hot-looking mustard-colored vest and small black cap came running over from the small shack next to the road.

"You can't just park here. How did you get past me?"

Tom smiled as he walked over to the person he now could see was probably sixteen or seventeen. He introduced himself and said they had reservations in the resort. The boy jogged back, checked his book and seemed ready to run back to them when Tom motioned him to stay.

"No need to run in this heat. Just point the right way," he called out.

The boy complied and they headed toward a nearby building.

Over fresh seafood cocktails and some northern Pacific halibut steaks—that they agreed was much better than what they could get in New York—they talked about Bud.

"He's got to be feeing like the king of the universe about now," Sandy said.

"I hope so," Tom told them. "He's had a few frustrating days recently with the failed flyers, so he deserves a bit of fun."

"And glory," Bashalli reminded them. "I heard that Mr. Gardner tell him he will be listed in the credits at the end as, 'with aerial stunts by B. Barclay.'"

Sandy groaned. "That's going to go to his head and I can see it now. We'll have ten copies of the movie and he'll drag it out at every occasion."

After lunch they headed back into the LA basin and flew above a lot of the different studio lots before Tom flew them over Beverly Hills.

Both Bashalli and Sandy were stunned to silence at the large size of many of the houses, and also how small some of them were.

"I always imagined it as one long street with palm trees on each side and all the huge mansions. It's mostly like a crowded neighborhood. How disappointing," Bashalli told her husband.

Bud radioed at about four. "We'll be finishing the last shots in ten minutes, skipper and then our junior director wants to get a few more takeoffs and landings. The crew needs to be released at five, so come pick me and the suit up then."

"Roger. See you in an hour."

The atomicar was just touching down when Bud brought the suit to the ground a few feet away. The hot downdraft buffeted the car and its inhabitants.

"Trying to singe your wife, sister-in-law and best friend?" Tom inquired when Bud's visor came up.

"Oops! Sorry. I forgot all about that. Well, give the rig five minutes to cool down and then let's get out of here. Tomorrow is a travel day but I told them we'd get there, with the suit, our own way. Wes Norris likes that idea."

The first thing to do was return the suit to the safety of the cargo jet. Then, after Bud had a chance for a shower at the hotel, they headed for a restaurant down near Disneyland. The menu stated it had been around more than eighty years and specialized in big portions, cornbread and ten-inch-tall pies.

They ate as much as they could and took their pie slices to go.

"They'll make good eating on the trip down tomorrow."

The flight was fine until they arrived in El Cajon and stopped to ask for directions.

"Well," the service station attendant said eyeing the atomicar and trying to figure out if it might need gasoline, and where it would go, "that place is a bit farther east of here. You gotta get back the Eight Freeway and head east. Maybe, oh, thirty miles to a highway number Seventy-Nine, then take that north about a mile. You'll see Riverside Drive on the left and then Camp Oliver a quarter mile along on the right. Can't miss it."

Tom thanked the man and pulled around to the side of the station where it would hopefully attract less attention when the atomicar rose into the air.

They followed the indicated roads and got to the camp with several hours to spare.

One of the studio trucks had arrived the evening before and a large tent featuring plastic side windows had been erected in the open field.

A young woman started to come over, probably to say it was a restricted area, but she smiled when she recognized them.

"Hello, Emily," Tom greeted her.

She stopped. "You... you know my name?" She seemed very surprised.

"Of course. I don't recall who told me, but Emily *is* your name, right?"

She nodded. "Yes, but nobody remembers it. Most of the time I'm 'that water girl,' or 'the gopher.' Golly. Thank you for remembering."

After checking her clipboard she asked if they wanted anything.

"No, not for now. We got here very early and just wanted to wander around."

Emily left them to go count all the shipping containers that had arrived, most containing food and costumes.

Several men were erecting two other tents, these looking as if they were divided into many small rooms. Another worker said they were the dressing room for the cast plus makeup, costume repair and the quarters for the crew overnight.

Things were slow and boring and the girls suggested they might have waited to come down until that evening.

"Couldn't," Bud told them. "Just as soon as the crew and director get here we have to start blocking all the flying scenes."

Things began getting more exciting an hour later as the first truck pulled in. A swarm of men, women and moving dollies scurried around putting up the set pieces that would be building exteriors.

In another hour the small collection of false-fronted buildings were up and ready.

Things remained busy well into the afternoon when the final group arrived. Bud went over to work with the crew on how and where he would be flying the next couple days.

A helicopter with an outside camera mount came in throwing up a lot of dust and dead grass. It was, as Tom surmised, the way they would get the real flying scenes.

While light was available, a test flight was arranged, Bud got into the *Sky Streaker*, and he and the camera helicopter took off before five o'clock.

Thirty minutes later they were back and the cameraman and second unit director did not look happy.

"They can't keep up with me and the shots don't look good if I fly at their slow speed," Bud told Tom off to one side. He described some of the maneuvers and how the camera could barely be moved around to keep him in frame. "I feel sorry for them, Tom, but shouldn't they have thought about this?"

Tom patted his friend on the arm. "I have an idea."

He walked over to the director, spoke with him a moment before the man's face went from angry to enthusiastic, and then came back.

"I knew we'd packed something just in case, and now I am going to fly back to the airport and get it. Sandy, will you come with me to fly the atomicar back here? Bud, while we're gone make sure Bash doesn't get in the way."

"What is it you are going to get?"

Tom smiled. "The *Kangaroo Kub*. Put the cameraman in the rear seat we installed last year and we can more than keep up with you. We might even match some of your aerobatics."

Sandy arrived back at the small municipal airfield in El Cajon ten minutes behind Tom. He had already arranged for fueling services and a secure tie-down place.

They got back to the movie camp at eight. Everyone had eaten but Bud and Bashalli had arranged for some sandwiches for the two pilots.

Next morning things were set to start at eight, so Sandy flew Tom and the cameraman with his gear back to El Cajon where they picked up the *Kub*.

"Tight fit but that'll give me some extra stability," Danny, the camera operator said. "Can you demo what this little bird will do so I can plan around anything unexpected?"

By the time they arrived over the camp Danny was finding it hard to describe how enthusiastic he was.

Bud called them by radio. "Tom? We're three minutes away from the first take off and level flight. The director wants you to stay to the west of me until I get about three hundred feet, then come along my left side. Not too close but level with me. The shot will last about twenty seconds before I roll right and shoot up. Don't follow me; let the camera do that."

Tom confirmed that he understood and soon the ground and air cameras were rolling.

Everything went well and by the time Tom had to go back to the airport for fuel, they had eight of the twenty-nine shots scheduled "in the can."

He radioed their return as they left El Cajon again and Bud reported he would be ready for some of the altitude shots.

"Meet me at about ten thousand feet."

"Will do," Tom replied.

The camera behind him clicked into action as Bud announced his takeoff. Danny asked it Tom could roll to the right to catch the suit coming up, and Tom complied having to tilt the nose up a little to keep from losing any altitude.

This shot was to include a series of left to right and back again swings and would end when Bud rolled the suit on its back before heading higher up.

The first take didn't go as planned and Danny asked for three minutes to make an adjustment to his camera.

They were half way through the second take when Tom glanced at his small RADAR screen. He did not like what he saw. A small pip, racing in at an almost intersect angle, had just come on the screen.

"Bud," he radioed. "We have company. Might just be sightseers but watch out on your four o'clock. Whatever it is, is coming up from about seven thousand feet. I'll call them."

He switched to the general aviation frequency. "Swift camera jet calling unidentified aircraft rising up from Pine Valley area. This is a temporarily restricted movie airspace. Please veer off and traverse to our south. I repeat veer off and pass to our south."

There was no answer. The dot didn't waver and now Tom felt a chill run down his spine.

"Bud. No joy. They either don't have their ears on, don't care, or don't have any good intentions. Suggest you drop down and head for the camp while I try to sort this joker out."

"Skipper. I can avoid him as long as you can give me some bearings to watch. I'd hate to get us behind schedule if it turns out to be a joyrider up here."

They both turned to the north and flew in formation. All the while Danny was getting more and more footage of the flying suit and often giggling at what he explained was the "...sheer quality of this stuff!"

The other jet streaked below them by fewer than a hundred feet. The turbulence from his jet caused Bud's suit to spin out of control for a moment before his skill had him back in level flight.

The next pass came on Tom's left side.

"Flyboy? That's another of those old French fighter jets like the two that attacked us over New Mexico. I think we've got trouble."

"Roger. Shield me until he moves off then I'll go down. You'd better call in the Marines."

Tom turned his head to the side.

"Danny? We've got an enemy intruder out there who may try to attack us. Put the camera on the floor between your feet and hold on tight. I'm going to be making some pretty tight turns."

"Are you kidding me? This footage is like gold. I can sell it as stock footage for a quarter million, easily. You concentrate on the flying and I'll be back here making my retirement fund!"

Tom couldn't say anything as the jet now bore down on them from overhead. It looked like the pilot intended to crush down on them. He watched as it approached before flipping the left wing down and spiraling out of the way.

"Hit the dirt, Bud!" he called out.

"Danny, this had better not be some movie stunt Howard Gardner is pulling. If it is I'm shutting this picture down!"

CHAPTER 20 /
HAPPY, HOLLYWOOD-STYLE, ENDING

THE CAMERA operator swore it wasn't anything planned.

The other jet pilot evidently underestimated the *Kub's* maneuverability and speed. Time and again as it tried to get past Tom to go after Bud the inventor was able to get in the way and force the attacking jet into a sharp turn, dive or climb. Several times the jet nearly went into a stall keeping from ramming Tom's jet.

Over and over Tom dodged, side-slipped, rolled and even looped out of harm's way only to have the other jet, built to be a high-speed fighter, come around for another run.

"I'm on the ground," Bud reported.

Good, Tom thought as he counted down to his next maneuver. *I hope Sandy has taken Bash into the tent. I really don't want her seeing this if it goes bad.*

"Man is this ever great stuff!" Danny said.

"Stop it! Stop it right now. Can't you see we might die up here? That is no stunt pilot and this is no lighthearted matter. If I can't keep us from letting him get into attack position... he has missiles and I doubt he'll have any problems using them on us."

Danny gulped. "I'm sorry. I've been around Hollywood too long. Everything is magic this and misdirection the other thing. Guess I've lost a sense of the real world. I'll shut up now."

Tom knew he hadn't stopped filming but had no time to say anything more; the other jet was screaming in from their right. He knew that if a missile attack was going to happen, it might just be now.

But, rather than loose fiery death, the other jet made a sharp turn so it was flying next to the *Kub*. For a second, the pilot raised his shaded helmet visor and grinned at Tom. His next move wasn't so friendly. He ran his right index finger across his throat in a slashing motion. Suddenly, the attacking jet slowed down and Tom knew he was trying to line up far enough behind to get a missile lock on.

"Can't let you do that," he muttered as he also slowed the *Kub*. "Danny. I need you to be my eyes behind us. Turn around and tell me how far that jet is behind us."

For the first time the cameraman could be heard setting his equipment in the floor. His body movements jiggled the tiny jet as he positioned himself.

"Maybe a hundred yards back there and just above us a few yards. He's moving back more."

"Keep it coming, Danny. Every ten seconds at the very least. More often when he maneuvers."

For five more minutes Tom did everything he could to stay within the safe range. The missiles he believed their enemy to be carrying needed a full thousand yards clearance or they would not arm and lock onto their target.

"He's doing a whatchamacallit. A loop. Going straight up."

Tom matched the maneuver coming over the top a few degrees so he could see the other jet. Now, they were flying just two hundred feet apart with Tom slightly behind.

Tom hadn't looked at his RADAR so he was surprised when four shapes zoomed past them perhaps five hundred feet below.

"Swift Jet. Identify yourself so we know who the bad guy is."

The inventor keyed his microphone. "Waiving now," he reported as he wiggled his wings several times.

"Got it. Assume the other playmate is *not* friendly."

"Affirmative. Similar jets tried to down us a few weeks ago. Tell me what to do."

"Head down and let your friendly neighborhood U.S. Navy handle this. By the way, we are out of Miramar NAS."

Tom pointed the nose down but also turned around so they could see what was going on the enemy jet and the newly arrived Navy fighters.

As two of the fighters swept wide the other two went high and low on the now retreating jet. Although technically capable of mach-2, the old jet had never hit the sound barrier. Now it seemed to be struggling to remain in the air.

An uncharacteristic puff of black smoke from the Mirage told the inventor one of the compressors in his engine had just ceased working.

As Tom and Danny—now with the movie camera back to his eye—watched, one of the sweeper jets pulled along side the attacker's right wing. The enemy pilot must be in a panic because he fired off one of his missiles. Fortunately for everyone, it faltered a few seconds later and dropped straight down.

Doubly fortunate was it was dropping into a completely unoccupied part of the hills.

The Navy pilot was unhappy about this turn of events and moved closer getting his wing under the wing of the Mirage F-1. With a little flip up, he sent the Mirage into a spiral the pilot could not pull up from. By the time he almost got control he slammed into the hillside in a ball of flame.

Tom relaxed and realized his neck and shoulders were so tense he could barely turn his head.

He pulled the throttle back a little allowing the small jet to slow down to about four hundred knots. He took a few deep breaths and tried to roll his shoulders. Eventually things began to loosen and he keyed his microphone.

"Navy squadron leader. This is Swift Two.

"Go."

"Don't want to bother, but how did you know to come to the rescue?"

"Easy, Swift Two. Base got a 9-1-1 call from a Swift Three. The woman said what was going on and that you needed help pronto. Glad to have been of service. Are there any other unfriendlies around?"

"Haven't seen anything else. If you would escort us to El Cajon we'd appreciate it."

By the time the squadron left them Tom learned from them that Wes Norris had requested a standby squadron in case of trouble, so the jets had been ready to roll when Sandy's call came in. He also found out that the reason the Navy jets had not fired on the Mirage was they were in a no-fire zone with population centers too near for safety.

As first Tom and then his cameraman climbed up and out of the small jet, Bashalli came running from the parked atomicar and threw herself into his arms squeezing him so tightly that he felt a slight pop as his spine realigned. It felt so good his legs nearly collapsed under both of them. He realized Bud and Sandy were standing next to them so he reached out with one arm and brought his sister into the hug.

"Thanks, San," he whispered. "I hear you saved the day for all of us."

"You've had Bud's back and my back so much I owed you at least this little save."

They returned to the movie site but only after Tom spent a half hour sitting in the atomicar on the radio with his father. In the end Mr. Swift advised continued caution but had some good news.

"As nearly as Harlan can figure out there were three Mirage F1 jets that were part of a nineteen plane purchase by Libya back in the late nineteen-seventies that have been unaccounted for over nearly a decade. We know for certain twelve of the nineteen were shot down in various raids and that four are decommissioned and sit in a rusting cluster at the airport in Tripoli. That leaves those missing three. We're guessing the jets you have run afoul of are those same aircraft. At least the one forced down at Nellis in Las Vegas had many parts from one of those jets."

The final days of location shooting went very well with even more action sequences being quickly added once everyone appreciated the excellent job their pilot was doing.

Lawrence Laurent came to the site on the final day of shooting. He watched, silently, as the last five flying scenes were staged and filmed, requesting only to be allowed to run the camera from the *Kub*'s back seat for one extra scene.

"I've been watching the dailies and the one thing we don't have is the," and he made finger quotes, "'hero flies off into the sunset and the audience knows that everything is perfect and happy' bit. Here's what I imagine…"

He described the shot to Tom and Bud who agreed it was possible to shoot it at the appropriate time of day.

"A little corny," Bud stated, but the director didn't seem to hear him.

"I brought the dailies from what you've already done if the two of you would be interested in seeing them."

"Absolutely. Can our wives see them with us?"

"Sure, Mr. Swift. Only they need to promise to not discuss them with anyone. Not until the picture comes out. Oh, and just so you know, the whole multi-part serial idea has gone out the door in favor of making this a single, three-hour epic movie. So. I've got a couple things to do but, umm, that gopher girl—"

"Emily," Tom told him firmly.

Laurent gulped. "Yeah. Emily will get you all set up in one of the rooms in tent two and show you those shots."

He wandered off to go speak with the woman.

She came over, a smile on her face.

"He actually called me by my first name," she said in wonder. "Neat! Well, give me ten minutes and I'll come get you."

The boys went to talk with Bashalli and Sandy who had been lounging around with Brian Pemberly. He'd arrived to film a few scenes where his character comes in for a landing in a fairly wide shot, featuring Bud, then in close-up—and standing in exactly the same spot and pose—where he either flips his visor up or removes the entire helmet to deliver one or more lines.

"They wanted me to do this in the studio but I said it is much easier to match how Bud is standing when he lands if I can be right here to see it. Besides, I'm already in the fake rig so I just walk over and we swap places. Magic!" He smiled up at Tom and Bud. "Sorry about calling it a 'fake' rig. Only, I don't know what else to call it."

Tom replied, "Fake is as good as anything." To the wives he said, "We've been invited to see the daily footage of what Bud has been doing. Interested?"

The women shot to their feet. "Are we? Try to stop us!" declared Sandy.

Brian rose. "Think I might horn in on that?"

Emily came over to get them. When she heard the star was joining them, and he also called her by name—Tom had a quiet word in the actor's ear about that—she enthusiastically agreed to bring in another chair.

In all there was more than an hour of flying scenes to watch. And, these were just the ones the director had declared as being what was wanted.

"It is so much more vivid seeing Bud in the air than from down here on the ground," Bashalli remarked.

"It *is* more vivid on the screen than it was being up there," Tom responded.

"Trick of the digital filming process. You can dial the camera to give better than real life results," Brian told them. He named several of the settings that in years past had to be manually accomplished in the developing and printing of the film.

"Incredible" was the joint opinion of them all.

"Bud, you make me look exceptionally good. If I ever have any role requiring flying, I want you to double me!"

The final scene was to be made just as the sun was going down so Sandy, the director and Tom headed for the airport to retrieve the *Kub* an hour early.

As the director described what he needed as footage, Tom was envisioning his positioning. It was going to be a tricky shot.

"You do realize that to get that we are going to need to come in quite low and make a snap turn into a climb. Then, so your camera can see Bud it will need to be upside down and pointing straight up through the canopy." He had to explain the physics a couple times before Laurent understood, but finally he agreed on the technique required.

"If we can take the shot up to about five thousand feet before your man levels out and heads directly into the sun, it'll make cinematography history."

"It's going to mean Tom has to stand the jet on its tail and hover for you," Sandy said, sounding unhappy.

"Oh. Can't that happen?"

"It can but the jet will vibrate a bit," Tom replied.

"We've got a stabilization circuit in the camera that can take care of that. Let's go."

Tom was on the radio giving Bud the countdown and description of what he needed to do before they were off the ground. When they arrived and circled around the camp, Bud was ready on top of a nearby hill, poised to fly.

The *Kub* came in low and slow from the east until they were half a mile away. After warning Laurent Tom flipped the jet upside down. Bud soared skyward followed by Tom now in a vertical climb at about the same rate, the cockpit facing the *Sky Streaker*.

The completion of the scene was perfect. At the agreed altitude, Tom told Bud to level off and head into the setting sun. The *Kub* remained standing upright in mid air for more than a minute to get the complete shot.

Laurent was ecstatic. "Got it! We got it, Swift! We got it!"

Tom nosed over and picked up enough forward speed to stay in the air as they spiraled down to a lower altitude.

"Tell that amazing pilot of yours to come on back. That wraps the flying scenes."

Bud met them at the airport where he shucked the *Sky Streaker* back pack—but remained in the flying suit—and the men put it in the back of the atomicar for the trip back to the camp.

Laurent was giddy with glee when they arrived telling everyone how it was the perfect Hollywood ending and would have audiences cheering at the end of the film.

Having heard a lot of that sort of talk over the years, many rolled their eyes and wandered off. Only the actual audiences would see if his prediction came true.

With the sun now down it was decided that everyone would have a good meal and stay at the camp for the evening. Even Brian accepted that he would be roughing it and took it with good grace.

Three days later the Shopton four were saying their goodbyes at the soundstage when Howard Gardner came over to speak to Tom.

A few minutes later and after giving the producer a reluctant nod, he explained what was going on.

"Mr. Gardner believes there are a few more scenes that require the *Streaker*. Not the flying one, but he is begging to keep the non-functional one for another two weeks until they wrap everything. I've agreed pending approval by Wes and from dad. Hang on for a bit."

He walked over to the FBI agents who had decided their standard dark suits were totally unnecessary and unproductive so they were sitting in a small group in their shirtsleeves, rolled up because the outside temperature had reached ninety.

The agent had no problems with the suit staying.

"Nobody knows if that pilot the Navy brought down was Mirov, so I have to ask you if you believe it was him."

"I can't be certain, Wes. The pilot did bring his visor up and I did see most of his face, but it was quick, from a sixty feet away, and I was waiting to see if I had to maneuver the heck away. But… yeah. It sort of looked like Streffan Mirov."

"Okay. Then I can tell you there were some discernible remains located at the crash site and they have been tested out. They were a partial match with Mirov's brother and his mother, both samples are in our databases. It is the agency's opinion that there is a ninety-seven percent probability it was Streffan Mirov. In that case, we believe the threat is past. Just as long as you are leaving the non-working suit, we will draw down our presence to a single agent until the end."

"Can I ask you a question, Wes?"

"Shoot."

"Okay. How is it an FBI agent from Cleveland ends up back in Shopton and then all the way out here and is seemingly everywhere this project has gone?"

Norris smiled and leaned in so only Tom could hear his answer.

"Because there are some very big plans afoot for your suit. Why do you think the Navy was so happy to come at a moment's notice?" He patted the inventor on the shoulder.

Tom promised to come back for the final day to pick up the stand-in suit.

A small lunchtime celebration had been arranged by Emily— with the director's and producer's permission, of course—starting twenty minutes later. Hand shakes, kisses and hugs were exchanged with all the people they had worked with. Even their one-time guide, Bonnie, came to give her well wishes to the ladies.

Before they left, Brian came over to shake hands with Tom and Bud one more time.

"I have to tell you this has been an experience," he said. "You two are the best, well, *outsiders* I've ever worked around or with. I appreciate all you've done. You, especially, Bud. I'll look great on screen because of you."

He gave the girls one more kiss before turning away, what looked like tears coming to his eyes.

The last man to come see them was Danny, Tom's cameraman from the location flights. He handed the inventor a video disc.

"That's all the stuff I probably should not have taken. The stuff where you were saving our skins. I wanted you to have a copy. Let me know if there is anything you think is taboo from my using in the future."

With the real suit already locked up in the cargo jet, all they had were a few souvenirs the ladies had been given. Tom pulled out of the soundstage and stopped near the guard table.

"Walter? You take care of this movie and yourself," Tom told the older man with a smile.

Walter got up and reached over the top of the door to shake hands.

"You too, Mr. Swift. Mr. Stunt guy and ladies. Oh, and do yourself a big favor. Try to forget all this stuff behind the scenes or else you'll never enjoy another movie." He tapped the side of his nose with an index finger in a knowing way and winked.

Tom lifted the atomicar off from the road about fifty feet away and turned to the north.

"Farewell, Hollywood," Sandy said.

"It has been... interesting," Bashalli added.

Tom and Bud just took deep breaths, glad it was over.

The Swifts and the Barclays sat around the back yard table finishing their Marionberry cobbler and enjoying the warmth of the early autumn breeze that wafted through the neighborhood. It brought with it the aromas of perhaps a dozen other families enjoying a barbecue on the final weekend of October. Halloween would be coming in five days along with predicted rain.

"Now that I am back to full steam," Damon was telling them, "I intend to take a firmer hand in what you get yourselves involved in, boys!" He was looking pointedly at Tom and Bud. "Speaking of which, do you have any idea what is next on your calendar?"

Tom finished swallowing his last bite of desert before answering.

"Well, Bash and I were talking just last night about me taking that vacation I sort of promised her once we got you on the road to recovery nearly four months ago." He grinned. "It also hit me that, back when I was working on those nanosurgery robots, I received a request from the European Resources Commission to investigate our coming up with a truly viable way to connect Europe with North America."

He wanted to say more but he still had little reason to suspect that in a matter of weeks he would embark on the most ambitious construction project he and Swift Enterprises had ever undertaken as he would be developing his Atlantean HydroWay!

Anne *tutted* and spoke up, saying, "I think that is just about the end of work conversation for now. You two need to have an off switch built in so we women in your lives can shut you up about space *this* and ocean *that* and get you to just talk to us like civilized people!"

She sat back and kept a straight face for about two seconds before she, and everyone else at the table, broke into laughter.

Even little Bart laughed and clapped his hands.

"Go to space!" he declared, but not quite loudly enough for anyone else to hear.

Made in the USA
Monee, IL
08 November 2022

17308255R00115